The Psychics' Seaport Murder

By Lynn Marron

A Witch Triplets Mystic Mystery

Book Designer: Leonard J. Bloom, Jr.
Published by Kear Press
Stratford, CT
LIBRARY OF CONGRESS: 2015939715
ISBN: Paperback 978-1-942888-05-5
ISBN: E-Book 978-1-942888-06-2

Rev 1 _ 7/18

This book is dedicated to

Anne and Carl Larsen

Who–among other good things--

have given us the

Creative Jonathan, Brilliant Nathan,
and Magical Elizabeth

Chapter 1

The cries of drowning sailors assailed her. It must be coming from that fifteen foot high, black iron anchor set upright before the Mystic Seaport Museum's admission booths. The seaport's ghosts cried out to her, but she should be at a table in the McDonald's waiting to meet 'them.'   But she couldn't find the McDonald's. It must be after one p.m., but Holly Corey had misplaced her watch. How could she always use her powers as a witch to find jewelry for other people, but she could never find her own stuff?

She'd stopped here to get directions and calm down a bit. Now the wailing, weeping dead were confusing her more. There were tourists all around, and she just wanted to hide. Holly found a wooden bench and sat down. She should be having her reunion–the most important meeting of her twenty-two years, but she wasn't ready. Her curly, shoulder length, blonde hair wasn't cut because she couldn't afford it. Those retro, red eyeglass frames which had seemed so fashionable two years ago looked stupid now. She didn't have a job or a college degree. It was mid-September in New England, but these nylon cargo pants were too hot for today. They'd see her looking hot and smelly, without money or a job. What if they just rejected her out right? She dreamed about this reunion for years. What if they never showed up? What if she couldn't find them?

Holly's eyes started to fill up. Only a baby would bawl; she bit her lip. Maybe she should just run away again. Go back to the parking lot and drive away as she did her first year of college. Ran away like she did from her last job. No. She would do this! Holly stood up, and she started to walk resolutely back to the sidewalk.

"Miss. Miss!"

A voice calling. She glanced back, seeing a tallish, blond-haired man, in the blue shirt of a Seaport Village

Museum guide, holding up her handbag, which she had left on the wooden bench. Her aunt was right; she was always a scatterbrain. Holly hurried back and took the bag from him. "I'm sorry." Feeling a bit sick-stomached, she just stood still for a moment. Anything to keep from going to that dreaded rendezvous at McDonald's.

The tour guide had a sweet, lopsided smile and a white embroidered sperm whale tail on his cobalt-blue shirt. "You okay? You don't look so good. Maybe you should sit here, while I get you a bottle of water from the Ship's Chandlery?" He indicated a store in that row of white shops on the other side of the paved courtyard.

Obediently, Holly sat down, but she had no money to waste on water bottles at tourist prices from what was really a glorified souvenir shop. "No–thank you. I'll be all right."

Holly looked up into blue-green eyes like her own. He had a laughing, gentle smile as if this young man knew something funny that she didn't. She started to explain, "I've got go. To the McDonald's. Do you know where it is? I'm meeting someone—maybe. If they show up."

Uninvited he sat down beside her. "They're men?"

"Boys, no..." Her brothers were men now. So many years lost. Years that could never be made up. They had grown so far away from her. "Yes..men-men now."

"They'll show up for a pretty girl like you," he said that like he knew it was an undisputable fact.

The happy fizzy feeling of his fun vibrations made Holly want to giggle. "Especially with my old style glasses." His aura was so clear. So strong, so familiar, in her embarrassment, she hadn't read him, but now, as always, Holly studied this stranger's emanations: this man gave off colorful auras of friendly loving green light, white power, a tinge of dark blue sadness, and a touch of black--fear. Strangely his emanations were almost perfectly in tune with hers.

In total amazement, she burst out at him. "Y-y-you're my b-brother!"

He laughed outright, making him look younger and even a little elvish with that slight slant of his ears. "Of course. Didn't you sense me?"

"W-w-which one are you?"

"You can't guess?" he teased.

"Umm." She wanted to hit him and hug him. Tears were forming again–of happiness.

"Since I work here at the Seaport, near where I live?" he prompted.

"You're Frosty Christmas Corey!" she finished triumphantly.

"Yep. Frost." He stopped, his aura going from green love, to creative orange, then darkening to a strong purple of intuition. "When we were kids you used to call me Frosty after the snowman. I'd forgotten that."

"Do–d-d-do you like me?" Holly begged. "I mean you don't know me–but-but- do you think you might like me?"

He smiled. "I don't know you? You like dogs that swim. Love to wear the color pink. Everything pink. Your favorite ice cream is pecan, and oddly, you get happy in thunderstorms. Of course, I know you!"

"You remembered after all these years," she said softly. "Frosty, you love Halloween, Bar-be-que chicken, and dirty old tools, and smelly workshops." Again, she felt the drowned spirits calling out from the anchor. She looked toward them. "Don't they bother you?"

"The tourists walking around? They pay for my salary."

Holly shook her head. "The spirits. The d–d-drowned ones."

He seemed to stop and think about that. "I don't hear them that much. Not like you seem to. I kinda see them as friends that whine a lot. There's a lot of ghost voices here at the Seaport. I'll have to give you a tour someday. But shouldn't we go get lunch and meet brother, Noel? It isn't every day; long-lost triplets are reunited."

"Do you think he'll like me?"

Frost looked back at her and studied her carefully, then shook his head. "No. I don't think he'll like you." He reached over and kissed her forehead. "I think he'll love you. Like I do!" Then he stood up. "I can't give you a ride. I just take my bike to work."

"You don't drive?"

"Well, Ben left me a truck, but I never got a license for driving a car. I've got my Boat Captain's license. Do you have a car?"

"Sort of." Holly definitely had wanted her brothers to get to know her a bit, before they saw her transportation. "It's in the parking lot," she said reluctantly. "Can't we walk? Where is the McDonald's? I didn't see it driving in."

"It's on Coogan, up the hill. The second left turn on Greenmanville as you come off of the Thruway. We're about a mile away. We could walk it, but that will cut into the time we have together because I've got to be back to lead a tour at two."

She wanted them to have all the time together they could. "Then I'll have to drive. My-my—it's in the p-pa-parking lot."

He nodded and turned to the road they had to cross. Holly shyly walked beside him, unconsciously holding out her hand by her side. Without even looking, Frost took it and reassuringly held it in his warm, callused hand as they walked out to the sidewalk.

Across the road, there were lots of cars. All ones Holly wished she had, especially when Frost blurted out, "Look at that old time hearse! Wide tail fins and velvet drapes in the back windows. Must be the 1950's? Somebody's actually driving that old heap!" Then he looked at her, and his face changed. "Oh, my God–is that yours?"

Apologetically she said, "It's a 1956. I got it at a really good price. The ghost in the back kept screaming when other people tried to drive it."

He studied it. "A spirit from one of the coffins they transported?"

"No. The former driver, Bernie. He loved driving a Cadillac so much; he bought it when the funeral home upgraded. Then after he died, he just stayed."

"Can't you get rid of him?"

"I've never tried. Bernie's a nice soul. He moans to remind me to add oil since the gauge is broken." Holly wished she had rolled up her messy sleeping bag in the back.

They slid in on opposite sides of the wide, red-leather bench seat. Frost looked at the red plush that lined all the interior, the ultramarine blue drapes in the back windows, the ivory steering wheel and the chrome railings in the back. Then he actually smiled. "This is pretty cool!"

With him giving directions, she pulled out of the parking lot hanging a right. Alongside them to the left the Atlantic ocean harbor melding into a river mouth. They passed a fancy cemetery. Funny, she rarely, if ever, heard a ghostly voice calling to her from a cemetery.

On her right, small stores, laundry, antique shops and a store selling ship's brasses, then at the light, a big sign for the Seaport 'Olde Village Shopping'. They turned right and headed up the hill.

"McDonald's on your right," Frost directed.

She was so excited Holly had trouble parking the long hearse. She expected her other triplet would be slender, about Frost's 5'11" with blond hair and blue-green eyes, like Frost and herself. Inside the fast food restaurant, they looked around. Standard McDonald's with a seaport theme. There were nautical map designs embedded in the tables and sandblasted into the glass partitions. A number of couples, families, and truck drivers were sitting at tables, but nobody is looking like what she expected. Her hopes started sinking. Maybe Noel wasn't coming?

Frost walked ahead and ordered a fish sandwich meal. Holly wondered if he was going to pay for hers. But no, he paid for his own and then went to look for a table. This wasn't a date, and she figured tour guides didn't make that much. She ordered from the value menu, just a burger, no soda or fries and joined him at a large round table in the back corner.

As she looked out the windows to the parking lot, Holly's stomach churned too much for her to eat. She just left her burger there in its yellow wrappings. "Noel should be here. Maybe he isn't coming?"

"Course he is." Frost's appetite didn't seem affected at all. But seeing Holly's nervousness, he leaned back and closed his eyes for a moment. "He's near. Angry."

"Because I was late?"

Frost shook his head. "No. He's angry at being late himself."

"You've seen him already?" she said softly.

"Not since we were separated at five years old. But I feel him–I feel you sometimes too–but it's easier with him." His blue-green eyes opened, but seemed unfocused, as if he was staring a great distance beyond her. His voice had a detached sound. "Sometimes when Noel's emotions are strong, I can even know what he is reacting too." Coming out of his reverie, Frost looked back at her, face reddening.

"You blush easy, too," she said.

Flushing darker, he looked down at the untouched burger in front of Holly. "C'mon, eat something. Didn't you get a soda? Hydration is important! Here, take some of mine."

"N-no. I don't..."

"Holly, you are scaring me. You look so pale, and your hands are trembling."

She kept staring at the doors. "What if Noel was on

time and didn't see us and just left?"

"Look at the clock over there. We were only three minutes late."

"What if he comes here and doesn't like us?"

"Worst comes to worst; we'll all just meet and move on." Frost shrugged. "But that's not going to happen."

"It could. He could just have lunch and never want to see us again."

"Since we've all inherited a share of the house, we'll have to stay together to work that out."

"I-I-I remember a house out of town, near cow fields, with tall, white columns in the front and so many, m-many rooms. It's a huge m-m-mansion, isn't it?"

"Yeah." He gave that lopsided grin she remembered all those years. "But it's falling down around my ears. The real estate lady said we should pull it down and sell just the property."

"Don't tear it down until I've seen it!" she begged.

Frost laughed. "The mansion's lasted over two hundred years; I think it'll make it through today."

She took a bite of her burger, which actually tasted quite good. Well, she had driven through the night to get here, slept in her car on the parkway and hadn't eaten any breakfast.

He pushed his soda cup closer to her again. "You need hydration. I had a lady faint on the dock during one of my tours last week."

Holly obediently took a sip. It was unsweetened ice tea; she was expecting soda. "You like tea too?"

"Where do you work?" her brother asked.

Holly twisted her lips. "I-I-I.."

He finished for her. "Stutter when you're nervous."

She smiled. Took a breath. "Odd jobs. Temporary." Holly wanted off the subject of her failed life. "W-what is it like to work at the Seaport?"

But his eyes were now unfocused again. Staring into

space beyond her. Was he having some kind of fit? In a moment Frost spoke in that distant sounding voice again. "He's near. In the parking lot—no, coming in." Suddenly back as himself, Frost turned to the doorway as a blue-suited, twentyish man, with white blond hair was walking in. Stopping. The stranger closed his eyes for a brief second, then turned his head in their direction. Staring right at them.

Holly half rose, waving one hand high, shouting, **"Noel! Over here!"**

Both her brothers winced at her loudness. Seeing people looked at them, Holly sat down, blushing a deep red. Both her brothers, with the same fair skin, were reddening too. Noel turned from them and started walking away.

"He's leaving?" whispered Holly in despair.

"No—silly! He's going up to the counter to order."

She relaxed and smiled, as she watched Noel—her brother—order food. After so many, many years of dreaming about the three of them reuniting it was perfect.

Finally, bringing his tray over, Noel joined them. As he sat down, Holly brightly explained, "I'm Holly Christmas Corey, and he's Frost Christmas Corey." Oh, God. That was so lame. He could figure out which was his brother and which was his sister.

Noel sat down, saying formally, "N. C. Corey." Then he just started to unwrap his chicken sandwich and eat, as if this happened every day.

"If our mother worshiped the Earth Goddess, even if we were born on December 25th, why name us after a Christian holiday?" Holly wondered.

As he laid out his food, N.C. carefully squired out some ketchup and recited, "They've actually never known the date of Christ's birthday. The church settled on December 25th, because it was near 'Mirthra's' solstice celebrations and they were also trying to supersede the Roman worship of 'Sol Invictus.' That god's traditional birthday of December 25th."

Frost was studying his blue silk tie. "You always wear that monkey suit in ninety-five degrees?"

His brother reddened. "I had a job interview. The Mystic Aquarium has one of the best marine mammal study programs on the East Coast. They have beluga whales, seal shows, and access to the Atlantic. I thought if I could get into their trainer program, maybe I could work it into my doctorate. I'd like my thesis to be on the captive belugas' reception to human speech."

"Did they hire you?" asked Holly eagerly.

The dark psychic wash of his heavy, utter disappointment pressed down on her, even before he spoke. "The big boss, Dr. Morjessky, was out on a research boat. The three guys I spoke to didn't seem too impressed with me." N.C. slammed a fist down. "I always do real lousy on interviews. That aquarium has the best beluga program in the country! They've got four whales in three interlocking pools–I could have done all my research there... and I blew the interview!"

Frost seemed unaware of Noel's deadening pessimistic aura. "If you get the position, you plan to live here?"

Noel looked embarrassed. "I'd have to. But I didn't get the job. I can't go back to my university; my grant ended there. I'll have to find another place. Connecticut's awfully expensive."

"Tell me about it," said Frost, taking another sip from their shared tea. "Unfortunately I got to be back at the Seaport. We're short-handed, so I'm leading another tour at 2:00." He looked at his bare wrist. "I keep misplacing my wristwatches." He looked up at the restaurant clock.

"**Don't go!** " cried out Holly. "We just met!" Both her brothers started flushing and looked with embarrassment to see that other people were looking at them again. Before taking another bite of his burger, Noel turned his wrist.

"You've got thirty-five minutes."

"I'll need fifteen to jog back."

"No," Holly interrupted. "I'll drive you back. N.C. can stay here and finish eating. I'll come back for him."

Frost nodded. "Then we've got fifteen minutes more. Twenty-minutes to sum up twenty years. My name is Frost. Or to Holly--Frosty." Noel frowned at this, but his brother smilingly continued, "When we were split up, I stayed in Mystic, living with our grandparents and then my great uncle, Benjamin Corey, who lived here in the family mansion..."

"Did he like you?" Holly asked hopefully.

Frost shrugged. "Fed me. Taught me carpentry. Bought me toy ships, shoes and school books. Enrolled me in the Boy Scouts." He looked from Holly to Noel and seemed not to need to modify the truth. "But he was a man who would have preferred to live alone. As I got older, Ben kept more and more to himself. We lived in the same house, but I didn't see him for weeks at a time."

"How is that possible?" asked Noel.

"You'll understand when you see Witch House again."

"Witch House?" Holly faintly remembered that unpleasant name.

"Well, the Captain Corey Mansion. Kids used to call it 'Witch House' when I was young, because of the horror of what had happened there."

No one spoke for a time; then Holly had to break the silence. "That was kind. Enrolling you in the Boy Scouts."

Frost smiled wryly, while her other brother looked at her. "You were with our mother' sister. Was Aunt Maureen *kind*?"

"I-I-I was a duty to her." Holly looked down at her thin hands clasped in her lap. "She-she did her duty."

"And nothing more?" Noel said coldly. "That's what I got from Major Scofield. He raised me because he was our father's cousin."

"Did he talk about Daddy?" Holly asked, so desperate to know.

Noel just suddenly got interested in his french fries, and Frost gave him an out by asking, "You were raised at West Point?"

"When the major taught there."

"He was a major?"

"Retired. Major Kermit Scofield. When he taught military strategy at West Point, I had the run of the place."

"Could you have gone to West Point?" Holly prompted.

Noel looked sad. "Had the grades too. Got a letter from my Congressman. Just didn't do well in the interviews and nobody was pulling for me, I guess."

"Didn't the Major push for you?" she asked.

N.C. made a sour face. "He never thought I was West Point material. And the Major died the summer I graduated from High School."

"But you went to college anyway?" Holly said.

"Princeton. Yeah, against the Major's advice. He always thought college would be wasted on me. And that I'd run up a lot of debt I couldn't pay. He was right. But now, I've got my Masters in Marine Biology. I'm trying to set up a doctorate program focusing on belugas. Well, if I can't get access to whales, it will be large marine mammals."

"You're young for a doctorate," said Frost admiringly.

"But I've run up enough debt to pay off until I'm ninety-nine years old. And I have no job," said N.C. sounding discouraged. "You go college, Frost?"

"Naw. Didn't need to. I've been learning a lot at the Seaport."

"As a tour guide?" Noel's voice had a touch of disdain.

Holly wondered if his tone was perhaps an echo of his late Uncle Kermit–he was their Uncle Kermit.

"The tour guide part is a living–not much of one. Can't keep up the mansion on my salary." His voice took on a deep excitement. "But I'm a volunteer marine carpenter. Also, I'm working with Tarus, who is teaching me ancient methods of navigation. He's sailed all over the Pacific Ocean without G.P.S., and at the Seaport Museum, I'm kinda an unofficial curator," he finished proudly.

"That a higher pay level?" Noel asked.

Frost flushed but ignored that. "I've designed and built the Connecticut tobacco trade display that is currently running in one of the galleries."

"What has tobacco got to do with a New England seaport?" Holly asked.

"Tobacco was and still is a big Connecticut crop. I've gotten stereopticon slides of the sailing ships that transported tobacco from this seaport! Original tobacco cans. Photographs of local barns painted with cigarette advertisements. Old Cuban cigars with Connecticut wrappers. Some hand rolling equipment for those cigars. I built the cabinet, painted the background. You guys have got to come see it!"

"Oh–I want to!" said Holly. "How much does it cost to get in?"

Frost thought about that little problem. "Let me see if I can get passes." He looked at the clock on the wall again. "Holly, I'll need you to drive me back."

"You have a car here?" Noel asked.

She thought of the haunted hearse. "Sort of."

"Yep, she's got something alright." Delight at Noel's surprise to come glowed in Frost's mischievous aqua eyes. "Wait till you see it!"

Chapter 2

Noel looked at Frost. "Why didn't you drive?"

"I peddle to work on the bike. Uncle left me the truck. It's mothballed in the garage because I never learned to drive, but I've got my Small Craft Captain's license. The bike's been okay; it's only a bit hard food shopping with only a backpack." Frost looked up at the wall clock. "But I've got to go earn my bread and clam chowder." He started to stand up.

"**No!**" said Holly. We've just met! When will I see you again..."

"Where are you two staying?" Frost asked.

"I-I" Noel stuttered a little too. "The airport limo left me off at the Mystic motel down the hill. I've got a room tonight. But the prices are high." He looked at Holly. "Do you have a room?"

She shook her head. "Coming here I just slept in the back of my car at rest stops on the Thruway. I can use the restrooms there all night. Saves some money."

Frost was cleaning up his yellow food wrappers. "You'll stay with me at my house. Well, our house. The both of you."

"I've already registered for tonight–so I'll have to pay the motel," Noel finished with a hangdog resignation.

Frost shook his head. "Not if Alice is on the desk. The red-haired lady manager. Tell her you're a friend of mine, well, my brother. She'll let you out of the reservation."

"You'll let us stay at your house?" Holly asked.

"It's two thirds ours," pointed out Noel as he started wrapping up his uneaten food.

She protested. "Noel–N.C.–you stay and keep eating. I'll drop Frost off and come back here."

"Okay," organized Noel. "Holly and I will do the tourist bit, walking around here until you're done with work. When is that?"

"Five twenty."

"We will try not update ourselves until we are with you again. We'll meet you at 1730." A Holly's questioning look, he further explained, "That's military for 5:30 p.m. Where do we meet?"

"Use the Seaport village parking. We'll meet in the courtyard, before the museum admission booths. You know, Holly, where we first met?"

Leaving Noel to finish his lunch, Holly drove Frost back to the museum. Anxiously she asked, "W-w-what do you think Noel will say when he sees the hearse?"

With that lopsided grin of his, Frost just chuckled out loud. "I don't know, but I wish I could see it!"

Coming back to McDonald's, Holly again parked in the back out of sight. She found herself anxious as she hurried in, half afraid that Noel would be gone. But still wearing his hot suit jacket, he had gotten himself another tea and was waiting at their table. Slipping in the curve of the booth bench Holly started, "Where did you live before West Point?"

Noel put up a staying hand. "No questions, until Frost is with us." And he kept saying that at every eager query that Holly could not help spilling out during the afternoon. When Noel finished drinking his tea, they walked down the hill and crossed the street on the river, over to a two-story motel. Obviously, both her brothers had the same financial problems as herself so that she couldn't borrow money from them. What was she going to do next? Could she find a job here? And as usual, lose that job here? When Noel entered the A-shaped building that served as the Mystic motel lobby, he straightened his back and marched over to the desk.

A petite, bright red-headed, fortyish woman looked up and smiled. "Can I help you?"

"Are you Alice the manager?"

"Yes."

"I'd like to cancel my room today," he said stiffly.

"For tomorrow?"

"No, today."

"I'm sorry, you've already checked in. And I've sent your credit card through." The woman looked concerned. "Was there something wrong with the room?"

"I just wanted to get my money back, if I could."

"Sorry." She shook her head. Shoulders sagging a bit, Noel started to turn away.

Holly pushed forward. "He doesn't need the room because we're staying with our brother, Frosty Corey."

"Frost?" Alice looked at the stiff-backed Noel. "Oh, that explains it!" She looked at her screen. "N.C. Corey. When I first saw you, I thought it was Frost coming in the door, but I was so busy with all the limo people checking in. Still, I should've connected that name." The manager keyed something in on her computer screen, as she looked back to Holly saying curiously, "I didn't even know Frost had a brother and sister?"

"We're triplets."

Alice's eyes widened, as she looked at them questioningly. "He never mentioned it?"

To Holly that meant Alice wasn't originally from around here or she would've remembered the horror of their mother's death. "W-w-we were separated as children," she said, realizing that opened a lot more unanswered questions.

Alice looked at her computer. "You know, with the fall foliage tourists and the convention at the museum, we should have a full house tonight." She started typing. "You clear out the room and bring the keycard back. My maid's in the hospital, so I'll have to clean it up. I can't promise, but with the leaves starting to turn, I probably will be able to rent that room tonight. If I can, your credit card will be refunded." She smiled at Noel. "Tell Frost he's got to drop by and explain himself!"

Holly loved that she and Noel said, "Thank you," at

the same time. They climbed up the outside staircase to the second floor of the motel room block. For a moment Holly breathed in a water-mellony smell as she looked to trees that covered where the river joined the sea. This was a nice town to live in.

The neat room on the second-floor balcony was decorated in reds and oranges, with stylistic paintings of modern sailing ships. The only sign of Noel being in there was black laptop case and three huge, old, beat-up leather suitcases. Holly tried to lift the middle one. God, it was heavy! "What do you carry in this--barbells?"

Noel reddened. "Books. School papers. Pretty much everything I've got."

Holly thought about the pathetic mound of cardboard boxes in her hearse alongside her sleeping bag, and that single, brown-paper-wrapped oil painting. All she had been able to salvage from her life of twenty-two years. "You save all your old papers?"

"Nope, just the ones I'm working on for my doctorate. The rest had to go into the dumpster when I left my dorm room."

After straightening up the bedspread, they carried the bags outside and down to the manager's office. Alice smiled when they walked in. "Already got a reservation for your room. Your credit card has been refunded." Noel looked relieved as he handed the keycard to Alice. Back outside Noel put his overstuffed bags down on the parking lot tarmac. "These bags are heavy. Why don't you go back up the hill and get your car?"

Holly wanted to put off doing that for as long as possible. Somehow she didn't think Noel would have the same fun reaction to her hearse as Frosty did. And she didn't want Frost's friend, Alice, to see it from the office windows. Holly just hefted the solid weight of his third bag and laptop case and said, "It's not a long walk. C'mon." She started across the street and up the hill.

Not looking too happy Noel lifted up his heavier load and followed. At the McDonald's parking lot, Holly figured she had to get this over with. She marched over to her hearse and set down the bags to catch her breath.

Behind her Noel stopped dead, asking in horror, "You drive a hearse?"

"I got it for a great price–it's haunted too, by the shade of this poor driver..."

Her brother eyed the long, black Cadillac without enthusiasm. Then he nervously looked around to see if anyone was watching them. "Let's get this stuff in fast." The hearse had four doors in the front and a wide one in the back. Noel opened the one behind the driver. Her boxes and painting were all loaded in the casket section, on to one side only, so that she could sleep in the sleeping bag on the other. Closing his eyes in pain, Noel shoved his bags in and then hurried away from her offending hearse.

With hours to kill, they walked back down to the road. Noel stood looking sadly down a series of modern style white buildings in the distance. "What's that?" Holly asked.

"The Mystic Aquarium. They've got a full acre of beluga pools outdoors. Inside they have shark and jellyfish tanks, a 4-D movie theater, an indoor marine theater where the dolphins, seals, and sea lions perform. In the back acreage, they have a New England style lake habitat, seal caves, and a penguins' habitat. All sorts of great exhibits." The initial enthusiasm in his voice drained away. "Dr. Morjessky's work is there breeding sea mammals is world famous. I wanted to study her procedures."

"We could go over and see the Aquarium?"

"Costs a lot to get in."

Yeah, he didn't have much money either. "If you don't get the job here, what are you going to do?"

He shrugged. "There's an aquarium in Norwalk with

a smaller, but interesting seal program. But living here in Connecticut is so expensive."

Which means he would be going away. They were just reunited, and she was being left again! Helplessly, she looked about. "What's down there?"

"A bunch of tourist traps. 'Ye olde village' type."

"We've got time to kill. And it doesn't cost anything to just shop." Holly eagerly looked to the small 'olde village' collection of one story cottages centered around a duck pond. "I'd love to look there?" She started to slip her arm into to his, but a self-conscious Noel pulled away. He was not as touchy-feely as Frost evidently was, but Noel headed down the hill with her.

The mystic olde village was a collection of cottage stores, selling jewelry, baked goods, casual clothing, books and toys, all laid out like a little New England town, with a duck pond around a 'mill' wheel building. Holly started with Nordic sweaters and worked her way through a shop of kids toys.

Noel just kept looking at his watch.

Soon Holly too found herself looking at the fancy clock high on a post. Still, an hour and thirty-five minutes until they could go pick up Frost–and find out more. Noel saw her looking at a Bearclaw in the bakery window. He went in and bought one. Splitting it, Noel handed her a half.

"D-d-delicious," she said. "Thank you."

As they walked, Holly looked up, seeing an elegant, scroll-shaped, hand-carved wooden sign, with *Rainbow Realm* scrawled in beautifully painted letters. "Can we go in?"

Noel looked dubiously at the store window displaying silver pentagrams, tarot cards, prisms and Wiccan books. "We don't have time–you've got to drive back to the museum."

She reached out. Putting her hand on the Tutor styled diamond pained glass of the Rainbow Realm's front windows. A mixture of sensations washed over her: warm happiness; the smell of sandalwood incense; the soft smoothness of velvet. Inside this store, something waited for her. But a warning echoed from Aunt Maureen; *You keep daydreaming about those weird witch things, they'll put you away!* Holly followed Noel.

Just after she parked, Frost found the hearse. By pushing her boxes and Noel's suitcases forward, the three of them also loaded Frost's bike in the rear on top of everything. "You got a lot of room in there," Frost marveled.

The three of them easily fit on the single front bench seat. Frost directed them through town, under I-95 and out to a more rural area. Here houses alternated with small farms.

Finally, they reached a yard, hidden by fir trees and overgrown lilac bushes. Over them, Holly could just make out the white roof line of a two-story house. There was a large central building, with four columns and a pair of smaller one-story wings, also with columned porches.

Holly turned off on to a gravel driveway that curved through the bushes. She could see more here. "It's a mansion!"

"Not the front drive," Frost directed her away from the graceful crescent driveway that curved before the front columns. "We'll park in the back."

Noel sounded impressed. "Greek revival. Probably built in the Federalist period."

"The front is a fancier addition to the two-story house in back that partly dates back from a pre-revolutionary farmhouse," Frost explained.

Slowly Holly got out of the hearse. Yes. The white paint was grayish and peeling, but it was a real, two-story mansion with tall 'Greek' columns and all. Not waiting for her brothers, Holly hurried ahead, following on a brick pathway between the seven-foot-high lilacs bushes.

The attack came suddenly.

A huge, black dog burst from the bushes; jaws open

savagely, his spittle hit her. Holly recoiled in fear. She had no defense. Terrified she fell back, raising her arms to protect her face. Teeth bared, the brute was crouching low for a leap at her throat.

Someone shoved her away hard, as a commanding voice ordered. "**Sit!**"

Arms over her face, eyes closed, Holly heard the dog snarling viciously. But the dog's growling wasn't getting closer, so Holly opened her eyes and slowly lowered her arms.

Noel's blue suit bent between Holly and the dog's savagely bared teeth. Her brother was too close! The massive dog was still shuddering with its vicious growling, but strangely the beast was sitting obediently before Noel. Holly moved to the side. Now she could better see the dog; he was black and tan. A massive rottweiler, with his ribs showing. Suddenly Holly felt pity for the frightened, starved looked animal.

"Is this dog yours?" Holly asked Frost who was coming up behind her.

He had moved to the bushes where the dog came from. "No. The dog isn't mine. Neither is that dead body on the other side of the hedge."

Chapter 3

Frost knelt down, reaching out to touch the guy's neck. "Cold."

"D-d-don-t t-touch--he might be s-sick!" Holly warned.

Noel moved to the body's other side. "Not sick. He's stiff."

Frost had gone dead white; Noel looked closely at his brother. "You know him?"

"I think it's Rolf. Rolf Van Hom. He works at the Seaport."

"A friend of yours?"

"Not really."

"He visits you often?"

"Never."

"I'll call 911." Noel used his cell phone.

Soon the police were outside, measuring things in the bushes, taking pictures and searching through the overgrown gardens. As the trees cut off the setting sun, it started getting darker and cooler. The three of them stood by her hearse, watching. Finally, Frost said, "That dog's growling at the policewoman."

Noel whistled. The Rottweiler trotted to him. "Sit!" He commanded. The dog obeyed.

"Do you think this was his dog?" Holly asked.

Frost just shrugged. "Could be. Could be a stray."

"The cops should take the dog," said Noel.

"They don't seem too interested," added Frost.

They looked at each other.

Frost finished, "I've told them it might be his dog, but they don't seem to care. Let's just go inside." He led them past the police to a small back, covered porch on one of the wings. The dog just followed close to Noel, whimpering and looking up at them with fear-whitened eyes.

Holly found herself reaching down to pet him. He didn't growl, just looked frightened.

They entered in the North wing, a one-story building that had a porch in the front, one on the end and a small walk up porch they were using now. Frost lead the way, with Noel following. Last, Holly started to block the doorway, but the dog whimpered, and she just let him follow her in.

It had been a grand mansion at one time. In this north wing, they entered to a room-sized pantry, with an old wringer washing machine. All the walls had shelving for canned goods, now mostly bare. Then a door opened to an eight-foot-high ceiling kitchen. A true country kitchen, one room, bigger than any apartment Holly'd ever had. In the corner was a yellow linoleum-topped table with four chairs, set in a windowed alcove, and still holding one lonely plate of food. A heavy-legged work table dominated the center near an old, but big, six burner commercial sized stove. That set across from the big brick fireplace that once must have been the original cooking area. Holly moved to the narrow, modern refrigerator.

"Why did you bring that dog in?" Noel demanded.

"He might bite one of the policemen. We could be liable as owners of the property," Frost covered for her. "He'll just stay in here until the police go away."

Holly was softly touching the worn wooden counters under glass-pained china cabinets. Right now, one-third of this was hers. She never owned a house in her life, and even if this was going to be sold, right now one-third of all this was hers! "That poor dog must be hungry."

Frost looked about. "Don't have any food for a dog."

On the table was the remains of breakfast. A full plate of eggs, bacon, and toast. "You left your breakfast?"

Frost reddened. "Made it as usual, but with meeting you guys and everything, I just didn't feel like eating."

His sister raised the tin plate to her nose. "Still smells

okay. Should be fine for a dog." Holly put the plate down on the floor.

The dog hugged close by Noel's leg, seemed afraid to leave him. With a reassuring smile, Noel reached down and scratched his head. "Go for it, fella."

Claws clicking on the yellow linoleum floor, the rottweiler padded over and in two huge bites had swallowed the meal. "We'll need a name for him–he's got a collar? Frost reached down towards the dog's neck, apparently moving too fast. The Rottweiler bared sizable yellow teeth, growled menacingly. Going very slowly, Frost raised his hands flat up as he pulled back. "Okay. You want your space. I understand."

Moving more carefully, Noel walked over and knelt by the dog's side. "Easy fellow," he said softly. The dog's eyes were showing white edges; he still growling deeply, but he let Noel slowly touch and rub his neck, then scratch his ears. Slowly, the dog's long, uncropped tail started to thump hesitantly on the wood plank flooring, and Noel rubbed him from head to back. "No collar. No dog tags. If somebody had him, they weren't feeding him much."

Noel knelt there, closing his eyes. "I don't think the dog was with our guy in the backyard. The dog's terrified. I don't feel a home."

"Can you ask the dog what his name is?" whispered Holly.

Eyes open again, Noel shook his head, flushing with embarrassment. "I don't talk to animals." The huge Rottweiler reached over and licked his face. Noel let him, rubbing the massive head, as he continued, "I just kind of feel what they're thinking. Whether hurt or hungry or scared or wanting to get away. And they seem to understand I'm not here to eat or deliberately hurt them."

"But that dog obeys you?" Frost said.

"Animals don't obey me as such–they sometimes

seem to understand what I want. If it's not too complicated or too hard to do, they try to please me. They know I'm there for them." Noel stood up, lightly slapping the side of the dog, who reacted by wagging his tail again.

Frost shook his head in admiration. "You should get that Aquarium job! You'd be great with the animals they have there."

"How can he pet fish?" Holly asked

"They've got the belugas whales and sea lions, seals, penguins, parakeets. There's a good-sized stream and New England wildlife pond. How are you with painted turtles?" joked Frost.

"It would have been a great place to study," Noel finished regretfully. "But, as usual, I blew the interview."

A thoughtful look on his face, Frost pointed outside. "You guys go out and bring in your suitcases. I've got someone to call. The only phone here is in the front parlor."

The police were loading the body bag into a shiny new hearse when Holly and Noel came out. It made her feel sick, but she is searching she felt no spirit lingering. She longed to explore the property–was the swimming pool still there? The carriage house? Then she remembered that chilling corner at the back of the property. The old, stone mill. Two stories high burned out by the horror within. Would her mother's spirit still be there? Drawn Holly looked at the overgrown thicket of trees.

"Don't even think about it!" ordered Noel. Holly lowered her eyes to the ground and walked to her own hearse to unload. They got out Noel's suitcases, and then he started helping her with her stuff. There were five cardboard boxes, a suitcase, sleeping bag and the brown paper wrapped painting in the back of a 1956 Cadillac hearse, all her worldly possessions. She had more than Noel, who only had three suitcases and a laptop. Between the three of them, they didn't have much, but Holly turned around and looked at that high, white house. The paint was peeling, but still, they each owned one-third of a genuine mansion!

Back inside the kitchen, Frost was opening a can of hash.

"Dinner?" Noel asked.

"For the dog. We'll eat canned soup and eggs until we can go shopping. Which, if I'm buying, will not be until payday this Thursday."

Noel turned to Holly. "Can you make dinner for us."

"Sure!" Holly said. "B-but Aunt Maureen didn't like anyone else working in her kitchen, so all I can do microwave dinners and canned soup."

"We don't have a microwave," said Frost.

A hesitant Holly looked at the stove. "If you tell me what to do?"

"I'll make scrambled eggs for us tonight. N.C., can you cook?"

"Yes," he said.

"Well–we'll take turns teaching Holly," suggested Frost.

She was focusing on the dog. "What will we call him? Blackie? Lucky?"

"We're not keeping him," said Noel.

"How about a more manly name," mused Frost. "Charla-mange? Fur-ton?"

"Furton?" asked Holly.

"The Seaport Museum has built a working tourist boat, with a replica of Fulton's steam engine. So we could call him Robert Fur-ton?"

"You haven't outgrown bad puns?" Noel asked with a superior attitude.

"Aren't Rottweilers a Germanic breed–how about Thor?" Holly suggested.

Frost looked down at the dog. "You like 'Thor'?"

The dog looked from him to Noel. Noel nodded to the

dog and Thor thumped his tail.

"Thor it is!" Frost set down a full can of hash on a plate. The Rottweiler again finished the meal in two bites while Frost continued talking. "I called Herald Gustav. He's the captain that takes out the Aquarium's sea watch tours. He's also the relief captain of the seaport's paddlewheel rides on the steamboat."

"That sounds familiar," his brother said. "I think he was one of the three that interviewed me?"

"Yhep. He was. And you're right. You don't interview well. He said you kinda come across as stiff. Cold. A bit superior."

Noel hung his head. "Damn! I really wanted that job."

"Don't tell him that!" Holly protested.

"Hey," Frost continued, "It's feedback. N.C. needs it for his next interview there. You've got to come across as a team player."

"There isn't another interview," Noel said in a flat voice.

"I said they thought your interviewing technique was bad–not that they thought you were bad."

"They want to hire me?" started Noel hopefully.

"Not hire you, yet. With your background, you made the short list. You write a good application, but, unfortunately, there are three more candidates. All with roughly the same qualifications in the field as you, but two of the other guys have had some working experience at aquariums. One guy's already got his doctorate, going for a job that pays peanuts. Employment sucks around here."

"Working with Dr. Morjessky--I would have paid them, if I could have gotten it," Noel trailed off.

"You weren't ruled out," Frost continued. "Gustav said they phoned you to make an appointment when Dr. Morjessky can do the final interviewing. But you haven't gotten back to them yet?"

Blushing, Noel opened his suit jacket and reached for the case on his belt. Pulling out his cell phone. "I put it on 'silent' before the meeting, and I forgot to turn it back on."

"Call them," said Frost.

"Nobody will be there in the office this late," argued his brother.

"Leave a message!" said an exasperated Holly.

While Noel was on his cell phone, the landline was ringing outside the kitchen door. Frost's lips thinned. "That will be the newspapers. We don't want to talk to them."

Holly was looking to that closed door. It must lead to the main wing and rest of her house. Her grandmother's house. Where they had all once lived together as a family, Her mother, father, grandmother, Uncle Benjamin, Frosty, Noel and her. She wanted so to go walk in there. See if the rooms were still as she remembered them. Yet her feet felt glued to the kitchen floor.

As usual, Noel took the lead. "Where will we be sleeping?"

Frost thought about that. "Well, when I got older I took to sleeping here, in the housekeeper's room, in this kitchen wing. It's got a bathroom and large bedroom with a small wood stove. Come winter, the oil bills here are terrible. We keep it pretty cold and burn a lot of wood. But between the fireplace and stoves, it's okay in here. We shut off the water to most of the bathrooms, so the pipes don't freeze."

"Bathrooms–how many?" asked Noel.

"There are seven full bathrooms and two half baths."

"Nine in a house from the 1800's? That's a lot," said a surprised Noel.

"The back wing dates from pre-Revolutionary war. It's two stories. With three bedrooms upstairs, a small galley kitchen and parlor. Ben kept his office there. You guys would have to feed the wood stove to keep it warm on cold nights."

Holly frowned, trying to remember. "Didn't each of

the upstairs bedrooms have bathrooms?"

"Yhep. In the 1930's our great-grandmother, Julia Corey converted the house into The Captain Corey's Bed and Breakfast. Her daughter-in-law–our grandmother, Helen, kept running it as one until she died in 1986. Then her son, Uncle Benjamin, just closed it down.

Most of Holly's years here were a total blank. Just a feeling that horrible things had happened. Holly clenched her hand. "Ca-ca-can we see it?"

Frost shrugged and led the way. The door to the kitchen had a small round port-hole type window, and the door swung both ways for serving the dining room.

From it, Holly stepped into a seaport. Literally–an old whaling port was painted all over the room's walls, with amazing color and detail. A floor to ceiling mural of an early eighteen hundreds dock, with its windjammers and whalers and hand-carts of cargo. "That was painted by Warren Johns Thomas. We've got a painting of his at the Seaport Museum. The seaport's one is only 24" by 36," but it's valued at over $100,000."

"Could we sell this?" asked Noel eagerly.

"Naw. It's painted into the plaster. It'll crumble if you try to take the wall out.

Holly saw a long table that seated twelve. Beside it was a sideboard, elaborately carved with game-birds and leaves. There were also two built-in corner cabins filled with China. But moving ahead, Frost was already leading into a formal parlor, with its carved white marble fireplace and Victorian furniture. Holly saw a dusty, upright rosewood player piano on the worn oriental carpet. There was a jade inlaid oriental screen, was it once carried from Cathay in the hold of a Yankee clipper? More sea-themed paintings and some photographs. Was there one of their mother, Hester? Holly only had one picture. And nothing of their father. What did she remember about him? Daddy holding her hand on the beach, as Frosty and Noel ran ahead?

"That entrance back there leads to the suite Uncle Benjamin lived in. Let's see it."

When they entered, Holly saw it was like a good-sized house of its own. Frost said, "He died here–in that chair over there. Do you feel him?"

Holly stopped, closed her eyes in concentration. "No. He's gone on."

"That's what I felt too," confirmed Frost.

"We ought to get rid of that chair," said Noel walking through a small office and smaller kitchen and a large bathroom with a clawed tub. Climbing an old wooden staircase that did three sharp turns, they went to the second floor. A parlor landing and three small bedrooms. This house had lower ceilings, age wavy window glass, and dusty sheets over most of the furniture.

They went back downstairs and into the main house front parlor. "To your right, that's the door to the Library wing. That's got a full bath and was used as a rental in the Bed and Breakfast. It's got a recessed porch just to look cool in the front, and a real sitting porch on the south side end. The library also has a fireplace. Not as efficient as the wood stoves. One of you could take the back suite and the other the library?" Frost suggested.

By herself, Holly was walking to the front of the building. To the tall, two-story entrance hall she remembered so well. The floor with its inlaid compass rose medallion and keystone border in wood. The high side windows and glass fantail window over the great double doors that opened to the curved driveway from the road.

Red stained the view. Outside she could see the flashing lights from the police cars. Picturing the man's dead body laying in the lilac hedges, Holly averted her eyes from the windows to look around the foyer with its impossibly curved staircase.

As if in a trance, she started climbing it, more of those beautiful murals beside her. Here was pale blue-green sky with clouds and a view of land from out at sea followed the curved staircase upstairs. She rested her hand on the polished banister that her dad once held her to slide down, then released her into her laughing mother's loving arms.

Upstairs, more dust. Rooms to the right and behind the stairs, a small sitting area, that was decorated with 1940's deeply padded leather chairs. She looked in each of the bedrooms: the Rose suite with its sleigh bed; the gold room with its carved Chinese enclosed bed with hangings embroidered with birds of paradise; and the Greenroom with its ivy figured wallpaper in the front of the house.

There was one door she hadn't opened, just above the curved staircase landing. It wasn't original; it must have been added when the mansion was remodeled for the bed-and-breakfast. Taking a deep breath to center herself, Holly opened it. Behind the door, another staircase was calling to her. What was up there frightened her, but Holly had to ascend. The staircase was steep with uncarpeted wooden steps; she remembered starting to climb it as a child, then falling. Holly moved toward it. Some flash of memory. Being carried up? Her memory. Her mother's? She started upwards. A door at the top.

She opened it. Only an attic room really, with dirt and cobwebs everywhere, worse here than below. A musty smell from a room long closed. But also a faint sweet aroma, a familiar scent of spring nights, honeysuckle. Holly took a deep breath, but it was gone.

Holly was in a big room, that ran the entire length of the attic. Light still came from the lace-curtained windows overlooking the front drive. The opposite end held two doors; she'd have to look inside. To the sides, the ceiling walls slanted sharply up, along the roof lines. In the center stood a solid mahogany four poster bed that was stripped of hangings and linens with only a blue striped mattress remaining. Holly turned around. Against the wall, a Victorian bureau with a beveled-glass mirror. A dusty rose velvet-covered chair, with a small cherry writing desk in front of it. And in the center, an even steeper staircase, going almost straight up. Almost robotically, Holly walked to it. Muffled voices from below were calling to her. "Holly! The police want to talk to us."

But she just kept climbing up to the white light.

Chapter 4

Bright light assailed her. Its brilliance made her blink painfully, but slowly Holly opened her eyes. She was inside a huge, white wood cupola, windowed on all four sides. The staircase trap door opened to a platform only seven-foot square, set on high on the roof of the mansion. From the multi-paned windows, she could see 360 degrees, over the cedar shingled roof, above the lower trees, houses, and farmland. She could even make out the distant silver shining glimpses of the Atlantic's water horizon. When the trees lost their leaves, she might even see the seaport itself.

She scanned all around. At the edge of woods, she saw another shine of water through the trees. A small lake? Could she see the mill pond and its horrors from here? She'd asked Frost where it was, but he evaded answering. And Noel had forbidden her to go there. If she wanted to see where their mother died, she would have to go alone.

All around the four directions of the cupola, up two feet from the floor platform on four sides, were window seats, covered with faded, rose pink-velvet cushions. Holly moved closer to the glass and sat down, drawing her knees tightly up to her chin. Like she had done as a child. She had come up here with mommy, in the darkness. To sit, quietly waiting as the sky lightened the world below. Sitting with the clouds, to mentally float above all. To raise their arms high in appreciation for being given the gift of another day and to greet the sun joyously with upstretched hands. Honeysuckle seemed to flood the air.

Again those annoying muffled voices from below, tying her to the earth.

"Holly?" A worried Frost was calling out in the room below her.

Followed by an annoyed sounding Noel. "Where is she? Where do those stairs lead to?"

Those pestering voices are drawing closer, stealing her peace.

A blond head came up the center stairwell. Noel. "You okay?" He looked around. "That your perfume? It's awfully strong."

She had to tear her vision off the peaceful horizon and the river running to the endless sea.

When she didn't answer, he put more command into his voice. "The police want us downstairs. On the double!" Not looking back to see if she was following, he headed down the staircase.

In the bedroom, a frowning Frosty stood waiting by the small, white Franklin wood stove. "Incredible views up there," he said softly.

"I've seen them before," she said, looking about the dusty room. "Those two doors?"

"Big walk-in closet and storage. And a bathroom."

She moved to open the left door. A bathroom with a small sink, old-style toilet, and a tall-back, lion-claw tub, with a metal ring above it, but no shower curtain hanging from it. There was a high, round window over the tub.

"This will be my room," Holly said.

"Way up here? I'll have to turn the water back on. You'll have to carry the wood up for the stove because I'm not," he said as she followed him downstairs.

The police were in the front parlor. Two officers came over to Frost. "Sir, we'd like you to show us where you were standing when you found the body."

Holly started to follow them out the front door. A tall, sandy-haired police sergeant was moving to intersect her. "Excuse me, Miss. Could you just join me over there."

She blinked nervously about. Noel was gone, and Frost was disappearing. They must want them in different areas to interrogate them separately. So then they could compare their stories to ferret out lies. "D-d-do." The speech teacher had said to stop, take a breath but, "You-you think w-we killed him?" How could he possibly think that Frosty or Noel or that she could kill a man?

"Ma'am, please. Calm down. Why don't you sit on that couch? Nobody said anybody killed anyone. The coroner hasn't even seen him yet."

Obediently Holly sat. Her eyes filling with frustrated tears, this was to have been the greatest day in her life, and now she was being accused of murder.

He was looking concerned. "Miss–is there somewhere I could get you a drink of water?"

"The-the- kit-kit..." She just pointed through the dining room arch that leads to the kitchen door. He nodded and hurried away.

From inside came barking and growling, but the policeman disappeared. At least he had left her alone. She wasn't under arrest–yet.

Holly had a little more control when he came back, with a tin coffee mug filled with tepid water from the kitchen faucet. She didn't want a drink, but to put off questioning, Holly drank it all.

The policeman looked a bit kind. He was six foot four, with a craggy face, and he was dressed in a navy blue uniform with sergeant's stripes. She just had to calm down and talk to him, but Holly didn't want to put the mug down and make a wet ring on the polished end table next to her. Because of his height, he loomed above her 5' 9", but he had considerately stepped back a bit.

"Please, sit down," she offered.

He looked doubtfully at the small, empire chair near him, but he sat down, across from her.

"Y-you think he died naturally?" she asked hopefully.

He didn't actually answer, asking instead, "did you know him?"

Frost said he recognized him, but would Frost tell that

to the police? She shook her head and put the water down on the carpet near her foot. Hopefully, she wouldn't do her usual clumsy bit, forget and kick it. "We just came home a-a-and h-he..." She couldn't finish, twisting her hands in her lap.

The policeman tried again saying gently, "I'm Sgt. Travinski."

"Holly C-c-corey."

"The others?"

"My brothers."

"You all live here?"

Did she live here? Well, she didn't live anywhere else. "Y-yes. Sort of." Holly could hear Thor barking. Noel must have shut him up in the housekeeper's room off the kitchen. Where were the others? Were they under arrest? Would she be arrested? The policeman asked a few more questions, then to her relief, Noel walked back from the kitchen with another of the police, a woman who must have been taking his statement. The tall policeman stood up, telling her, "That will be all for now. Please call us if you think of anything else." He left a card that said 'Sgt. Paul Travinsky'.

The two police left as Frost was walking in the front door, saying, "We fed the dog, but never got around to making dinner for our selves."

Holly followed her brothers into the kitchen. The dog mournfully whimpered and scratched from the other side of Frost's bedroom door, until Noel opened it and began rubbing his neck. Holly was taking tin plates out of the cabinet. That's all they seemed to have here, tin or blue spotted enamel plates. Finding a drawer full of mixed flatware, she started setting the small kitchen table for three. "Did you tell the police you knew him?"

"Van Hom? I said he worked where I worked. That I didn't really know him, and I have no idea why he would be on this property."

She watched as Frost put a black iron frying pan on

the stove to heat and started breaking eggs into a bowl. Drawing closer, Holly saw something was wrong. "Those are bad!"

"What..."

"There's blood streaks in them!"

He smiled widely, as he is cracking more eggs into the milk. "City girl. These hens have a rooster in with them. These are fertilized eggs. I buy fresh eggs, vegetables and sometimes goat's milk from the Hoyt sisters. They have a farm down the road. I'll have to buy some more if we're all eating here."

"Do you think the Aquarium will hire him tomorrow?"

"N.C.?" Frost shrugged. "I don't know. Gustav said three of those other candidates have better credentials. And he's had no real experience."

Soon the eggs sizzled on the hot pan. The mouthwatering smell of food filled the air, and Holly realized how hungry she had become, but she still had to push. "If he could get a job there and I could get hired at the Seaport Museum with you, we could all keep living here together..."

Not meeting her eyes, Frost scraped at the eggs. "The seaport village is basically an outdoor exhibit. End of October the tourism drops off, and the museum cuts back on staff. And Holly, even with the three of us working, on low-level salaries we can't afford to keep this place up."

Chapter 5

The next day at the Mystic Aquarium, they had Noel's name on a list at the ticket booth. The ticket taking woman smiled at him. "You're a bit early. Just go to conference room B." He walked away on a cloud. His name was on the list! But so must those other three candidates and they had more experience than he. His new brother said he should act 'more friendly.' Be a team player. Uncle Kermit said Noel held himself too sloppily. That he spent too much time thinking before he answered. Noel was starting to sweat. Would he smell?

Taking a deep breath, he quickly headed into a cobblestone paved, open courtyard. A few families with young kids were walking about. Cafeteria and souvenir shop were to his left, beyond that, there was an exhibit on the Titanic that he saw yesterday. Then straight ahead was the imposing Aquarium itself. Signs promoting the seal show and jellyfish exhibits, and the glass windowed shark tank.

Farther on the right, was an open-roofed pavilion, with the stingray petting tanks. Noel had been reading about this facility for years, knowing it would be a fantastic place to continue his marine studies. Beyond the petting, tanks lead a gravel pathway to the Aquarium's twenty-seven acres. He'd love to take that nature trail, past the New England marshes and pond, to the seal and walrus habitats and then to the ice water ponds of the penguin's pavilion.

Noel checked his watch. He was forty-seven minutes early.

He looked to the farthest right, to the beluga exhibit! A mock rock-carved cement embankment with five-by-five foot plexiglass windows, set in alcoves at various levels. Beyond those walls spread an acre of Northwest water, with four fabulous, monstrous white shadows swimming through the blue.

As if drawn by irresistible magnetic attraction, Noel headed to a lower pit, to get a fish eye view of the pools. Totally fascinated, he watched as the four behemoth beluga whales dived, rolled and rubbed against each other. Well, three of them. The fourth just listlessly floated in the center. Not seeming to notice anything.

Noel knocked a knuckle against the window.

Immediately--from the left–almost touching the glass, a massive shape eyed him as it barreled past. Fifteen feet of streamline white torpedo, bulbous head, clubby fins and a sculptured, recurve tail. Four of these gorgeous creatures–all for him to study every day--if he could just convince someone he was worth hiring!

He should be finding conference room B, but still entranced, Noel watched the water ballet before him. Then found himself focusing more and more on that one hovering, just below the water line. Whales were mammals. He must breathe, but diving belugas could slow their metabolism and stay underwater for thirty minutes. But usually, they only stayed under three to eight minutes.

Yet this one in the center wasn't diving. He wasn't sleeping, and he seemed to be ignoring the others. Pressing his hand against the window port, Noel got a brief flicker of hopelessness. It seemed that it was coming from the center of the tank. He tried to focus his concentration, calling the creature to him, but the great white animal never looked in his direction.

Frost glanced down at his watch. Only five minutes to his interview! Where had the time gone? Where was conference room B? Last time he had been interviewed in the cafeteria, just to the left of the admission booth. Frost climbed the wide, poured cement steps to the cobblestone ground level plaza.

A tallish woman, with dirty-blonde hair, was mopping the floor. She was dressed in blue denim shirt and jeans, not the red shirt of a guide but obviously, she worked here. She'd know where the conference rooms were.

"Ma'am, do you know where conference room B is? And I think one of your belugas is sick."

She snapped back at him. "Don't you look where you're going? You've stepped right into that mess! You'll track that blue glop all over!"

Reddening, Noel started scraping blue slush off his shoe on the courtyard paving stones.

She mopped it up. "They let them buy slushies in the canteen, and the little kids dump them on the floor. Somebody will come along, slip and sue us." She looked up at him her brown eyes searching him. "So you need conference room B, and you think one of the belugas is sick?"

"I was early for an interview and, I was watching them. The one in the center is not swimming. Not paying attention."

With a disgusted twist of her lip, the fortyish woman stuffed the mop back in her bucket, "Follow me." She walked down the cement stairs to the lowest window. Not knowing where the conference room was Frost just followed. They both watched as the ghostly behemoths swam past the glass. Well, three did. The fourth listlessly floated underwater in the center.

Seeming annoyed the woman ignored Noel and headed back to the reception courtyard.

There another blue dressed custodian was coming over carrying a yellow, *'Danger Slippery'* sign."

"Charlie, where were you?"

"I had to clean up vomit in the I-Max," he quickly explained.

"Finish this up!" She turned back at Noel. "Why do you think Koda is sick?"

He looked at his watch again. "I've got this interview with Dr. Morjessky..."

"Who is running late today. Let's see to this sick whale first." She turned and started walking toward the covered, open pavilion attached to the Aquarium. Here tourists and their children were dipping their hands into low petting tanks getting a thrill at the touch of velvet skinned skates, starfish, and horseshoe crabs.

Noel followed as the cleaning lady unlocked a door labeled 'staff only' to the Northwestern exhibit. They went inside a dark room, then out into blinding sun reflecting off a white, stone modeled concrete pavement that surrounded all three interlocking arctic pools.

"Trisa!"

A tall young girl in the red Aquarium staff T-shirt and blue pants hurried over. "Dr. Morjessky?"

Great. Noel was going to have his interview and be dismissed right now!

The doctor was continuing in a disbelieving tone, "This gentleman thinks one of our belugas is sick."

"No," Trisa said, shaking her head but looking nervously back to the tank. "At least I don't think so." She ran her fingers through her short red curls.

Noel felt he had to defend himself. "The one in the middle. He's not swimming. Staying away from the others."

Dr. Morjessky looked at Noel. "They do that sometimes. They've got bad days, just like us. Days they want to swim slowly and be alone."

Noel shook his head, as he walked to the edge of the pool. If he could have worked here...

The older woman reached for a clipboard with lined sheets. Studying it, she said to Trisa, "Koda didn't eat anything at," she flipped some pages, "the last four feedings?"

"He misses his regular trainer."

"Why didn't you tell me? Will's been gone a week. We've got to do a blood draw on Koda. Call him over."

The girl looked helpless. "Koda won't come. If he's

not hungry—he won't come."

The older woman glared at her. "He is trained..."

"Koda would come for Will, but now that Will's gone, he's not obeying. He would only present his tail for Will."

Noel looked in the sunlight splashed water. "Maybe he is just depressed now that the trainer he was familiar with is gone." But that feeling of despair, hopelessness washed over Noel. It was more than just missing a familiar fish giver.

"Try to call him in," said Dr. Morjessky briskly, turning back to Tricia. "Use the subsonic whistle."

The girl blew four silent blasts on a silver whistle. They watched. Nothing cut the crystal clear water in the center where a white shadow stayed below. The other three monestrous white shapes glided past their platform always checking for a stray fish.

Yet the one they called Koda, stayed with his tail to them, then dived to the bottom of the pool, Dr. Morjessky was obviously displeased with Trisa's performance.

Noel looked at Trisa. "Can I try?"

He took the whistle from her and turned toward the water. Quickly wiping the whistle on his suit coat, he stood with his black sneakers overlapping the edge of concrete apron on the pool. Blew the silent whistle four times, as she had. Then concentrated on the white shadow down at the bottom. Calling him up. No movement

The two women waited.

Then the great animal surfaced, breathed with a rasping bellow, twisted and flapped slowly. Koda did a shallow dive, then seeming to cruise wearily came up toward the surface. There he started hesitantly to turn toward the platform where Noel stood, but thirty feet before them Koda twisted away. Swimmingly listlessly toward the center again.

Trisa helpfully suggested, "Maybe if you blew the whistle again?"

Noel shook his head. "Be quiet! Please."

They watched the huge mammal start to swim in a growing circle, coming closer, then swimming away. Noel closed his eyes to concentrate more, trying to draw Koda to him.

Behind him, Dr. Morjessky quietly ordered, "Tricia, get a blood pack for me." The girl quickly moved to get something out of a built-in cabinet. In a moment Dr. Morjessky was pulling on surgeon's gloves, as she moved to Noel's side. Speaking in a very low tone, she said, "We need him to swim over and present his tail so I can get blood."

"He won't do it," Trisa said loudly.

"Quiet!" Dr. Morjessky glared at her. To Noel, she said, "If I can get the needle into his side we can take it there."

Seeming to ignore both of them Noel had knelt down and put his hand slowly into the cold water.

"He's not as tame as the others–with those teeth he might bite," warned Trisa.

At a distance, Koda raised his head out of the water. Seeming to watch them. Then he slowly sank beneath the wavelets to swim slowly away.

"We lost him?" Dr. Morjessky breathed.

"Not yet," said Noel. He dragged his hand back and forth in the water and concentrated harder. Willing Koda to come to him.

The massive creature raised his head and seemed to look in Noel's direction; then the white whale only slowly sank beneath the surface.

Chapter 6

In the morning, Noel hadn't wanted the hearse anywhere near the Aquarium, so Holly let him off in the parking lot of the Olde Shopping Village. If she wasn't in the lot later, he was to call her at home after his interview, for her to come back and pick him up there. Noel had no idea of how long it would take. Should she just wait? But then only he had a cell phone.

Not being able to make up her mind, Holly stayed in the parking lot. Then she thought of another thing she could do. The newspaper hadn't any jobs for her, but she walked out of the Olde Village parking lot and across its wandering brick pathways to the main road. There she crossed the street to the Mystic motel.

When she walked into the office, Alice looked up with a friendly smile. "Frost's new sister, Holly, isn't it? I heard you guys found Rolf's body in your backyard?" Alice was looking at her if she expected to learn more about the discovery,

"You knew him?"

"He's been renting a room here. The police have sealed it off. Tell me I can't rent it until they release it. I can't run a motel like that!"

Holly started. "Y–y–you said-said your maid was sick?"

"Dorrie had a gallstone removed, and now she's got an infection."

"Y–y-you need..."

"Need a maid?" Alice finished. "Well, I've been putting a note on the lobby door while I ran upstairs to clean. It's a real pain, but the temporary I hired for this morning showed up drunk. Yes, I could use someone-but only until Dorrie gets back. That will might be a week or so. Maybe three?"

"Fine," said Holly.

Alice sounded a bit doubtful. "Have you cleaned motel rooms before?"

What job hadn't Holly done to keep going? "Yes. Hotel. Wes-westin in Long Beach."

"Can you start at seven thirty tomorrow? I set up the complimentary breakfast, but then Dorrie would clean up afterward. Most of the business people will check out early. You should be done by two."

Holly nodded, as Alice handed her a job application to fill out.

After filling that out, she walked back to the hearse. Noel wasn't there. If they were still interviewing him, that was good news. With a maid's job, even only a temporary one, she would have some money to put her share into Witch house, and if she had to wait for Noel, it would give her some time to shop in the village.

Crossing the street, Holly headed back into the Olde Village. Most of the stores were shingled with weather grayed wood. She saw the store with Maine sweaters had one side covered with white and red wooden lobster buoys. Outside the kite maker's shop was a colorful garden of cloth dragons, swirling moons, and bright triangles. It wasn't October, but the costume store already had Halloween masks for Frankenstein, pirates, and zombies.

She thought of the cold, murdered body lying beside their back pathway at home. There must be a florist here where she could get some cleansing sage or a candle shop, where she could get a protective white one? Passing the brick oven pizza restaurant, she saw the wooden sign for the Rainbow Realm, with its Wiccan books and symbols in the window. They must have something that would help her!

Walking inside was like entering a young witch's dream world. Tables of silk scarves, rose carnelian beads, incense burners, and delicate resin fairies unfolding their diaphanous wings. Tall bookcases lined the walls and, entranced; Holly ran her finger over some. Books on sacred oils, brewing spells, aromatherapy, the Egyptian Book of the Dead and the magical properties of gemstones.

In the back of the jewelry counter, a petite woman was ringing up a long line of senior citizens. Her dark-bronze hair was smoothly chisel cut, and her eyebrows seemed to tilt up just a bit. Rapidly tapping sales into the computer, the storekeeper made eye contact with Holly and gave her a wide, welcoming smile. Finally, the line of shoppers left, and the saleswoman looked back to Holly. "Seniors' tour–they've all got to get back to the bus on time. Is there something I can help you find?"

"Just looking." Holly moved to study the glass-enclosed jewelry counter. Silver pentagrams, crystal drop pendants, Navajo turquoise squash blossom necklaces, and a wicked looking, double-bladed athame.

Athames were the ritual knives of witches. Did Holly's mother kill herself with a knife like this?

The shopkeeper cocked her head. "Are you alright, dear?" With her perfect skin, the woman only wore lipstick and thick kohl outlining her eyes. "I'm Skye Rainbow. This is my shop."

"H-H-Holly. Holly Corey."

"Tourist?"

"No, I-I-I lived here years ago. Just moved back."

"Yes," the proprietor said softly. "Corey. That's an old family name around here."

"Did you know of my parents, Hester and Gault Corey?"

The woman looked at her curiously. "I didn't think there any more Coreys were living at Witch house?"

Holly decided to let that pass. She was now looking among the small bottles of essences, oils, and the sacred candles. "We had a tragedy on our property. A death."

Skye held out a hand near Holly. "Not just a death–I sense something more. Something terribly wrong. Something evil. The papers said someone had been killed, murdered?"

"Is there something that w-w-would…"

"Return your environment to the harmony you seek? Violence is always a serious disruption of the natural flow of energy. But there are ways to restore accord."

The storekeeper slipped out from behind her counter. She wore a high necked, flowing silk blouse in tie-dyed shades of deep purple to pink violet. Holly followed as Skye moved to her counters. "You'll need a wand of sage. Some lemon juice. Some salt–sea salt is best. Sprinkle somewhere the body lay. Light a white–no a scarlet candle. Pray to the great Horned One to remove all vestiges of negative forces. Do you know how to do a cleansing ceremony?"

Holly shook her head, so Skye spent the next hour explaining it to her.

Much later, Holly was out of there with a bag of sage, peppermint oil, and a scarlet candle. God, she had to stop spending money like this.

It must be late, but she didn't see Noel. That should mean his job interview was going well or had she missed him and he had already started to walk home? He'd be angry with her.

Should she stay here in the Olde Village–or go home and wait for his call?

After standing there for a time, she drove home. There was a police Tahoe parked in the driveway, with that tall, sandy-haired sergeant typing in a report on his computer. Seeing her pull in, he got out.

She noted how good he looked in that trim, dark-blue uniform with his long legs and wide shoulders. Holly parked and walked over to him.

He was speaking to her. "The victim's name was Rolf Van Hom."

"I-I know. He worked at the Seaport."

He looked at her sharply. "So you know Van Holm? You said yesterday you didn't recognize him?"

She started flushing badly. Had Frost admitted he knew him? She didn't want to undercut her brother. "A-A-Alice told me."

"Alice?"

"At the m-motel. The Mystic."

"You know Alice Seymour?"

She didn't want to tell him she was going to be a motel maid, but, "I-I'm going to work for her."

"Replacing Dorrie?"

"T-temporarily. Alice said the police had sealed off Rolf's room?"

"Aaup. Alice knows everything, about everybody. But you still say you don't know the victim?" He was poised to write her answer down.

"N–n–o. I d-d-." She shook her head. Feeling like a liar, made her shuttering worse. Holly just shook her head, and he wrote something down on his pad. "V-v-victim?" she started.

"Van Holm was shot in the back. At close range." He said that while closely watching her reaction.

"Then he was m-murdered?" She'd seen blood on his shirt, but she still wondered if it was some sort of accident. Van Holm's spirit was not there lingering, like someone who did not believe he was suddenly dead.

"You still say you didn't know him?"

"N-no-no. I mean...yes, I didn't know him." She shook her head. Why did he think she would know him?

"He apparently was dating Miranda Talmadge?" The sergeant stopped again, still watching her closely.

"Mir-miranda?"

"You don't know her?" The sergeant was still watching her. "She also works as a guide at the Seaport

Museum with your brother. Rolf Van Holm was the ticket taker there."

"He did?"

"Hasn't your brother been dating Miranda Talmadge?"

"I don't know."

"Frost never left, mentioning he was taking Miranda to the movies? Or brought her home for dinner?"

"Until yesterday, I-I-I haven't seen my brothers since I was five years old."

He looked at her, then like a good cop, the sergeant immediately blinked past his surprise. "You hadn't seen them for seventeen years?"

"When my mother...su-su-su... died we were separated. Frost stayed here with our uncle; I went to California with our aunt and Noel was given to a cousin, a military man. They went overseas. Moved a lot."

"Noel?"

"N.C."

"That's Noel Corey? So you're Holly, Frost, and Noel?" He sounded a little like he just realized a joke had been played on him.

"We're triplets b-born on December 25th. All our middle names are 'Christmas' too." She tried to laugh. It fell flat. Those intense blue eyes stared at her, coolly evaluating. It made her feel like she looked guilty. "It's on my license if you want to see." She pulled it out of her handbag and showed it to him.

Sgt. Travinski took it from her and studied it for a while. "Your license and hearse are still listed at a California address. If you're living here now, Connecticut state law requires that after thirty days you must change your driver license and your vehicular registration must be updated after sixty days of residence."

"I–we may be selling this house. Then I don't know where I'm going."

He smiled, sounding less officious. "Just visiting's okay." Then he really stopped sounding like a cop and seemed to look at her as a woman. "Of course, Mystic's a real nice place. If you like us, you could stay."

She found herself giving a revealing blush when he said '*if you like us.*'

He was continuing back to business. "I'd like to talk to your brothers again?"

So that was the sum of his interest in her? Just another murder suspect to be questioned? "N.C. was going to call me from the Aquarium to pick him up. Of course, I haven't been here answering the phone. And Frost said after work; he'd bike back." She looked about. "I was supposed to pick up some eggs at a farm stand somewhere around here." She looked vaguely about.

"The Hoyt sisters. Down that road, take the first right on to Chestnut road. Number 185's on the mailbox." He put his book away. "I'll drop by later to speak to your brothers."

Sargent Travinski must work out. That body looked hard, and that rear end looked good. Holly watched him go, just savoring the long-legged, good looks of the man. What could she ever do to make him stay with her for a bit of time? Short of killing someone herself?

Chapter 7

No message from Noel on the phone. Thor was sniffing at her and wagging his tail hopefully. They needed food in the mansion. Witch house was on ten mostly wooded acres, so they didn't see many neighbors. She got back into the hearse and headed right on the Stone road, finally passing some newer houses closer together, and then open farmland again. She turned on to Chestnut Road.

The Hoyt sisters seemed to have quite a few more acres on both sides of the road. Their pastures spread out around their two-story wood frame house. An open, covered vegetable stand stood out front, with tomatoes, corn, and pumpkins--orange and bumpy red pumpkins. All vegetable prices were scraped in chalk on slate. Holly walked past the stand and saw an unlocked box with a note on top, '*Leave the money for vegetables inside. Knock on door for milk or eggs'*.

Holly opened the box out curiosity. There was cash in it, trusting people. She could see the remains of truck gardens in the back and an old style carriage house. Fancier than the Hoyt's two-story white clapboard farmhouse. Out front chickens were pecking at the grass. Holly walked up to the wide, coffin door and knocked. It was opened almost immediately as if someone was expecting her.

"I'm Holly Corey. I was wondering if I could get two dozen eggs?"

"Come in." A tall, fortyish looking woman with glossy chestnut hair called out to someone inside, "Sarah, Frost's sister is here." She spoke in a formal tone, not friendly but certainly not hostile.

Outside, the house could have passed for a white boarded farmstead from the 1830's. But once past the small, enclosed entry hall, the illusion of the 1800's was gone. The old house had been totally gutted, with the first floor being reconfigured into a wide open, old beamed floor plan. The front area was sparsely dotted with walnut and chrome tubed furniture, padded with nabbed, moss-green silk cushions.

In the nearly open floor, three fieldstone fireplaces still rose upwards. Besides the one that once heated this front room, then there were two other fireplaces: a huge walk-in one in the back area that remained the kitchen; and a smaller fireplace to one side that must have been in a bedroom in the original house. To the left in the back was what looked like a door to a bathroom or pantry that was still walled off, but the rest of the first floor was open with wide planked floors that were highly polished. She also noted the outer walls were filled with floor to ceiling bookcases, packed tightly with hundreds, maybe thousands of hardbound books and paperbacks.

Holly found herself focusing on the beauty of the six foot long, highly polished, burled cedar coffee table in front of the couch. There were two stark colonial staircases that rose from the front and back, still what dominated that room was a massive wooden floor loom, five foot high by seven foot long. Sitting on its bench was another fortyish looking woman, presumably the other Hoyt sister. She had strawberry blonde hair and was weaving a roll of green fabric over sixty inches in width.

The weaver smiled at her. "Holly, Frost told us you and your brother were coming home. I'm Sarah, and that's my sister, Abby."

"We heard you found someone dead on your property?" Abby asked thawing a bit.

Sarah shook her head as she operated the long foot pedals of her loom. "How dreadful. To have something like that happen near your home. Blood and smells of evil linger so."

"I went to the Rainbow Realm. Skye told me to sprinkle lemon juice, salt and hold a smoking stick of sage over it lit by a red candle to cleanse the site."

Something she said seemed to unsettle the Hoyt sisters. The smiles on their faces stayed the same, but for a brief minute, Holly detected something else–fear? hostility?-- Behind those frozen smiles. Then it was gone as if it had never been there.

"Did she recognize you, dear?" Sarah asked too casually. "The Goldsteins have been an old family around here. In Revolutionary times, they were quite wealthy Tories, who switched sides just in time. They've been scrambling for other people's money ever since."

An aloof Abby just stared at Holly.

"Goldstein?" Holly asked.

Sarah smiled brightly. "She was Marium Goldstein before she started styling herself 'Skye Rainbow.' Didn't you find that name highly unusual? Of course, perfect for the operator of a 'New Age' store." Her tone held a little contempt.

"I thought she might be Indian or her parents lived in a hippie commune," Holly responded.

"Not quite," said Abby frostily. "When the seaport was the home to the whaling ships, the Goldstein family was very wealthy."

"Socially prominent," Sarah corrected.

"That was in the 1830s?" Holly asked.

Abby exchanged a look with her sister. "Sarah is the local historian. She studies things like this."

"Then you must have known my parents, Hester and Gault Corey?"

A brief silence. The Sarah said carefully, "Not very well." She depressed two treadles and began running the shuttle through the loom's myriad strings.

Abby moved toward the open kitchen with its back door. "If you'll follow me, we keep the eggs and milk in the spring house. Now did you bring some herbs? Frost usually cuts some fresh thyme and basil for us."

"Do you give us a discount on the eggs for the herbs?" Holly asked.

Abby looked to Sarah in a surprised fashion.

Sarah looked down and said, "Uh, no. Frost just gave them to us. They grow wild about the mansion grounds." She looked up at Holly. "But I guess we could give you a dozen or so eggs for free for what we've gotten in the past." She looked at her sister. "That's only fair."

Abby raised an eyebrow but just turned a smiling face to Holly. "It has been unseasonably warm for September, but the temperatures are going to drop soon. We'll be having our first frost, probably by Friday?"

"How do you know?" Holly wondered.

Again Sarah looked to her lofty sister, Abby just quickly returned, *"The Farmer's Almanac.* They're often quite accurate. You can save your herbs by cutting them tomorrow morning. Tie them with string at the base of the stems, then hang them upside down in a dry cellar or from the rafters in that big kitchen of yours."

Sarah finished firmly, "But she won't know which plants in her yard are herbs."

"Actually–I do," said Holly. "I've always loved herbs. My aunt used to let me grow pots in the bay window. Thyme. Basil. I was always interested in plants that have aromas. The ones you can cook with or use as a healing tea..."

Softening a bit, Abby looked down at her. "You mother loved herbs. Hester could grow anything. I remember once a friend of hers had dried pussy willow branches on her piano..."

Sarah explained, "instead of palms, Russian Orthodox churches hand out pussy willow branches to commemorated Jesus's triumphant arrival into Jerusalem."

Her sister immediately picked up. "For a year those sticks were kept dead and dry in a vase in front of Tatiana's icons. When she got her new branches, your mother took the old sticks and just put them in water. They sprouted. When they got leaves, Hester planted them outside."

"They grew?"

"Oh, yes. They are still growing wild down by that little stream on your property. Your mother planted most of what is growing around the mansion today," called out Sarah from her loom.

Abby was already going out the back door, and reluctantly Holly followed. She was sure these women could tell her more about her mother. And why she died. She'd have to let the sisters get to know her better, but would she have time before the mansion was sold?

The spring house was behind the main house, a fieldstone structure that was dug low into the ground. Holly followed Abby down stone the steps, into the earth smelling structure. A heavy wood door opened to a stone room, with a cold spring bubbling inside a square of stone. It was lit from the weak light of high, narrow windows at ground level. Collecting eggs from two wire baskets, Abby filled two cardboard containers for her.

How much did these two sisters know of her mother? Holly asked, "Have you been inside the mansion?"

Before Abby could answer, Holly heard a high scream for help!

She turned racing out of the spring house, as Abby called after her, "Dear–it's not what you think."

Holly ran up the worn stone steps. Another high scream for help. She looked about and saw the screamer. An emerald green peacock, spreading his massive blue-eyed tail as he again screamed a distorted '*help.*'

Abby had come up to behind her. "That's Saladin. He's so vocal, and he does sound a bit like a woman screaming. We have a small flock of peacocks as pets."

In the front of the house, Holly gave Abby money for a basket of tomatoes, for the eggs Abby had given her credit for the herbs. Neither Abby or Sarah had said anything about her driving a hearse; they just seemed to accept the fact.

As she pulled out, Holly glanced up at the porch. A grim mouthed folded armed Abby stood watching her leave, like a guardian sentinel. And the curtain in the window closest to the door moved as if Sarah was watching too.

She'd have to stop home and put the eggs in the fridge; then she'd drive down to pick up Noel. Yet something was bothering Holly, nagging at her. Something was wrong, but what was making her so uneasy? Then she realized what it was; she couldn't read the sisters! Not a thought, not an aura, or not even a flash of shared feeling. And come to think about it, Holly had not been able to read that Wiccan shopkeeper Skye Rainbow either.

Was she losing her abilities? Or were the three of them deliberately blocking her?

Chapter 8

What did the Hoyt sisters know of her mother? Or her father? Did they know where he was living? Or if he is still alive? Opening the kitchen door, Holly heard Thor's deep, resounded barks. Would anybody be burglarizing them? When she opened the back door, Thor pushed past her running to find a bush to pee on. Then he started barking and crouching for her to come play with him. He was a big puppy. When she didn't join the game, he trotted away to circle the yard, sniffing bushes.

Holly headed through the pantry to stuff the two egg cartons into the refrigerator. Would the dog eat more eggs? Should she buy any food for him? Could she spare the money to buy food for him? Soon she wouldn't be able to buy food for herself. Well, for a time she had that temporary job at the motel.

She checked the phone messaging. No call from Noel.

More waiting, but alone she could walk around the house without her brothers monitoring her reactions. Holly walked through rooms, not finding much she really recognized, but still not feeling up to opening cabinets and closets, trying to peek into the past. The mansion looked like it had been remodeled many times. Still, some of the plumbing dated from the nineteen hundreds, and Noel had pointed out the sections still containing lead pipes. She walked back downstairs to the main parlor. Everything smelled of dust. She should open the windows and clean, but outside the sun shined so brightly.

Sound. Phone ringing. Holly ran to pick it up. "Noel? Did you get the job?"

Even more precise and clipped than usual, Noel answered carefully, "My interview is finished. They've offered to let me see the marine mammal show while I'm here. Can you pick me up in an hour and a half at the usual place?"

"But you don't know if you've got the job?"

"I will talk to you later." He said and then hung up.

Thor was still outside. She could leave him there until they got back–but what if it rained? Or if he ran off? Holly should get him inside before she left to pick up Noel. She went to the pantry door. "Thor. Thor! Here boy. Come on."

Perversely the Rottweiler ran a little toward her, then retreated in the bushes wanting to play his endless chase game. Annoyed Holly walked down the steps toward the bushes. As she did, she saw something red flashing in the sunlight behind some leaves. She reached down, pushed back a branch and saw a small red flannel bag had been tied by its pull cord to another branch. The bag was only three inches by two, filled with something soft. She untangled it. The flannel looked new, so it hadn't been out in the rain obviously. Holly smelled something spicy and musky. But she had to pick up Noel, and the dog was still running free. She stuffed the bag into her jacket pocket.

She should just leave Thor outside, and maybe he'd go back to his owner? Noel would be happier, and they wouldn't have the expense of feeding him. Still, Holly went back in the kitchen and looked quickly into the fridge. Not much. Some peanut butter. Some cheddar. Bacon. She dug off two sticky strips of bacon and headed for the door. "Thor?"

His black, tan muzzled head is peeking out the wild growing shrubbery, nose up, smelling the meat. Hesitating. Then Thor was bounding for the back door. Like an accomplished matador, Holly skillfully held the bacon in front of her, then neatly stepped to the side as the drooling Rottweiler charged up the steps and into the house. She tossed the bacon toward the kitchen floor as she slipped out, closing the door on her captive to the howls of his bitter betrayal.

Driving the hearse, she turned on to Stone Road but didn't get far. The front lawn ahead was spread with bikes, bureaus, and tables full of a jumble. She could never pass a yard sale. Holly pulled on to the grass and parked. Piles of worn toys, end tables and children's clothes, a toboggan, coffee grinder, birdcage and boxes of books. Holly dug in the book box: dreamy Hawaiian wildernesses; a book of dog photos; one of healing with herbs remedies. That Holly carefully thumbed through. Only fifty cents. She'd get that. As she stood by the woman's card table to pay she looked down and saw a box of cream colored china, old-fashionedly painted with small, red-stemmed bluebells and yellow buttercups. "Is that a full set?" she asked the woman.

"There are two boxes. It was my grandmother's. Almost complete service for sixteen, with hostess dishes and it's only twenty-five dollars." Going through the boxes, Holly could see they had a chip or two, but most were okay. She didn't have a long-term job and, she hadn't even started working at the motel, and most of her money was gone...but all the kitchen plates in Witch House were of chipped, blue-enameled tin, with matching mugs. Only men could live like that. "Would you take less?"

With the two boxes of plates in the back of the hearse, she pulled into the Olde Village parking lot. A blue-suited Noel was there, pacing restlessly, yet she saw some hope in his happy, light green aura! "Did they hire you?" she asked eagerly.

"Holly, I got to go in the staff entrance, walk out on the beluga pool platform. See all of them swimming by!"

"The job?"

To her frustration, he still didn't answer her question, only continuing, "One was sick, Koda. He wasn't swimming. Felt–depressed. Hopeless. Dr. Morjessky told the girl to call him in. They used the sonic whistle. He didn't come, so I put my hands in the water and called him with my mind."

"He answered you?"

Noel shrugged, "Maybe--I don't know." It was a

warm day, and he started pulling off his suit jacket. "But finally the whale swam over to the edge of the pool and swam right to me. Dr. Morjessky got a blood sample from his tail. And Koda took a fish from me–well, he spit it out." Noel smelled his fingers. "Gotta wash my hands. Trisa–she works there--gave me a tour of the whole Aquarium."

"They have to give you the job after that!"

His aura darkened. "No. They're still interviewing those other three. Dr. Morjessky said two of them have aquarium experience and one's got his doctorate. She said they would call."

"Give me your watch," she said.

"You need the time?" He checked it. "It's one p.m."

"I need your watch!" She repeated firmly. "Picture Dr. Morjessky, and then give me your watch."

He didn't hand it over, but he didn't resist as she pulled his watch off, only saying, "I'll probably have to get a new one soon. It's weird, watches only last three months on my wrist, then they die."

Holly decided not to explain about a psychic's energy radiation and just placed the watch between her hands. The metal links of its expanding band were warmed from his wrist. Closing her eyes tightly to shut out the distraction of the parking lot and distant tourist voices, she concentrated. She visualized Noel in a red shirt, standing at the edge of a pool, speaking. Speaking to whom? To the microphone around his neck and a distant crowd, as long, white shapes swam to him. Noel is tossing them fish from the white cooler at his feet as he explained something to the crowd. "What color are the uniforms the Aquarium people wear?" she asked.

"Red t-shirts, with a seal on the pocket, embroidered in black. Sometimes with blue pants."

"Yes," she stated confidently, "N.C., you will work for the Aquarium. I see it."

"They are giving me the job now?" he asked

incredulously.

Now Holly hesitated. "M-maybe." She hesitated. "You will work there–I can't tell you when. Time is strange in visions. Do you get visions?"

"No!"

Which meant even if he did see visions like she did, Noel would never admit it. Holly took a deep breath. It was always so hard to explain, "I see something. A vision. A picture like a moving photograph. It can be next week–or years from now. So I see you with the belugas here. Maybe you'll get this job, or maybe when you get your doctorate, you could come back and get Dr. Morjessky's job," she finished hopefully.

He looked away.

"Noel, my visions are usually correct. I may misinterpret what they are saying sometimes, especially about time frames, but I saw you in a red shirt, standing before a pool, and feeding white whales. You will be working there–or somewhere with belugas, which has red uniform shirts."

"Sometime? Somewhere? Great!" he said in a disgusted voice, still looking away from her.

She hated to see him so discouraged. "Noel, it's close to closing time. Let's go over to the seaport museum and see if we can give Frosty a ride."

He got into the front seat beside her and disagreeably said, "Don't call him 'Frosty'–that's babyish. And call me N.C.!"

Chapter 9

When they stopped, Noel got out of the hearse with her, but he just walked a bit away from it and stayed in the seaport parking lot while she went inside. A guard pointed the way to the employees' locker rooms. She soon saw Frost in front of the building, but his total attention was focused on a yellow-calico gowned woman before him. In that 1800's costume she obviously worked at the Seaport Museum, and just as obviously Frost was drowning in her eyes.

Holly stood watching. Frosty smiled and blushed and stared intently at her. The girl with long black hair smiled at him, but she also gave shooting glances to every male that passed. Finally, Holly walked up to them.

The girl's eyes pulled back from a tall, older man and when seeing Holly, she moved to slip her arm possessively in Frost's. "Hello," the woman said smiling cloying. "And who are you?"

Closer, Holly could see the meticulously applied make-up and the fine lines about the eyes. No, she wasn't a teenager or a twenty-year-old she acted like, and her body language affirmed that Frost was her property. Just as Holly assumed she would lay claim to any male within five feet of her."H-holly Corey." Why did she have to stammer in front of this woman?

"Corey?" The woman turned to look questioningly at Frost.

Without looking in Holly's direction, he said carelessly, "It's only my sister."

The woman pulled closer to Frost saying smugly, "I'm Miranda Talmadge. Frost must have spoken about me."

Holly nodded. "I heard you were dating the man who was killed, Rolf Van Hom?"

The smug smile on Miranda's face hardened, as she turned on Frost. "You told her that?"

Shocked he looked at Holly, then back to Miranda. "No! No, I didn't."

"Actually the police told me," Holly said, watching Miranda closely, "How well did you know Rolf?"

"Not well at all." Miranda had taken her hand out of Frost's arm and squared off before Holly. "He just worked here! I don't know why the police questioned me. All of us have gone out to lunch or dinner, as I have with Frost. That isn't dating." And she looked back appealingly to Holly's brother. "I must have been with Frost when Rolf was killed."

Frost looked about to say yes, when Holly intervened, "no you weren't. That day Frost was leading tours here at the Seaport. When he wasn't here, he was with me and his brother, N.C., so you'll need someone else for your alibi."

"She doesn't need an alibi! Nobody does," Frost protested.

Miranda just glared at Holly. After the unreadableness of Skye, Abby, and Sarah, Miranda's vibrations were an open book, written in large type. Every word the brunette had just said was a lie! She had been close to Rolf, closer to him than she was with Frost. Rolf and Miranda were partners in something, what Holly didn't know. The worse thing from Holly's standpoint was that Miranda merely saw Frost as nothing more than
a free evening out.

Restlessly Miranda was looking across the short grass square, toward a tallish man. "Excuse me; there is someone I must talk to."

As they walked back to the parking lot, Holly said, "You didn't ask if N.C. got the job?"

"I already know. If he had gotten the job, I would have sensed soaring happiness. I didn't. Still, I don't feel that total despair that he had yesterday. They probably said they would call. No news is always good news." Frost finished optimistically.

For dinner, Holly found her grandmother's dog-eared, Betty Crocker cookbook and planned delicate Crepe Suzettes. But one of the cans she thought was chunk chicken turned out to be tuna, and the batter mix thickened. When she tried to pour the bowl into the crepe pan, it came out more like thick pancakes. She couldn't wrap any of them around the filling.

While she was mixing mayo into the chicken-tuna filling, one of the pancakes started to burn. Smelling the smoke Frost and Noel came in. Practically Noel pointed out, "We can eat just the canned chicken filling."

As Frost asked, "Is that chicken? It smells kinda fishy?"

"Do you have Triple Sec?" Holly asked.

"What?"

"An orange cordial for the flaming sauce," she explained, peering at the book.

"Will a Budweiser do?" Frost suggested. "We got three beers left in the pantry."

"No," said Noel. "She needs a high-alcoholic brandy. Heated."

Holly looked at the mess. Frost picked up a platter to carry into the dining room. "C'mon. We eat what's here. The dog can have the leftovers."

She had decorated the dining room table beautifully, with a gold brocade cloth, and she washed up some of that newly bought china, leaving the rest in the box. And for the silver candlesticks, Holly had found dark red candles. As she reached out to light them, Holly started brightly. "I got a job today..."

"Where?" Frost asked.

"At the Mystic Motel."

"Manning the check-in desk?" Noel asked hopefully.

"N-no." Holly studied the plate before her. She had forgotten to cook the frozen peas to mix in the chicken-tuna salad. "Cleaning rooms." She looked her brothers apologetically. "I've done that before."

"Good for you!" said Frost proudly.

Noel said nothing more and looked down at his plate in an ashamed fashion.

"It-it's only until the regular maid returns," Holly apologized.

Frost nodded. "Well, you work hard for Alice and word will get around. And I got another job for both of you."

"Where?" Holly asked.

"The seaport is going to make a big thing about christening that Polynesian outrigger we've been hollowing out. They have a festival. They're gonna need extra guides for the day, and are asking for volunteers to dress up. They provide the garb."

"Unpaid volunteers? That's not a job," shot back Noel.

"Well, you'll get into see the museum, and you'll get a free lunch at the cafeteria."

"It'll be fun!" said Holly. "As soon as I'll finish my rooms, I'll be there."

"Then you can see my tobacco display," finished Frost proudly.

Holly looked at her other brother, filled with happiness. "Please N.C., we'll all be together."

"I'll think about it," said Noel. "But I'll need a real job soon–or I'll have to move on. When do you think we can sell this house?"

"We could wait awhile, couldn't we? Live here together." Holly looked from one to the other.

Both evaded her eyes, but finally, Frost said, "When Uncle Ben died that ended his pensions. Not that there was that much. Nothing to leave, but the house. To keep this house running, you have to pay for electricity, phone. We have to pump out the septic tank once in awhile and pray the well doesn't go dry. We've got oil heat–heating this white elephant, that's expensive! We just warm sections of it in the winter..." he trailed off sadly, seeing her face.

"How much do the taxes cost?" asked Noel. "And the outside needs a paint job."

Frost shrugged. "I don't even know what the taxes are; Ben took care of that."

"You'll have to find out," said Noel. "Gather all the bills. We'll have to set up a spreadsheet on my laptop."

Holly persisted, "b-b-but if all three of us got jobs, we could keep the mansion and live here?"

Frost said nothing, so it was left to Noel to destroy her happy dream. "If I get the job at the Aquarium, I'll need most of my salary to start paying off my college debt. I've got to try and get current on my loans, or I won't be allowed to go for my doctorate."

Holly still argued, "whether we sell or not–the porch boards need to be repaired. The rooms have to be cleaned up, and some of them painted. The windows need washing. If you want to get the best price, we have to clean up."

Frost looked to Noel, who looked at her. "Well, you're the woman. It's woman's job to clean up."

"Oh–no!" She might be shy, might prefer to withdraw than fight, but she wasn't putting up with that! "This mansion is a Corey **family** job!"

Frost found two buckets, a rag mop, and two brooms and a vacuum cleaner that looked like it came from the dark ages. Holly ripped up a rotting sheet into dust wipes, as Noel gathered the garbage cans. Holly wanted to just search through the mansion, but Noel ordered that they start cleaning in the public rooms so that they could get a real estate agent in. "One who appraises for free."

Holly started damp wiping the furniture, feeling down, knowing that the more work she got done, the sooner the house would sell and they would be parted. A fat spider ran across the desk before her; Noel raised broom to slam it.

"Don't kill it, please!" Holly begged.

"Yeah, Holly always liked spiders," called out Frost, as he chanted. "Remember the old poem:

A spider in the morning is a sign of sorrow;

A spider at noon brings worry for tomorrow;

A spider in the afternoon is a sign of a gift;

But a spider in the evening will all hopes uplift."

Holly smiled. "We've seen this spider in the evening, while we are cleaning our house. We'll get good luck!" She said out loud, as she thought to herself, *good luck to bring enough money to keep our family together in this mansion!*

Chapter 10

Up before dawn, Holly climbed to the top of the cupola. She should have worn a sweater over her nightgown, but she just wrapped her arms around herself, as she sat on the soft velvet cushion. Swinging her bare feet up on to it too, she resting her back against the cold wood, staring out into the darkness beyond.

The sky began graying the horizon. Content, Holly watched the darkness dissipate. Birds were starting to chirp, the sky pinking into a dome of gold, gilding the top of the trees before the ball of fire rose. Warmth and peace and the sweet smell of honeysuckle seemed to permeate her world as Holly snuggled down.

Looking out over her realm, she lounged on her wooden cloud hovering in the sky: South to the Mystic Harbor, the Museum and Aquarium; West to the river; East toward the old wing and the rising sun: and North to the parking lot and the hearse. Then Holly folded her arms tightly under her breasts and looked Northeast. That glimmer of silver--water. It was the mill pond. Suddenly, the sweet honeysuckle smell was gone, leaving only the memory of dust and death in its wake.

Realizing that she'd be late, Holly hurried back down to her room, washed up fast, and dressed in jeans and a shirt. She had to drive Noel to his volunteer job at the seaport museum, and then Frost too if he wanted it, and then she'd start her new job. Distant wild barking. Thor. Muffled. She started hurrying down the stairs. Sounds from the kitchen-- smashing of China.

Holly raced into the kitchen. All the cups, saucers and plates from the drain board were smashed on the floor. Body rigidly stiff, Thor was growling deeply but swinging his massive head from left to right, as if he did not know where the assault was coming from.

A tired looking Frost came out of his room, wiping his face with a towel, looking like he just finished shaving.

"D-did you hear it?" asked Holly.

"Yeah."

"Why didn't you c-come out?"

"Wouldn't have done any good."

"Could Thor have jumped up on the sink counter and knocked them off?"

"It wasn't the dog, Holly. See, the drain board rack is still set neatly by the sink."

Noel ran in and looked at the shattered plates on the floor. "Somebody broke in?"

"Nope. Go ahead and check, but that backdoor will still be locked. It always is. The other doors and windows will be closed, but any china or glass plates you put in this kitchen will be broken. If you take the rest of those plates out of the boxes, they will be smashed too."

"Our mother's spirit?" asked Holly, afraid to hear the answer.

"No. Ben said that the china smashing happened before our father was born. Grandma used to keep the good china in the dining room. It wouldn't get broken unless it comes back in here and Grandma left it unattended."

"The good china?" Noel asked.

"Those nice pieces in the corner cabinets. Some in boxes in the basement. Some nice pieces, some that came over on one of the China clippers, but I haven't seem 'em lately, so Ben must have sold them off years ago. Look, tin plates are just fine, whatever it is can throw the tin plates all they want. It can't break them."

Holly reached down and picked up a large piece of a smashed dinner platter. She held it with one hand, while she placed her other palm against it. Feeling the china's smoothness. Not coldness. Yet there was heat and terrible, unending fury.

"Holly! You might cut yourself. Don't trance while you are holding something sharp!" Frost had brought over a broom and dustpan and was starting to clean up.

"What threw this is not an 'it.' It's a human spirit. An angry human. A woman," said Holly.

"Any idea what she's angry about?" Frost asked.

Holly pressed harder against the plate. "No."

"Well. Whatever." Frost shrugged. "I heard that Great Grandma Julia had said the china smashing has been a problem since before the Civil War."

"We've got to have a seance to contact the dish breaker," said Holly.

Frost looked up. "You know how to run a seance?"

"N-no...Aunt Maureen disapproved of sinful dabbling. She that was what k-k-killed our mother." Holly looked from one to the other. "But I know our grandmother used to hold them here..."

"Until our mother died. Then grandmother's friends stopped visiting here," said Frost not looking happy.

That wasn't stopping Holly. "Well, we'll get a book, and we'll learn how to run a seance and find out why the plates are being thrown!"

Noel looked at her. "We aren't going to be living here long enough for that to matter."

"Yeah," said Frost sadly.

Noel was getting another broom. "In a house where plates fly across the room, maybe we shouldn't light decorative candles in the dining room?"

Frost sat down. "Naw, the dishes only get thrown in the kitchen."

"I felt a cold spot in the backyard, by the chestnut tree," Noel also started hesitantly.

"That's someone different. That's the Indian." Not bothering to explain that, Frost said, "Did we save any of Holly's pancakes for breakfast?"

"The dog got them," Noel answered.

Frost looked outside. "Looks like rain. Not too much fun on the bike, can Holly give you a ride today?'

"Sure," she nodded. "But Frost, you have to learn how to drive."

"Got my learner's permit while Ben was alive. But I don't know if the truck is driveable anymore, and I turned in the plates to save a few bucks."

"You can learn with the hearse," said Holly firmly.

"You teach me?" Frost's voice held a touch of disbelief.

"No, I will," said Noel finding oatmeal in the cabinet.

"The hearse is a standard transmission," Holly warned him.

"So is Ben's truck," said Frost.

"That's okay. I learned on a standard. The Major had a jeep," said Noel.

"Frost will get his license," Holly said firmly. "Then we'll see how much it takes to fix Uncle Ben's truck. Then we'll have three drivers and two vehicles."

Noel looked from Frost to her, then said carefully. "You will have your hearse, and Frost will have the truck when we sell this mansion and separate."

Feeling Holly's pain, Frost changed the topic. "Holly, you've got to go to the Hoyt sisters. Cut some herbs to take with you. I've put an order in for a fresh kill chicken."

"A chicken, with feathers?" What would Holly do with that?

"They'll pluck and clean it for us," Frost reassured.

"I don't know how to cook a-a..." she started.

"That's okay," said Frost. "I make a great fried chicken–if we can get some crumbs and buttermilk on the way home."

"Do we have eggs? I'll be making a quiche tomorrow," suggested Noel.

"We got enough, but pick up a basket of potatoes and a quart of goat's milk," Frost told her.

Holly looked up upset, "I-I-I don't have any money."

"The sisters will give us credit," Frost reassured her.

Holly frowned. "There is something strange with the Hoyt sisters. When I'm with them, I can't read them?"

"Read them?" Noel asked.

"Pick up on their emotions, wishes," Frost explained. "We can all do that, to a certain extent. Holly is just a little bit stronger on tuning in to what causes the emotions."

"But the Hoyt sisters..." she started.

"Can shield themselves," Frost finished for her.

"Shield?" Noel asked.

"Like the Enterprise on Star Trek, it puts up invisible force fields when it's under attack. Trained people can do that. Especially if they've got something to hide."

"Do the sisters ever drop their shields?" Holly asked.

Frost thought about it for a minute. "Not that I've ever sensed."

Noel looked from one to the other. "You've both got to stop talking like that! They'll put you away!"

Chapter 11

Frost had gotten Noel a day's paid work carrying lumber at the museum. After dropping her brothers off, she parked the hearse at the Mystic Motel. Apparently, Alice had already heard about the hearse because she didn't seem at all surprised to see it.

In jeans and a palm tree t-shirt, Holly started her first day as the Mystic Motel maid. Alice gave her a pass-key card, showed her the closets where the supplies carts were parked and the downstairs room with the huge commercial washer and drying machines. The first room Holly started with had some ruffled sheets on the bed but otherwise looked as neat as a pin. The remote was in place on top of the t-v, all the food wrappings and newspapers were carefully stowed in the wastebasket, with soda recyclables neatly lined up alongside. A fast change of towels and sheets, vacuuming and mopping up, and the room was sparkling. The neat family had also left her a tip of several dollars on the bed stand.

The next room was a filthy disaster. Empty beer bottles all over. Taco chips crunched under her shoes, as she picked up a dead pizza slice laying face down on the carpet. Holly sprayed the carpet with rug cleaner, letting it soak in, while she started on the bathroom to find somebody had vomited on the bathroom floor. Thank god the cart had some heavy rubber gloves. This one room took her three times longer to clean up than the other one, and the slobs left her no tip. For two floors of rooms, Holly did her cleaning and then had to drive back home to start cleaning again.

Back at the mansion, Holly went into the kitchen and Thor jumped up happily to see her, all his frustrations about being penned up were forgotten. She petted his soft-furred head while putting a kettle on for tea to take a break. She should start cleaning the upstairs, but it had been such a long time since Holly had a chance to go out and run. Well, she didn't have running shoes, but her leather loafers would do. She stuffed a bunch of fresh cut herbs into her backpack and whistled to Thor. "C'mon, boy. Will you stay with me?"

Released from the kitchen, the big black and tan dog barked and dived into the woods, rejoining Holly at the old stone rock wall that marked the end of their property's ten acres. From the side of the road, she picked up a stick and threw it ahead for Thor to chase, then bring back to her.

He growled fiercely when she tried to pull it out of his teeth, then jumped about eagerly like a puppy, for her to throw it again. They did this as she ran alongside some fields, then a few small, tacky looking contemporary houses, stuck close together, like a cluster of black shelled muscles at low tide. Finally, she and Thor turned off on to Chestnut road a narrower, older farm lane.

Ahead there was a blind curve, which Thor was running to. Seeing something beyond, he stopped, took a solid stance to hold his ground and started thunderous barking. Holly ran faster, but before she reached the turn, one of those green, three-wheeled, runner's baby carriages was bearing down on them. A blonde haired woman in a pink running suit pushed it from behind.

Holly commanded, "Thor, over here!" Obediently the Rottweiler ran back, taking a stance to protect Holly.

The running mother had rested a four-foot pole on top of the carriage's sunshade–to keep cars away? As Holly watched, a blue car came racing round the curve and had to slide over the center line to avoid hitting both mother and child.

When the mother reached her, Holly started to say something, but the other woman yelled, "keep that dog away!" Saying that the mother-of-the-year just pushed her carriage past, toward the main road, with its faster, more dangerous traffic.

"C'mon, Thor," Holly said, and they were off running

around the corner.

At the Hoyts' the plucked chicken with its head cut off looked bad; it was almost as silent and unreadable as the two Hoyt sisters. Abby dropped the pullet in a plastic bag, reused from the food store. Holly gave them their herbs, picked out some potatoes and cucumbers and paid. The sun was higher as she ran back, making her hotter and sweatier.

She should be tired, but Holly was filled with a restless energy. There was something she had to do when Frost and Noel were not around. Today? Noel had ordered her to stay away from the burnt mill building. Frost said he went there once and would never go again, but she had to see for herself.

Would she have enough time? Or should she wait for a day when the guys didn't need to be picked up? But if they were selling the mansion, she might never get there. She had to get this over with. Thor had gone over to his blanket and was curled up sleeping. She'd go, but she'd do it with a big strong Rottweiler at her side. "Thor!"

She headed to the North boundary of the property with its rock wall. At some time, this land was open grazing; now her fields were overgrown with sugar maples and young oaks. Thor took off to chase down a flash of brown--a rabbit? She could hear him barking, so it was still reassuring to know he was nearby.

Following the stone wall, it didn't take much time to find the deep ruts, remnants of the old wagons that used to haul wheat to the mill. She put her hand down in one of the depressions. How could it last this long, with rain and snow? But it did. Of course, there may have been car traffic on this road when her father and his coven had gathered here. On the dark nights, they must have come. Like the night her mother died here.

The thought sickened her- but she walked on. As if realizing she needed protection, Thor joined her as the woods gave way to a golden clearing of sunlight. Here a small river had been dammed to run the mill wheels, so now a serene shining mill pond spread before her. A red-winged blackbird flew out of the cattails growing at the water's edge. Water spilled over the dam's black rocks in white foaming rivets, build in the 1800's the dam still looked strong.

Holly slowly raised her eyes from spill run-up to the pond level. There it was. The burned ruins of the two-story stone mill. The ruins where her mother had killed herself. Abandoned her triplets. Abandoned life itself.

She slowly climbed the incline. From the front side, the round-stone building almost looked intact, but the fire had burned through the woodworks inside, destroying the roof.

Why had her mother done it?

After walking around the building and feeling nothing, she sat cross-legged in the wildflowers, above the cloud mirroring pond. A bullfrog blinked in the green scum then jumped away as iridescent winged dragonflies flitted over the cattails.

Channeling the energy of the warm earth through her calmed Holly. Finally, she was ready. She closed her eyes and sought her mother's spirit, sought to understand Hester's death. With arms placed on her legs, her thumbs resting loosely on her index fingers as she breathed slow and deep. Yet nothing came.

No brush of her mother's gentle spirit nor the screaming horror of her burning death.

Finally, Thor came over and insisted on licking her face with his big, rough, wet tongue. She had to get back to the real world and pick up her brothers from work.

*   *   *

Directly after picking up her brothers, Holly tried to get more mint and lemon verbena cut before dark, while Noel took Frost went off on a driving lesson.

It started going badly when Noel pointed out, "don't

turn on to the main road. I don't want to go where anyone can see us."

His brother found that ridiculous. "It's a public road–of course they'll see us."

"Turn here!" Noel commanded.

Frost tried, but Holly's hearse stalled for the eighth time when he couldn't get the proper coordination of the clutch and gas pedal.

"I keep telling you–let the clutch out slowly!"

"I know! I know!"

Noel knew a new driver shouldn't be trying to learn on a standard shift. The hearse was nearly double the length of most cars and when Frost was concentrating he didn't even seem to hear Noel.

A low sob. Noel looked at Frost. "Is that you?"

"No."

Noel twisted in his seat. Someone was crying in the empty back of the hearse. "What is that?"

"Bernie."

"What's a Bernie?" Noel asked.

"He owned the hearse before Holly bought it. The question is why is he crying?"

"That's pretty obvious! He doesn't like the way you're grinding those gears!"

"Look–this would go easier if you could shut up once in a while!"

Noel had enough. "**Stop the car!**"

Frost hit the brakes abruptly. The hearse jerked to a stop.

"**Stop but not in the middle of the road!**" yelled Noel.

"**You said stop!**" Frost yelled back.

"**Not here!**"

"That's it!" said Frost. "Get out!"

"I can't get out! I'm the licensed driver! You get out!"

Blue and red lights flashed in the rear view mirror at the same second the siren started. "Oh, shit." Noel sank down in the seat as the police Tahoe pulled up behind them.

Chapter 12

Holly was out cutting fragrant lemon verbena when the hearse pulled into the parking behind the house. They were early. Something had gone wrong with Frost's first driving lesson? Noel was at the wheel, struggling to park the long hearse, reversing it into some rambling, overgrown rose bushes still entwining a rotted-rail trellis.

Wild, agonized wails issued from the back of the hearse. Noel and Frost jumped out. "What the hell?!"

Holly rushed to check the paint on the back of the hearse. "Bernie! It's okay."

"**What's going on?**" screamed Noel over the rising, keening cries of pain.

"**It's the ghost!**" yelled Frost.

Noel whitened, but Holly consolingly made circular rubbings on the hearse's polished finish. "No damage! I'm sorry Bernie." she crooned soothingly. "N.C. will be more careful next time. I promise!"

"What the hell is that?" Noel demanded of Holly.

"The former owner is complaining about how you park," said Frost sounding smug. "He doesn't like your driving, Mr. Andretti."

Noel still glared at Holly. "It or he has been making soft sobbing sounds the whole time we were out!"

"Oh–the oil must be low. The oil gauge is broken. I have to get some and a new filter. But I'll need money." She looked at a hunched back Frost. "Why couldn't you drive the hearse home?"

"General Martinet there kept issuing too many orders!" complained Frost.

"Simple instructions-which you couldn't seem to follow! Then we got pulled over by a cop," Noel explained. "Your brother's learner's permit has expired a year ago."

"I didn't know permits expired," shrugged Frost.

Holly decided not to point out that Frost was Noel's brother too. "Did Frost get a ticket?"

"I'm the one who is in charge!" exploded Noel. "The driver with the license is responsible! They give the ticket to me!"

"Y-y-you got a ticket?" Holly asked anxiously.

Frost shrugged. "No. We got stopped by that tall cop. The one who likes you."

Holly felt herself reddening. "Sgt. Travinski? He d-doesn't really like me-he..."

Frost smiled at her. "Trust me. He's interested in you. You know I can tell."

Noel continued, "he gave us a warning. He told Frost he has to get a current learner's permit before he goes out on another driving lesson." He turned back to Holly. "And you have no registration or title in your hearse!"

"I do!"

"It's not in that glove compartment!"

Holly looked back to the hearse, where the ghost was still howling, but his moaning was winding down. "The papers aren't in the glove compartment. I put them in a ziplock bag and hide it under the passenger seat."

Noel stood there, looking at her incredulously. "Why?"

"Well, somebody might steal the hearse, then if they looked in the glove compartment, they'd have my title and registration."

Noel looked at Holly to Frost; then they all looked to the still howling hearse. "Somebody might steal...?" he repeated.

All three of them started laughing at the same time.

Chapter 13

Holly handed him a basket overflowing with cut herbs for Frost to carry in. "You're going to renew your learner's permit tomorrow! "

Frost didn't answer. Instead, he said to Holly, "You picked up the chicken?"

"Yes, I'll set the table."

"No, Noel will do it. You are learning how to fry a chicken. C'mon, sis."

"Okay, but afterward we need to tie up those herbs and hang them from the rafters in the pantry. I need string. Do you have nails for the beams?"

Noel pointed out, "we're not going to be living here very long."

Frost just reached for the breadcrumbs. "We could use Ben's fishing line. There are some nails in the beams already. Our mother used to hang bundles of herbs from them."

"Good."

In the kitchen, an excited Thor barked, crouched down and jumped up, running from one to another. Again Holly realized he wasn't much more than a big, overgrown puppy. Using buttermilk, an egg, olive oil, and bread crumbs Frost soon had a great fried chicken dinner, with a side of home fries. She had to admit his dishes were delicious, and that Noel could bake much better than she could. It made Holly feel even more inadequate as a sister and cook. But she just dug in, then noticed Noel was checking messages on his cell phone and his aura blanched. "What's a matter?" she asked.

"Nothing," Noel said.

Holly exchanged a look with Frost, who said, "C'mon, bro. We can read you."

Their brother sighed. "My school loans are overdue. Way overdue. They're warning me."

"Can't you make a payment schedule with them?"

Frost suggested.

"Already did. But without a job, I can't meet the payments."

Frost took another bite. "Well, at least they don't have debtors' prison anymore."

"They're threatening to garnish my pay."

His brother only shrugged. "No problem. You don't have a job."

That only got Noel's face closing tighter. "Hopefully I'm going to get one! But I won't keep it long, with that kind of trouble following me. And I'll have no credit. Until I'm at least current on my loans, I can't continue my studies. When do you think we could sell this house?"

Holly didn't want to hear that. "We've got to fix up the mansion first–so we can get a better price."

Frost didn't look too happy either. "Well, we may not own it ourselves soon, unless we get some money up..." He was interrupted when the phone rang. Frost got up and hurried to answer the old style phone tethered on the table in the front parlor. With the dining room door open they could hear him. "Yeah, he's here. One moment." Frost raised his voice, "N.C., it's for you."

Holly looked at her brother. "Does anybody know you're at this number?"

"Only the Aquarium," Noel said quietly as he got up.

"Then you got the job!" Holly cried joyously.

He didn't look that confident or eager to take the call. "Dr. Morjessky said they would call even if it was a rejection." As Holly followed, Noel walked straight-backed out of the kitchen, through the dining room. In the parlor, Noel turned his back on both them, as he talked into the phone. With only the weak, yellow light from one lamp, Holly couldn't see if Noel's aura was changing. As she followed Frost back to the kitchen table, she anxiously asked. "It must be the Aquarium center? What did they sound like?"

"A woman's voice. Sounded more annoyed then friendly."

"Did you get any feeling from the voice whether he got the job or not?" Frost was already back eating his fried chicken. He just shrugged. "Anytime it's been someone close to me, and something is really important to them, I have trouble reading it."

Holly sighed. She'd noticed that problem too. The call was short, and then Noel was headed back to the table, stiff-backed as usual. Desperately, Holly read strong emotions about him, mixed emotions, what did it mean? "Who was it?"

"That was Dr. Morjessky. The blood test for Koda came back positive for Erysipelothriy rhusiopathiae."

Holly started to stammer, "E-r-er-rr..."

Frost cut her off. "Holly–don't even try!" He looked to Noel. "What does that 'E' stuff mean?"

"It's a bacterium infection belugas are particularly susceptible to. Koda probably got from eating an infected fish. It can lead to septicemia. Untreated, it could've killed him, but they are administering ciprofloxacin." Noel spoke with a detached, clinical air.

"C-cip," Holly started.

"It's an antibiotic. He should be okay," Noel finished.

"What about your job?" Frost asked.

Noel blinked as if he still couldn't believe it himself. "I start tonight. Holly, can I borrow your hearse?"

"Sure."

"I go in, get my uniform shirts, fill out paperwork and then after the Aquarium closes, I'm supposed to try to call Koda over so they can give him his first dose of the medicine." The luminous green joy of his aura faded. "Only this time he probably won't come to me again, and I'll be fired on my first day."

She could sense Noel's deep fear. Despite his martinet front, she could feel her brother's deep insecurity in his abilities. "He will come," said Holly firmly. "Do what you did before. Get some fish. Go to the edge of the pool. Ignore everything around you and take a deep breath. Clear your mind. Picture Koda. Picture the fish in your hand. Picture him swimming to you. Picture him taking the fish from your hand. Keep repeating that over and over in your mind. He will come," she finished confidently.

Noel didn't look as positive.

This was the time to bring up her plan. "You've got a job. Frosty's got a job. I'll find work. Maybe we don't have to sell the mansion. Maybe we could open it as a bed and breakfast again? I could run it. Then we could all stay here and live, together. Forever," she finished happily.

When she finished, she looked from Frost to Noel. Noel was staring down at his plate. "Holly, I told you, before I can set up my doctorate program, I've got to get current on my loans."

"Yeah." Frost had to weigh in. "There is something I've kinda just let slip. I checked with the Town Hall at lunch. I knew it'd be bad news; I just didn't figure how bad." He took a piece of paper that was folded in half by his plate and opened it up. "The property taxes. I knew they'd be coming soon, but Ben didn't pay them last year." He passed the sheet first to Noel, who paled before he passed it to Holly, as Frost was continuing, "if we don't sell this property, the town is going to take it away from us."

Holly looked at the sheets. "So much?"

Frost made a wry face. "It's Connecticut, guys, and we've got over ten acres."

"How much time do you think we have?" asked Noel.

"I spoke with the town clerk. Explained that we're settling our great uncle's estate and that we're putting the property up for sale, so we'll pay everything as soon as it sells."

"What did they say?" Noel asked.

"A year delinquent, it better sell fast."

Noel took off for his new job, and Frost went to his rooms, leaving Holly to wash the plates and set them on the drainboard. Hearing a knocking at the front door, she wiped her hands and hurried to open it.

Two older men in suits stood outside. One held a small notebook in the palm of his hand. "Miss Corey?"

"Y-yes."

"Detective Harry Bristol and Detective Hiram Warren. We like to talk to your brother."

"Which one?"

Detective Warren looked at his tiny notebook. "Corey, Frost C."

"Please come inside."

They talked with Frost in the parlor. She could hear the murmur of voices, but not much of what they were saying, other than it was more questions about Rolf Van Hom's death. The fact that they only wanted to talk with Frost frightened her.

While the detectives questioned her brother, she decided to set up an experiment. Holly took out four of the new china dishes from the box in the dining room and spread them on the kitchen sink counter. She sprinkled rock salt in the first; lemon juice in the next; in the third, she lighted the stage bundle and let it burn a bit in the plate; the fourth was a combination of all three.

When the detectives left, she asked Frost what they wanted, he only shrugged and took Thor out for a walk. The only good news came when Noel returned home. Koda had come to him and taken a fish with the medicine. He had a job! Noel was off to his rooms to study the Aquarium's employee manual. Alone, Holly climbed up to her third-floor room. It was freezing. She tented wood in the Franklin stove and started a fire.

They'd need money. Besides the house, what did they

have to sell? She had a few small pieces of jewelry from her mother and grandmother. Holly opened the box now on the bureau, shifting through a three stoned, garnet ring, opal pendant, baby's tiny gold necklace, a bracelet of cut onyx, and a man's gold pinkie ring. Everything in that box was of great value–to her--to the rest of the world, it was stuff for the Good Will store. The hearse, this house and what was in this room was the sum total of her value for twenty-two years. Pretty worthless.

Wearily Holly climbed into her four-poster bed. Why were they still questioning Frosty? Why weren't they questioning someone who might know something? Like that Miranda Talmadge? Maybe Holly should do it? Worrying for her brother, she slipped off into a restless sleep.

When Holly finally awoke, outside was the black night. The Franklin stove in the room was down to white, popping embers. It was cold and way before dawn.

Why had she awakened? Something was wrong in the mansion. Holly fumbled for her glasses. Then pulling on her bathrobe, she headed barefoot downstairs. She was coming down from the second floor when she heard it: the muffled sound of smashing china.

Chapter 14

When she reached the kitchen, Thor was locked up in his bedroom, as Frost was sweeping up the broken china off the linoleum. "I don't know why these bowls were on the drainboard," he complained.

"I left four out, with salt and sage and lemon juice. I thought it would stop the breaking."

He shook his head. "You can't leave China in the kitchen. This happens every time. Don't want Thor getting broken slivers in his paw pads, and you go back to bed, you're in your bare feet!"

After a fast two weeks of working, it was payday for all of them. Holly'd have some money in her pocket again, and after she finished cleaning up the last rooms, she'd go over to the seaport museum and get fitted for her volunteer's outfit.

Hurrying the last motel rooms as fast as she could, Holly soon had the sheets running through the massive washing machines. The investigation was still ongoing, the room that Van Hom had rented was sealed off with yellow crime scene tape. Holly's pass key would work on that room, but no, she had better stay out of police business. Deliberately, Holly wanted to shut down her mind, experience no more vibrations! Finally, she could pack her cleaning cart away and head on down to the lobby.

Alice was cleaning up the complimentary breakfast bar, and Holly moved to help, taking out the coffee filter. "This is my job."

"We'll have a new delivery of danishes tomorrow. Want to take some of these home with you?" Alice asked. "You finish up here, and I'll write your paycheck up."

"Thank you." Holly spoke carefully, "Frost said you know just about everybody around here?"

"Didn't know about you and N.C.," said Alice with

just a touch of annoyance.

Holly tried to say this casually. "D–do-do you know Sgt. Travinski?"

"Paul? Oh, yes. Know him since he moved here from Boston. He stayed here for a time."

"I-is is he...I mean, mar-mar..."

"Married?" Alice smiled at her. "No. Came close once. They were engaged for the longest time. The day of the wedding, she ran off with the best man. Can't see why. Paul would be a real catch. But after Margaret took off, he just started focusing solely on his career." Alice looked sharply at her. "Is he interested in you?"

"As a murder suspect," Holly said sadly.

"Maybe, maybe not..." Then Alice looked a little concerned. "I hear the police questioned you guys again?"

How did Alice find those things out? "only Frost. I don't know why."

"I wouldn't worry about it too much. The police just don't have any leads, but Frost has a good reputation around here. "

"That end room on the second floor is still sealed with police tape?"

"Which means I can't rent it. Although I'm glad to see Van Hom gone."

"Why?"

"He had a lot of scrungy looking visitors. I wondered if he was buying or selling drugs?"

"Couldn't you throw him out?"

"Not without any proof, and I really didn't want the police to be swarming over here. But I was hoping he'd just leave." Alice handed a check to Holly saying regretfully, "Oh, and, Holly, I'm afraid this is going to have to be the last check."

"Was there anything wrong with my cleaning?"

"No! I'd hire you again." Alice looked genuinely

saddened. "You do a marvelous job, but Dorri says she's ready to come back to work. If I need someone again, I'll call. And do use me as a reference."

"T-t-thank you." Holly tried to say.

"And drop by just to talk sometimes. It gets lonely here, and I might have heard something about Paul."

Well, jobless again, but at least she had gotten two checks. And a volunteer job at the museum village.

The next day at the Mystic Seaport Museum, Holly's volunteer pass got her into the women's locker room, where she found a blue paisley gown with an apron and mop cap that fit loosely. The woman there gave her a red and white volunteer badge, and she was assigned to the Figurehead gallery.

Coming out of the locker room, Holly saw someone in 1800's clothing lounging against a stack of barrels. "Frosty! You sensed I'd be here?" She liked him better in his blousey, white linen docent shirt and slops trousers, than his modern, blue tour-guide outfit.

"Yhep." Frost frowned. "But I also sense something is making you sad?"

"My job at the motel finished," Holly confessed.

Always an optimist, Frost quickly smiled confidently. "You'll get something else–something better!"

There was clopping on the cobblestone road beside them. Holly looked up as two palomino draft horses pulled a long-wagon load of tourists past them. In the distance, she could see the three masts of the Seaport's great whaling ship moored at the dock. "I'm assigned to the Figurehead gallery."

"Yhep. That's back there along the river."

"Oh." she still wanted to look toward the docks, with the seaport's many boats. "Wish we had time to see everything."

Frost linked his arm in hers. "Nothing stops us from taking the scenic route."

As they walked about he explained the seaport village was actually a collection of period buildings gathered from all over New England and laid out as a Yankee whaling port road in the 1830's would have been. Frost was walking her down a cobblestone road, passed the tavern, with other small, one-story building alongside it: a one-room school, print shop, lock repair shop, pharmacy, and dressed stone bank.

"Over there, beyond the whaler. Those three buildings are where we repair or build ships." She could see one of gray wood that loomed five stories high. They walked on to the dock, nearer the huge ship, Frost said proudly, "That's the *Charles W. Morgan*, a real whaler ship built in 1841!"

A disbelieving Holly eyed the three master. "It lasted all this time?"

Frost shrugged. "It's just as original as George Washington's axe."

"Huh?"

"This guy owned George Washington's original axe. Course the axe head had been replaced twice. And the handle was replaced four times, but it was still George Washington's original axe," he teased. "That ship was originally built for a few thousand. We've done seven million dollars worth of renovation on it since 1968."

Holly smiled. Ahead, she saw crowds of tourists at the edges of a grassy green, where leather helmeted men where running some sort of relay race with a leather pail in each hand.

"Paid docents. They're re-enacting a fireman's bucket brigade. They do that three times a day." They kept walking and reached the bay. More boats. A Polynesian outrigger canoe was painted bright colors. "Captain Tarus painted protective totem eyes. Someday I'll get you a ride in it. The tourists ride the steam engine paddle wheeler. Herald Gustav is captaining her today. We'll also have to get you a ride on that some time."

Turning back they passed several larger buildings, a period house, and a planetarium advertising their star shows. Frost lead her inside the modern brick galleries. As they passed through a room of paintings of ships and period portraits in gilded frames, Holly stopped at one, seeing a bright painting of the harbor area she just walked, only instead of a few cloud reaching spars, the water looked like it floated a forest of masts. She studied the work carefully. It looked almost impressionist in some of the surface, photographic in other areas. It had a light cerulean sky, with high mares' tail clouds, and colorful windblown streamers from the ships' masts.

Frost approvingly noted her interest. "That was painted by Warren John Thomas. He lived near here in the seaport in the 1800s. He was famous for painting ships and seaport landscapes."

"The style-it resembles the murals at the mansion?"

"They're not signed, but I think they were painted by him or at least one of his students," Frost said proudly.

"How much is this painting worth?"

"It was donated from the Carson estate, but it would have sold in six figures."

That would solve all their problems! "Are you sure we can't get the murals off the walls in the dining room?"

"Holly, if we ripped off the plaster, they'd be destroyed." He was already pushing on. "The next building connected to this is the Figurehead gallery. It has my tobacco display. Where you'll be standing guard."

They went down concrete stairs to the Figurehead gallery. The room was probably three stories high, but the ceiling was too dark to see. The gallery was dramatically darkened, with just strong spotlighting on the bigger than life-sized figureheads: a wooden, bare-breasted mermaid; a Napoleon hatted naval man; a prim Victorian woman, and a huge sweeping gold-gilded eagle. Some smaller ones were about alongside other samples of swirling, elaborate, decorative, marine carvings taken off old ships.

The gallery was impressive. Frost let her look around a bit, and then he leads her over to the side wall by the steps. There was a large glass case about seven foot long and eight foot high. As she looked at the wide board mahogany case frame, Holly realized something. "It's carved in a repeating design, that resembles the curved 'v' of a whale's tail?"

"Yhep. Tarus gave me that idea." Frost puffed up proudly.

"You carved the wood framing?"

"And built the cabinet."

She touched the deep, stained cuts that swirled around. Then she looked inside the lighted cabinet as Frost was over her shoulder, pointing out, "I painted the background landscape to look like an 1850's tobacco farm."

He was talented as a cabinet maker, painter and as an exhibit designer. At the top the case, she saw wide, sheafs of dried brown leaves with their stems tied hanging upside down as they would dry in a tobacco barn. Different levels of shelving displayed various tobacco tools: pipe tampers, snuff cans, wooden cigar rollers, and early cutting knives. Frost had enlarged photographs of stereopticon cards and early sepias of leaf harvesting and masted sailing ships at anchor alongside a busy dock. "That's old Mystic Harbor," her brother explained with pride. "I found those photos in the town library. And that's a genuine Indian peace pipe and wampum that I talked one of the museum's directors into lending," he finished proudly.

At the bottom, Holly studied a yellowed ship's log spread open, with its bales of tobacco cargo meticulously listed in faded, spidery handwriting. Touching her fingers to the glass case, she briefly felt the residue of some seaman clerk's pride in his new position and his dreams of the future.

Frost was talking to her, "You can hide your water

bottle back here. Read some of the cards under the exhibits so that you can answer tourists' questions. If you have any trouble, like somebody getting sick, call the guard. You should find the guard upstairs in the portrait gallery or just pick up that in-house phone over there. The museum operator will answer. I'll be back to pick you up for lunch at two, okay?"

As Holly nodded to him, she became aware of a disturbing presence drawing closer. Not a spirit. A living human. That woman she had seen before, Miranda. The slender but well-endowed woman was walking toward them, with a deep swing of her hips. The lady's seaport period gown really fit, extenuating her hourglass figure, while the perfume that proceeded her was oriental and musky. Five foot six inches of woman that expected to be watched, wearing her black hair, long and hanging, with a very non-period streak of neon green running from her widow' peak.

The lady moved in possessively tucking Frost's arm in her own. Her eyes boldly challenged any female that stood near 'her man,' but Holly had a distinct feeling that 'her man' was any nearby male who could do her some favor.

"Oh, this is your little sister?" the woman asked, obviously measuring the perceived competition with her eyes, seeming not to realize that 'his little sister' was taller than her.

With her arm in his, Frost reddened with pleasure. Holly could even see his aura brighten in the dim lighting of this display gallery. "Miranda, we're going out for a pizza after the museum closes. You want to join us?"

Miranda smiled with her lips only. "Perhaps. I'll let you know." She leaned confidently against him. "And I've got to run an errand today–I'll need someone to cover in the school room. Can you slip away and do it? At two?"

"Sure," her well-trained puppy pronounced.

Holly spoke up, "Frost, we were going to have lunch then."

"Uh–you can eat alone, can't you, sis? Just go down to the cafeteria? Show them your badge. You get a free hot dog or hamburger, a can of soda, and a bag of chips."

Having won, Miranda smiled and leaned up to peck Frost's cheek and then hurried off.

Frost watched longingly as Miranda walked away.

More tourists were coming down the gallery steps, as a thin, blonde, thirtyish woman with two dark-haired kids in tow walked towards them and stopped at Frost's exhibit. She wrinkled her nose in distaste. "Tobacco." She looked at the kids. "That is a horrible exhibit! Smoking is very, very bad for you! It stinks!" She looked up at Holly. "You shouldn't have displays like this that kids can see. It glorifies the use of a disgusting, cancer-causing drug."

Holly hurt for her brother, but Frost only nodded in agreement. "Yeah. It's a horrible habit."

When the woman moved on to complain about the indecency of the braless mermaid figurehead being displayed in front of children, Frost leaned his head toward Holly and whispered down to her, "thank god the chief curator is a heavy smoker."

Holly smiled back in honest admiration. "Frosty, it's really a great display."

Smiling he left.

Then came hours of standing. Reading exhibit cards. Standing. Warning children not to touch. Not to run. Standing. Being asked where the ladies' room was. Where the cafeteria was. More standing, on feet, getting very sore. Bored, Holly tried to tune into a spirit to commune with but could find no ghosts here. Not even much of the residual energy of the marine craftsmen who had created these immense, practical, but totally artistic sculptures. But the masters' impressions she was seeking had been overlaid by decades of tourists' emanations, as patrons dutifully marched past following their museum guides.

At two, she had her burnt hamburger, cheese doodles and sipped a can of Seven-up alone. Then Holly returned early to her post to free up her replacement. She didn't take the long route, because without Frost beside her, touring the village museum wasn't that much fun.

A guard came to lock up the gallery at five and Holly went back to the women's locker room and changed out of her costume. Outside, she looked around. Where was Frost? Had Miranda decided she needed someone to take her out to dinner and Frost had just forgotten about Holly?

Chapter 15

She walked past the one-roomed, square cut stone bank and the wide wooden porched souvenir shop. Where was her brother? Holly tried to tune in on his vibrations but couldn't. Beside the whaler and some smaller boats was a forty foot steam paddle-wheeler, returning with its last load of tourists. The tall, blond-bearded captain docked it expertly. A dock hand threw a rope loop over the pier posts; then the captain climbed down the stairs to help swing the gangplank up to the pier. Seeing her stand watching, the handsome older man gave Holly a smile and a wink, as tourists started to disembark.

Blushing Holly moved on until she saw the guard who had locked up the Figurehead gallery. "I'm looking for Frost Corey?"

"Try the Boatbuilding barns." He indicated the end of the museum, along the water. She hiked over.

These shipbuilding barns were immense spaces, supported by the external structure, leaving the interior free of obstructions for the boats to be rolled in. The barn ahead was five stories in height and fully open to the outside, for ships to be built or repaired. As she walked closer, Holly smelled sawdust mixing with rank, low tide mud, as she passed huge stacks of lumber and barrels of tar. A decapitated torso of a huge Y shaped oak tree lay on its side right before the door; from its massive girth, the tree must have been over three hundred years old. Frost told her curators went out after hurricanes asking for donations of downed trees of unique proportions.

She walked just within the yawning opening of the first shed. A flash of white blond hair ahead. Frost was busy planning a twelve-foot board for a Cub Scout troop. "You have to narrow it here–you just keep shaving away a little wood at a time. Again and again."

A kid with short black curls asked, "wouldn't it be faster with an electric tool?"

Frost laughed. "Sure would! But we try to repair these old ships with the tools and methods their original shipwrights would have used."

As he answered questions and displayed antique tools, Holly just watched. Her brother seemed so happy here. He didn't need college. Frost needed to work with his hands creating works of useable art. Finally, the Cub Scout Master looked at his watch. "Boys, we have to go."

Returning to the real world, Frost seemed happy to see her. "Holly, we're closed?"

"Yes. Is Miranda joining us for pizza?"

"No. She couldn't, but she had a bag of laundry in her car. She wants me to drop it off at her dry cleaners. Also, pick her up a carton of cigarettes."

"Miranda gave you the money for that?"

He looked away. "She's paying me later. We can drop them off at her apartment on the way home." Before she could answer, Frost was continuing, "there's someone I want you to meet. Tarus. He's kind of my mentor here. I'm learning an awful lot from him. C'mon."

Holly followed her brother into the building shed, under one of the lofts. She immediately sensed a massive presence. A dominating mind. A powerful male. As her eyes adjusted to the inside darkness, Holly looked around for this man with his strong emanations.

At first, she didn't see anyone, but Holly smelled cigarette smoke. She looked down. Squatting on the ground was a shriveled little man, wearing just a pair of dirty white shorts, a cigarette dangled between his fingers. He smiled widely at her, with yellowed teeth, but those black eyes stared at her with a burning intensity that seeming to pierce her very soul.

"Your sister..." He spoke with a high, lilting sing-song

like accent. "Is very powerful. More than she knows, but she is so untrained." He seemed about to say more, then those penetrating eyes shifted off to the side of Holly, as he called out, "Gustav! You honor my lodge?"

"Well, I saw a new young lady headed your way. I had to introduce myself," said the hearty voice of the man entering.

Frost piped up, "she's my sister, Holly Corey."

The tall sandy bearded man Holly had seen docking the steamboat walked over. Standing hands in his pockets, Captain Gustav seemed to be studying her, head to toe, as Frost introduced him to Holly. "This is Herald Gustav. He alternates captaining the weekend runs of the paddle wheeler for the Seaport Museum. He also takes out the Aquarium's research vessels, and he runs his sport-fishing fleet off his own dock."

"Gustav likes riches. He works much for them," laughed Tarus. Holly had the distinct feeling that Tarus and Captain Gustav didn't like each other and it was more than two males wanting to pee against the same tree.

Frost seemed to miss the byplay totally. "Gustav had interviewed N.C. for the Aquarium job."

"You guys are twins?" the captain asked. From the way he was eyeing her, Holly knew that Captain Gustav considered himself quite the ladies' gift.

"Actually, with Holly here, we're triplets," answered Frost.

"Shame about the Aquarium job," said Gustav regretfully. "The other guys had more experience..."

"But Noel-N.C. got it!" finished Holly.

"Dr. Morjessky hired your brother?" Gustav sounded surprised. "Well, I did try to put in a really good word for him."

"N.C. noticed one of her whales was sick and saved him."

As if estimating their potential, Tarus looked from brother to sister. "Frost has the connection. You have it too, very strong. The third one must have it also."

"Connection?" asked a puzzled Gustav.

Tarus had stood up and was now busying himself lighting his next cigarette. "More ships sneak into the harbor. Why are you not busy visiting your friends, Gustav?"

Captain Gustav smiled tightly. He was over six foot tall, wide of chest with hard muscles under that nylon jacket. When Tarus stood up, Holly guessed the brown, wrinkled, ageless man, was barely over five foot, yet she had the distinct feeling that Tarus was the dominant one.

Gustav turned to Frost. "Want to earn some money Sunday? I'm short a fishing crew for a corporate party, if they haul in anything decent, there should be some nice tips. Could use your brother too, if he's free?"

Frost looked happy. "I'm in. I'll let you know about N.C."

Holly perked up. "If you need crew, I could...?"

"Seamen always hold that women are bad luck on ships," Gustav started off solemnly, then laughed. "But what I truly need are males bodies to cook, clean fish, and haul a lot of heavy beer cases and ice chests. When we're all not working, have Frost bring you and your brother around and I'll take us out fishing, just ourselves."

When Gustav left, Tarus stayed focused on him, watching the captain until he disappeared around the next building.

Holly would have liked to have questioned Tarus more on her triplet 'connections,' but Frost was hurrying her. "We've got to get Miranda's stuff in before the dry cleaners close. See you later, Tarus."

The Captain's pizza was first on the route, then Holly sat impatiently waiting in the hearse at the dry cleaners and then while Frost popped into a convenience store for

Miranda's cigarettes. Miranda's apartment wasn't on *'the way home,'* it was actually in the opposite direction, twenty minutes out of town. Frost directed her to a series of new, white-painted brick condominiums that overlooked the water. They looked expensive. Holly wondered how a tour guide's salary paid for something like this? She would have liked to see the apartment, but Frost told her to wait outside for just a minute, while he ran the cigarettes upstairs.

Since Holly was driving her hearse, technically she was running Miranda's errands, which didn't make her too happy, and she bet Miranda wouldn't remember to pay Frost for the carton of cigarettes. That feeling of annoyance grew as the *'minute'* upstairs stretched into a long fifty-five minutes by the hearse' clock. Just as Holly decided to go upstairs, she saw Frost coming back, and she muttered, "Bernie, I don't like that woman. She's not for Frost."

A ghostly sigh came from the back of the empty hearse.

Chapter 16

Right after their pizza, Holly handed over the keys for Noel to take Frost out on his second driving lesson. Then she went out to harvest the herbs that clumped all around the parking area behind the mansion. It had once been a large square of asphalt here, paved for the bed and breakfast guests of years ago, now only cracked areas remain with verbena growing up between the cracks. She loved the smell of verbena's lemony green leaves. Holly hoped they would dry well and retain their smell into the winter. She has to take some more over to the Hoyt sisters, the mansion had a huge amount growing wild, and a frost must be coming soon.

From the front of the house, Thor started his deep, thunderous barking. Oh, God, some salesman would be suing them. Picking up her basket she hurried on the remnants of the brick path around the house. Parked on the curving front driveway, was a black and white Tahoe with the license plate '609'. That SUV had been here the night they found the body. She stopped. That tall policeman was being blocked from the porch steps by a barking, growling Rottweiler.

"Thor, sit!" Holly said, automatically smoothing her hopeless hair and wished she had worn anything else but faded jeans and an old, untucked, plaid-shirt. The man's bright blue eyes turned on her. Oh, when that craggy face relaxed, he had such amazing blue eyes, they made her weak in the knees when he looked at her, and from his aura, she determined he liked what he was seeing. She started, "I-I'm sorry. About the dog..."

"He's guarding," he finished. "When a woman lives way out here, it's good to have a formidable dog protecting you."

"You've come to speak to Frost? He's not here."

"No..." he started.

But she cut him off, asking hopefully, "Did you find

out who killed Rolf Van Hom?"

That didn't seem to be something he wanted to get into. "I can't discuss an open case. That's not what I came out for. Actually, I wanted to talk with you."

"Me?" This hunk wanted to talk to her? "Do you want to come in?" Holly asked eagerly. "I've made some molasses cookies." Actually, Noel baked them, but the sergeant wouldn't know that.

He hesitated. The strong male red and loving-spring green of his aura shifted into darker grays. This obviously was an unpleasant duty to him. "I afraid this is official business. There was a complaint made."

"About Frost?"

"No. You."

"M-m-me?"

"You go out running in the morning?"

"I like to do that in the morning. Is that illegal?"

"No, I like to do that myself."

"But...?"

"You had the dog with you."

"Thor? Yes."

"He menaced a baby in a carriage."

That was so unfair! "He barked at a woman running along the road. She's always out there, pushing that baby carriage. I mean she's running down a narrow, curving, blind road with a baby. It's dangerous! She's got this long pole set on top of the carriage shade to keep cars away I guess, but she shouldn't do that. Cars were having trouble passing her. These roads narrow down so much..."

"Miss Corey,..."

"Please. It's Holly. Call me Holly! I-I've seen her a number of times. Thor barks, but he never close to them."

"Holly, legally your dog should be on a leash, and he's not wearing a collar, with a town registration tag."

Thor had stiffly walked over, plopped down

protectively between Holly and Paul. "He's not my dog," she said weakly.

Sgt. Travinsky looked at her in askance.

"W-when we found that body–the man–Rolf Van Hom, the dog was there. We thought it was his."

"Mr. Van Hom lived in the Mystic Motel. He didn't have a dog there."

"My brother, Frost, said he'd never seen this dog before. We thought the police would take him away, but you didn't. There was no collar." She reached down and scratched Thor's ear. "He was hungry. I know he sounds frightening, but he's a sweet dog. I think the baby's carriage scares him. He just barked. It wasn't an angry bark. When I call, he comes back beside me. Right away."

"Do you think you could get him a leash when you have him on the road?"

"Wouldn't that be stealing somebody else's property?"

Paul looked down at Thor. "He looks purebred with good conformation. A young dog. That would make him valuable property, but I haven't heard of anyone around here missing a Rottweiler. The owner should have had a collar on him with a town tag. I'll check if anyone has reported Thor missing."

"His name isn't Thor. I named him that."

The sandy-haired sergeant gave a wry grin. With those smiling blue eyes, that craggy, angular face was so handsome. "Aaup. If no one claims him, I guess he's yours."

"Do you have a dog?"

He seemed surprised she asked. "Sally. A border collie, and a retired seeing eye dog. Her muzzle's getting as gray as her fur and she can't make the stairs to my apartment anymore. She's living at my captain's place–lots of land to roam." Holly hoped he'd talk more, but he was back to lecturing, "if Thor's on the roads you must have him leashed for his own protection." The small radio on his belt was giving out a jumbled voice. He reached down for it as he still looked at her. "If you keep him, then you need to get him a rabies shot, then a dog tag from the town. Aaup?"

She nodded. He said something into the radio and then started to turn to leave, but stopped, looking back with a concerned expression to Thor. "He's probably still growing out of puppyhood. From those showing ribs, he was hungry for a long time, but he's still an awfully powerful dog. You'd better get him one of those special collars for controlling a large animal."

"I'm strong. Very strong." She bent her arm up in a muscle to show him.

He smiled briefly and left.

What a stupid thing to say! Coming across as a body-builder to that handsome hunk. Oh, why could she never be smooth and seductive, like that operator Miranda?

Losing daylight, she had gone back to cutting herbs, when the hearse finally pulled in. From her brothers' body language it didn't look good. Noel was getting out of the driver's seat. "How'd it go?"

Noel was furious. "He drives like a maniac! Doesn't listen to commands!"

"No, I don't, Herr Hitler!" Frost switched to an exaggerated German accent. "I'm not 'just following orders'!"

"Making stupid jokes isn't getting you anywhere! If you would just listen. Follow carefully; you'd learn something!"

"I'm not listening to you at all!"

"That works–cause I'm not teaching you anymore!" He and Frost were nose to nose.

Holly tried to push between them, saying reasonably to Noel, "Frost has to learn to drive. You have to teach him."

But Noel said flatly, "He's never going to learn to drive. It's impossible for anyone to teach him! And I'm not going to try again!"

"That works for me!" shot back Frost.

Chapter 17

Noel said that tonight after work he'd buy a sack of dog kibble, a collar, and leash for Thor on his credit card. Holly could pay him back when she could, or he takes it out of what he was going to be paying her for gas. Holly dropped him off in the Olde Village parking lot. She actually missed the long morning of cleaning out motel rooms, or at least knowing she would get a check out of it. Still, the idea that when Holly got home, she'd have to start cleaning the mansion didn't thrill her at all. It was one thing to clean motels for money; it was another to clean a house to sell when she didn't really want to sell it.

Since she was here in the Olde Village parking lot and didn't feel like going home, she could window shop. There were all those rustic, tourist shops she loved. So Holly couldn't buy anything, it didn't cost anything to just look. She stopped in the Nordic shop with its soft Icelander sweaters, canned cookies, and stuffed toy sheep. Walked past the invitingly smelling bakery. Leather Goods. Then ahead Holly spied the shop she had really been looking for the Rainbow Realm.

The small brass bell above the door tinkled when she entered, but Holly didn't see anyone in the large room of bookshelves and counters crowded with mixing bottles and incense burners. That was fine since she just wanted to browse. The great front window was multi-paned with clear diamond shapes like a colonial shop might have been. Inside it was hung with various stained-glass sun catchers and light-bending prisms that cast dancing rainbows all over the room.

She walked past the jewelry and silk scarves. That man had died in their backyard and now every time she walked past the overgrown lilac bushes where they found the body, she felt uncomfortable. Even burning the red candle and sage, the land still felt unclean, soiled, and she couldn't leave

China in the kitchen without another angry spirit smashing it all. Something here must be able to free the mansion from its destructive spirits.

She walked over to a counter of plastic bagged leaves holding thyme and vanilla bean. Holly wondered if she could sell some of the mansion's wild herbs here? She looked over at another table of candles. Tall saint's candles-with each glass holder displaying a picture of the saint and a prayer to appeal for their mercy.

Holly had moved from the candles to the decks of tarot cards. She briefly had visions of her Grandmother's tattered, reading deck. Playing cards laboriously marked with pen ink. Triple the size of a normal deck. Holly reverently picked up a Ryder tarot. Maybe she should buy one since Aunt Maureen couldn't stop her anymore? Well, after she got a steady job and paid for repairs to the mansion.

Skye and a thin man bustled out from a door that must lead to an office or stock room in the back.

They both reacted with surprise to seeing Holly standing there, then Skye said, "Oh. I'm sorry. I didn't hear anyone coming in." She turned to the goateed man beside her. "Chew two whenever you feel very tired. It'll help, and that energy massage should get you some sleep tonight," she finished brightly. As he nodded and left, as she turned to Holly. "I didn't hear the bell?"

Why did she feel like a sneak thief? "J-j-just looking."

"It's Holly, isn't it? Please do look."

Holly did as the woman busied herself behind her jewelry counter in the back, seeming to watch Holly, and then said, "Do you have a problem?"

"P-problem?"

"You're looking at the success oils? A boyfriend straying? A need for money?"

Holly smiled wistfully. "I just lost my job. But it was

only a temporary job."

"Oh, that's a shame. Where were you working?"

"The Mystic Motel." Holly picked up a half-ounce bottle; an amber tinted essence of sandalwood. "My mother worked with herbs and oils."

Skye smiled approvingly at Holly. "Did she?"

"S-sh-she believed in reading the cards. Using herbs for good health."

"Then she was a witch!" Skye spoke as if being a witch was the greatest gift in the world. "She must have cast spells?"

Skye was speaking of Hester in the past tense. What did this radiant woman know of Holly's mother? In these small towns, people remembered long-term scandals. "Did you know my mother, Hester Farrington Corey?"

"Hester. She's passed." Skye seemed surprised. "Yes, I did know of her. That was a long time ago. I was younger than her, but I had heard of her healings and her work with plants. I always wished we could have compared Books of Shadows."

"Book of shadows?"

"A book a witch or warlock saves their spells in. It's sort of a mix of cookbook, herb registry, journal. I had heard that Hester was practicing and that people came to her to cure their illnesses. Find their lost cats. But," Skye's face darkened, "then she died so young. So tragically."

"My aunt said that her dealings in the arcane killed her?"

"I can't believe that! Your mother had such a strong life force. Have you found her Book of Shadows?"

"I haven't found a Book of Shadows, but there's so much to look through at the mansion. I'll let you know."

She started to turn to go.

"Wait," Skye said. "It's nearly October. Halloween is a big tourist event around here, and then there will be the

Christmas shopping. I could use someone in the store." Holly looked up. "It'll only be part-time at first, and I can't pay that much. But if you wanted a job?"

Holly was delighted. "Yes. W-w-when do I start."

"Tomorrow. Come in at 9:30. Use the back entrance to the storeroom. I open at 10."

"Thank you."

"How did the sage I sold you work out?"

Holly thought about it. "I feel a little better when I walk past that spot where we found... but we do have a problem. And dishes keep getting smashed in the kitchen."

"They fall? Or slip from your hands?"

"They smash in the room by themselves. They must rise up, fly, then smash to the ground."

Skye looked surprised. "That's odd. Most ghosts can't move things, much less throw them. You have a very active, angry spirit, a poltergeist." She frowned. "They can be a little frightening. Oh, don't worry about it." Skye smiled brightly. "When you come to work here, we'll figure out a way that the problem can be dealt with. What is your birthday, dear?" Skye was reaching into the jewelry case.

"December 25th."

"That's Capricorn, the fish-tailed goat in the western zodiac. The seeker of knowledge. And the December birthstone is Blue Topaz or Tanzanite."

Skye took a silver chain out of the case with a small, bright-blue jeweled pendant, saying,"Here, wear this. Tanzanite is thought to be calming to the wearer and believed to aid in overcoming communication difficulties."

Holly shook her head. "I can't buy anything today."

"This is a gift, from me to you. Wear it about your neck. The silver chain will protect you."

"I-I couldn't take that..."

"It's really inexpensive, and we're going to be working together."

Holly looked at the chain in her hands. "I thought silver was a defense against witches?"

"You're a good witch. This silver will protect you."

"T-t-thank you." Holly let Skye put the necklace on her neck, feeling so blessed that someone--who she really had just met--would give her such a kind gift.

Stopping at home, Holly gathered up some more of her cut herbs for the Hoyt sisters and then drove down to their farm. At the wooden farm stand by the road, she picked out some cucumbers, green beans, and strawberries, but since they also needed eggs, she'd have to go inside. Holly counted her money-she had just enough. She climbed the porch and knocked on the door.

Again, it was opened almost instantly by tall Abby, as if she was expected. Sara sat at her loom, weaving a blue and green rug.

Holly started, "I needed to pick up two dozen eggs. And I've brought some lemon verbena, lavender, and thyme for you."

"We hear you're working as a maid at the Mystic motel?" Sarah said.

Someone else might have mentioned her being a motel maid as a put-down, but Holly had the impression--like all true New Englanders--the Hoyt sisters felt any honest way of earning a living was a thing to be proud of. "I was, but their regular maid is returning."

"Oh. Too bad," Sarah said. "Well, you'll find something else."

Her sister seemed to be staring at Holly's neck. Holly forgot why until Abby asked, "That necklace–where did you get it?"

"It was a gift. From the owner of the Rainbow Realm. She just gave it to me."

"Why would a storekeeper give away merchandise?" Abby asked suspiciously.

"Because we had that murdered man in the backyard. And she just hired me to work there part-time."

Abby looked at Sarah, whose eyes appeared to hardened. But that passed instantly, and Sarah slipped back into her warm, friendly smile. "Abby, it's a bit of a chill outside. Could you make us some of your special cider tea?" Sarah got up and walked toward the couch as Abby moved back to the kitchen. With the open floor plan, Holly could see Abby putting on a large, copper tea kettle and opening a solid door cabinet, covered inside with row after row of silver-capped herb jars. Sarah indicated the couch. "Abby mixes the most interesting teas. Please do join me, dear."

Holly should have been scrubbing the mansion hours ago or at least cleaning up the breakfast dishes before Noel and Frost got home, but these women obviously lived alone and needed to talk to someone. Obediently she moved forward to sit on the chrome-tubed framed chairs.

But as she sat down, Sarah reached out her hand toward Holly's neck. "This is quite a lovely blue stone." Delicately she was lifting it with her two fingers. Suddenly Holly realized what the woman was doing–Sarah was reading something from the necklace. Something that causes a brief frown to flicker across her face, then it was gone. "Yes. Quite lovely. Please indulge us; it's so nice to have a neighbor visiting. Just sit down for a little while, soon we'll have the fireplaces going, it's getting colder, and the leaves are beginning to turn, but as I told you before we will be getting a frost soon." Abby was working in the kitchen and there as a silence, then Sarah said casually, "So you will be working with Skye at the Rainbow Realm?"

"She knows all about spells and spirits. She thinks my mother might have had a Book of Shadows. Skye wants to see it."

While the kettle heated, Abby was carrying over a glass plate filled with homemade pecan cookies and appeared to nearly drop it. "You won't show her? That'd be wrong!" An outraged Abby's voice had deepened.

The vehement reaction of the normally taciturn sister surprised Holly.

With a quick look, Sarah just silenced her sister and turned back to Holly. "The term Book of Shadows is modern. It dates from the 1940's with Gerald Gardner and his Wiccan movement."

"But," Abby protested, "There's always been medicine books, recipes, and guides for prayers. The listing of herbs and their effects. But those were private books! Passed from mother to daughter or used by sisters. That is not something you exhibit openly at a shopping mall!"

Sarah looked up at her sister, saying mildly, "Abby dear, your kettle should be boiling." Abby looked at her and then walked back to the open kitchen, behind the massive old fieldstone fireplace. Sarah continued to Holly, "Skye said she gave you that necklace for protection? Why did she think you needed it?"

"We're having a problem. Any china left in the kitchen gets broken."

Sarah seemed to think about that. "That's an old problem at the mansion. I remember your grandmother mentioning it. It came even before her time. Your great-grandmother believed it was a restless spirit."

"A ghost?"

Chapter 18

Sarah inclined her head. "Well, there are many things that can get called 'ghost.' Sometimes it's a spirit that doesn't realize he is dead. That resents anyone that comes into his residence. Often it's an accident victim, a murdered woman or a suicide who seems to have trouble crossing over. Most spirits generally linger a short time and then move on. A ghost is bound somehow. The longer they are here they seem to lose what reasoning they ever had."

"Do they ever leave?"

"Sometimes. Especially if they can be reasoned with. But there are other phenomena, a scene of great energy, which imprints itself upon the land. And then like a recording, it replays, again and again, that is why I think people see things like the Battle of the Little Big Horn or a reappearing, sunken square rigger sailing its old waters."

"Is there intelligence connected to those visions?"

"I don't think so. No more than there is intelligence connected to a rainbow."

"What of smells—of perfume that seems to come and go?"

Sarah sat back. "Usually that's connected with a visitation. A spirit is trying to contact. Is it a pleasant aroma?"

"Yes. Honeysuckle."

"A woman. Perhaps she is trying to reassure you?"

"But the ghost in our house throws china across the kitchen?"

"Your mansion has been home to many people over its long life. But a poltergeist, that's rare for the spirit to have both the anger and the power to destroy. That can be a dangerous entity, and it's highly unusual that there was a spirit in that mansion that your great-grandmother, grandmother or mother couldn't placate or exorcize. They were masterful practitioners."

"Were they witches?"

She didn't seem to like the question, but Sarah answered carefully, "Witch has become a pejorative term to some and a commercialized schtick to others. Both sides of your family had extraordinary sensitivity, abilities to communicate at higher levels, and the desire to study and learn. Your mother particularly excelled at the growing and utilization of plants."

"My father was Gault Corey. Do you know if he is still alive?"

The opening with Sarah closed. "You should concentrate on dealing with the problems you are facing now. The spirit giving you a problem is in the kitchen. Your great grandmother Julia felt the china breaking spirit was female. A departed slave perhaps?"

"They had slaves in New England?" That surprised Holly.

"Not many. Our rocky soils and short growing season don't lend themselves to a plantation system." Sarah smiled wryly. "Of course the apprenticeship and millwork was a form of slavery, without the obligation to care for the individual after they lived past usefulness. Still, the Abolition movement was very strong in New England, and several houses around here, including yours, were stations on the underground railroad."

"That's people who hid escaping slaves and guided them North to freedom in Canada?"

"Yes."

Holly could hear the whistling of the tea kettle and the rattling of porcelain cups as Abby prepared the tea in the kitchen. The huge room filled with a delightful aroma of hot cider and cinnamon. Still, she said, "There's a mill pond on our property. I walked to it the other day."

Sarah stiffened. "You did?"

"My mother died there."

"Then it sounds like a sad place to go," Sarah commented coolly.

"Do you know why she committed suicide?"

"I don't know why it should even matter. You should be worrying more about the present and your future, not what can not be changed from the past. If you intend to remain living at the mansion, do not awaken things that should be allowed to stay sleeping."

Abby was returning with three gold trimmed cups and saucers and an empty plate on a large glassed tray. The tray had a beautiful, iridescent neon-blue pattern beneath the glass. Holly studied it and then asked, "Butterfly wings?"

Abby nodded her head. "Morpho Melelaus." Each of the cups had a metal tea ball in it, filled with loose tea and spices. "You should wait two minutes to let the dried herbs seep, then put your ball on the central plate."

"It smells wonderful," said Holly taking one of the shortbread-like pecan cookies that were made with a lot of butter. When she finally tasted it, the cider tea warmed her. Mentally, Holly tried to parse out the herbs: beside the tart apple cider, cinnamon, and anisette, cardamom? A bit of allspice? Some pepper? It was an interesting tea, with depths she could not completely decode.

Soon she followed Abby out the kitchen door to the spring house for two dozen eggs. Without Holly mentioning it, Sarah gave them credit for the herbs she brought when they added up her bill. Holly had just enough time to rush home, put the eggs and veggies in the refrigerator before she had to race out to pick up her brothers. She passed a police car on the way. Was it Paul's? She almost wanted to floor the gas; speed so he would pull her over and look at her with those handsome blue eyes. God, he was such a hunk.

After picking her brothers up, Holly told Noel and then Frost about the job at the Rainbow Realm. Noel seemed happy that she wasn't a maid anymore, but said, "People will see you working as just a salesgirl."

"Around here, that's fine," Frost finished. "I just wish she was getting more money. Well, you'll get experience. And maybe Noel or I can get you a full-time job at the Aquarium or Museum."

They took a short detour back to town, over the bridge to Green's Feed and Supply store. Noel came out carrying a huge bag of dog kibble. "It's cheaper if you buy fifty pounds." He had bought a long windup leash and collar and, "Let the ghost break this," a steel dog bowl–a big one.

When they got home, Noel showed them the collar. "It's for controlling a powerful dog. See if he does what you want, it's perfectly comfortable. But if he starts to pull, you yank back, and those spines dig into his neck, and he learns to stop running."

Holly looked at the collar, with what looked like a snake skeleton of small, steel spines, that would painfully stick into Thor's neck.

"Sit." Thor obeyed, as Noel started to fasten the collar on him.

"That looks cruel!" said Holly.

"It won't hurt him unless he pulls against it."

"Does seems kind mean," Frost muttered sadly.

"Look," Noel reasoned. "Thor's strong and getting stronger. He's put on at least ten pounds since we've been feeding him. If he decided to attack another dog or person, Frost or I might not be able to hold him back! Holly, you wouldn't have a chance. With this collar, if he pulls, it'll hurt, and he'll learn not to disobey. It will be better for him too." Noel looked down to Thor. "You understand?"

The dog looked back at them with sad, brown eyes.

Chapter 19

Before work, Holly made time to take Thor for a walk. As they left the house, he bounded forward, and when that leash pulled tautly the cruel collar dug into the fur about his neck, but instead of stopping, Thor just pulled against it more. "Stop! You fool!" she cried out.

Stubbornly, Thor pulled against his cutting collar, choking, looking back at her with reproachful eyes. Holly dropped the leash, and Thor ran off, but she knew if he hooked that trailing chain on a log, he'd strangle himself to death. "Thor! Come to me."

As if she had been beating him, he ran away from her. Holly squatted to the ground, begging, "Please! I've got to get that collar off you." Finally, slowly he came to her, and she could unbuckle it. "I'll carry your tags until we get another collar."

Still kneeling on the ground, she looked to the side and saw a flash of red. Holly moved to it. Hanging on a low branch was another one of those red flannel bags. She took it off. It was wet from the morning dew but again looked like it hadn't been out there more than a day. She tried to pick up the emanations from it. Who sewed it? She couldn't get anything. Nor could she feel the thrust of the curse. Was it for one of them or all the Corey family in general? Maybe the bag was made by the poltergeist from the kitchen? Ridiculous–spirits don't sew. And she had no time to deal with this now.

Holly slipped the bag into her pants pocket. Whoever was trying to curse them was obviously incompetent. She didn't so much mind the harmless-feeling little bags, but it disturbed her to know that someone who hated them was free to sneak on to the property. And they were getting bolder, leaving their little red flannel curses closer and closer to the house. Why hadn't Thor started barking when someone came near the house?

Her brothers were up in the kitchen when she returned. She smelled brown sugared oatmeal and male sweat. She had to get Frosty to take more showers! But it was so, so nice to be a family, to be together again. Frost took his bike, but she drove Noel to the Olde Village parking lot.

First day on the job for her. That always made her so nervous. She hurried to the front door of The Rainbow Realm, but it was locked, of course. Holly knocked on the diamond-shaped, lead caned glass front window, and from inside she saw Skye turn and come over to unlock the door. "Tomorrow, come in the back storeroom door. Look for the leprechaun sculpture," her new boss said smiling.

Skye had told her that before, and she'd forgotten. Holly scanned the counters: Candles; Oils; Books; Necklaces, would everything have prices on it? Skye was showing her the computer screen and how to ring up cash, then credit cards. At ten a.m. she was unlocking the front door to a group of seniors, and as they headed toward her jewelry counter, Holly felt like Custer at the Little Bighorn.

Her first day was like all first days, crazy, but by the end of the week, Holly was getting a little confidence. The waves of seniors and Japanese tourists only came with the buses, and the buses were generally finished about one.

New merchandise was unpacked by Skye in the storage room in the back, and she insisted on opening up all the boxes herself. Holly would go back and pick up merchandise to be shelved out front. The large storeroom was divided in half by two Celtic patterned bedspreads. The back area, with no windows, had merchandise boxes piled high on the floor and shelves. At the back, the door opened out on to the shrubbery screen before the parking lot. Holly would recognize it from the others by a leprechaun statue and Skye's plantings against the building.

The other half of the storeroom was furnished with

Skye's desk, a work table for the craft classes, with a ring of chairs and to the side, a high massage table was set up. "I teach yoga and give massages. When I do the therapeutic massages, you'll have to watch the store alone. I injured my back in the skiing accident. The doctor put me on Oxycodone, but I was still in terrible pain. Then I went to a naturopath, and she cured me with her shiatsu massages, so I learned how to give them."

It was a beautiful place to work. When it was slow, Holly could look through the books. Skye saw her and smiled. "Try one of the Scott Cunningham books, if you want to work with oils and brews." Holly had an employee discount, and she badly wanted some of the jewelry. Still couldn't buy luxury items now, but part of her first check was going for some essence oils.

On Friday, Skye was ringing her up. "Patchouli oil and Orris root? You have Cinnamon I guess? For a love charm?"

Holly blushed. "Yes."

"Good, you're learning. Think of your man and put out a small paper square. Then pour one part Cinnamon and one part Orris on it. Sprinkle a few drops of the patchouli oil, then burn this in a brazier and he will be drawn to you."

Holly closed her hand on her the bag. No harm in burning some homemade incense and just thinking of a tall policeman.

They soon had a routine, with Holly taking over the store while Syke is counseling her clients. Elderly women coming in for massages to help their rheumatism, younger women with pimples coming in for Skye's facial masks, and two young men that come for what Skye confided was a 'chakra' massage to cure their drug addiction.

At lunch, Holly put her purse on the jewelry counter and dug through to see how much money she had left. She took out eye-glass wipes, paperback book and that little, red flannel bag she had found and had forgotten. As Skye walked past carrying a box of artesian honey, she looked at the red flannel bag and abruptly stopped. "Where did that come from?"

"I found it in the bushes."

"Here?" Skye looked concerned.

"No. At home, in the backyard, near the kitchen door." Holly started to hand the bag to Skye.

But her boss stepped back, as if afraid to be touched by it. "Some one's putting a curse on you!"

Holly pressed it between her fingertips. "It has a peaceful feel."

"Your spell caster was incompetent! He or she tried to do a classic misfortune spell and didn't get the proportions right or tried to substitute ingredients. Most people can't find patchouly or yerba santa. And the spell books I carry are very politically correct about not printing the true curse formulas!"

Not willing to admit she didn't know what 'yerba santa' was, Holly untied the bag and emptied its contents out on to the glass counter. Purple lavender, allspice, rosemary, something that looked like the mummy's tana leaves and some dark berries...

"What are you doing?" Skye yelled. "I don't want bad vibes in my shop! Clean that stuff up–and throw it away. Not in the store! Take it to the rubbish can in front of the Nordic shop!" Skye ordered as she headed back into her office store room.

Holly should have thought of that. She used the edge of her hand to wipe the contents into her other hand, then tried to fit it back into its bag, which she stuffed back into her purse. She wanted Frost and Noel to look at it. And she wondered why Skye, as a skilled practitioner, didn't suggest a counter-charm that Holly could make.

That evening, Holly was upstairs at the mansion, dusting the mirrors in the second floor Rose guest room.

Furniture here was old but decent. If they were going to rent this out, she'd have to get new bedding and maybe new wallpaper. She was moving the vacuum to the next room when she sensed someone in the house. An outsider.

Holly straightened. Listened. Muffled voices below?

She headed down the curving front stairs. Noel was standing in the front parlor talking to a woman. They were facing away from Holly. The woman was wearing high heels and a short-skirted, blue pinstriped suit. Her blonde hair was drawn up in a neat French twist. Was this a girlfriend of Noel's? Or his boss, Dr. Morjessky? Realizing her glasses were streaked with dust and that she was only in worn jeans, Holly walked to meet this mystery lady of Noel's, who was giving her some bad vibrations.

Chapter 20

"Hello, I'm Holly Corey."

Obviously, Noel had expected her to be out running as usual, and now he looked like he'd been caught at something.

The fashionably dressed woman was also a bit of a surprise. Yes, she had great makeup, perfect hair, but instead of a twentyish girlfriend for Noel, Holly was staring at a forty plus woman, who smiled at her professionally. "How do you do. I'm Laura Bentine of Bentine Realty." Smilingly, the woman held out her hand to shake.

Holly left it hanging in the air, as she rudely asked, "What are you doing here?"

Her perfect veneer wrinkling a tiny bit, Laura looked to Noel. When he didn't say anything, Laura turned back and explained, "Your brother wanted to get an appraisal on this property." She looked about. "It's quite an amazing place. I understand that it belongs to the three of you?"

Holly looked directly at Noel, as she asked angrily, "Did you tell her that?"

Not giving him a chance to answer, Laura responded for him. "Actually, we hadn't reached that point yet. Before I came out, I looked up the town property records."

Still ignoring the realtor, Holly stared at Noel. "Does Frosty kn-kn-know about this?"

A reluctant voice came from the dining room. His shoulders hunched over a bit, Frost walked into the parlor. "Yeah, N.C. and I talked about it. We know you are against selling the mansion, Holly, but we feel you aren't facing reality."

That they both could do this behind her back, hurt the most!

Looking ashamed, Frost was trying to reason, "We need an appraisal...for estate taxes. Mrs. Bentine had agreed to do it for free."

When nobody spoke, Laura started again, "Perhaps you three should speak about it this. I could come back another day?"

"No," said Frost sadly.

"Holly, it's got to be done," Noel finished. "We own two-thirds of the mansion. No way are you going to get enough money to buy us out. If you keep opposing us, we'll have to take you to court, and you'll lose. Frost and I are sorry about this. We don't want to make you unhappy, sis, but, Holly, the mansion's got to be sold."

Laura had the false sympathetic-instant friendship of a good saleswoman. "Dear, tax records are public information, and I saw that the payments on this house are behind. I can imagine the running expenses are quite heavy, especially in the winter. You'll all be in a better financial situation if you can sell, rather then lose your equity through an unfortunate tax foreclosure."

Holly just looked at her with pure hatred.

Frost moved to put a gentle hand on her arm; Holly yanked her arm away from him.

Noel's mouth was set tight and grim. Her brother had a granite hardness she hadn't ever seen before. "Holly, maybe you ought to go out for awhile. Laura is going to look through the house. The entire house, right **now!**" he said.

She looked to Frost. His saying nothing, had greater meaning.

Not wanting them to see her cry, she hurried past them into the kitchen, grabbed her keys off the counter and was out the back door. She didn't bring a jacket. The wind chill cooled her body, not her mind. For seventeen years she had dreamed of coming back here and being a family again with her brothers, forgetting about what went wrong! Making it all right together. If they sold the mansion, they would lose their last chance, and her brothers didn't even care!

In the hearse with tears streaming down her face, Holly had to maneuver past Laura's silver Lexus. She hit the gas and burnt rubber pulling out on to the main road.

With Bernie moaning softly behind her on a too narrow back road, Holly was doing sixty when she blew past the black and white Chevy Tahoe going the other way. Crying, Holly didn't give damn, not even slowing, until she heard the sirens behind her. Suddenly drained, she took her time slowing down and pulled off the road. Trying to get control and turning to get her license out Holly realized she'd left it in her handbag back in the kitchen. With her tissues. Hastily Holly wiped her running nose with the back of her right hand as she started cranking the window down with her left.

Oh, course it had to be him. The tall, sandy-haired police sergeant, Paul Travinsky. "Miss Corey? Any idea how fast you were going?"

"Too fast," she said and sniffed drip from her nose.

"License?"

She closed her eyes. "I-I left my handbag home."

"Aaup." He frowned. "And still haven't found your registration?"

"It was in here all the time! Under the front seat." She reached over to feel under the seat on the passenger side, and of course, there was no damn plastic bag! She slid over farther along the wide bench seat feeling under the seat.

"No seatbelt, Miss Corey?"

"This hearse was built in 1956. It's grandfathered seatbeltless." Holly still felt frantically under the front seat.

"Most people put it in the glove compartment," he commented drily.

To show him it wasn't there; she opened the glove compartment. The registration with its plastic bag fell out. "Noel must've moved it there." She handed him the zip-loc bag with its registration, title, California oil change coupon and an unopened tampax.

He was writing up her information to give her a ticket she couldn't afford. They were selling her house against her will. Holly would never see Frost or Noel again, and it was all her fault because she couldn't find a decent paying job! Tears were starting again.

He spoke in a comforting voice. "Miss Corey. Holly, the worse thing that's going to happen if you're getting a speeding ticket. Do you have any other moving violations?"

"No." She wiped her nose again and willed herself to stop crying.

"Then this shouldn't affect your insurance."

"They're selling the mansion."

"Your house?"

She sobbed, "Yes."

"Who's selling it?"

"My rotten, bastard brothers! They have a realtor going through the house now! They did that without telling me! They surprised me with that sanctimonious realtor bitch!"

"Can they sell without you?"

In misery, she said, "I don't have money to buy them out."

"Uh, huh. Stay here. I'm going back to my car to check your registration."

Mercifully he walked away, giving Holly time to grab the wheel hard and get control. "Bernie–please–please stay quiet!"

When Paul came back, he was putting his pen back his shirt pocket. "Okay, you have a clean record. You've still got the license and registration in California, but you've got time before you must change it. Now, I'm just going off duty, and I really don't want to write this up. I'll give you a warning this time. Just turn around, and **slowly** go back down the road to Goodman's deli and park for a while, before you drive again. Get yourself a cup of coffee."

"D-don't like coffee. Drink tea," she said miserably.

"Tea. Fine. Just cool off."

"Are you asking me for a date?"

He seemed shocked. "No! I just want you to calm down before you rocket up the road."

"Could you come? To the deli?" she asked.

The way he spoke, he couldn't believe her. "Mam, they don't put me out here to stop speeders and ask for dates."

"You didn't ask me. I'm asking you. I just want to talk someone, and you're the only one I know around here. Please?"

"Well." He seemed to be studying her; maybe he liked green eyes, light blonde hair and a cute, upturned nose cherry-red from crying. Sgt. Travinski looked at his watch. "I've been off duty for about twenty minutes. Go to the deli, buy yourself some tea and I'll meet you there. I can listen a little." When he wasn't glaring at her, Paul had an incredible lopsided smile.

With a lot of tough wheel twisting, she turned around, and soon was parking the hearse near the old hardware store that was now Goodman's deli. The Sergeant had pulled his patrol car up to park near her, but as she started to walk in to get herself a tea, Holly halted.

That tall policeman was coming up behind her. "What's the matter?"

"I left my handbag home. N-n-no money."

"Aaup," he said as he expected it. "Save the picnic table over there. How do you take tea?"

"Oh, you d-don't have to...just get yours. Then we can talk?" She felt herself flushing and looked down at the ground again.

"Milk or sugar?" he repeated firmly.

"Black with lemon, if they have it."

She got the table in the pale sun, and shivered a little

as the early fall breezes cooled her, but waiting for him gave her happiness she couldn't even understand. He really didn't care who she was, but sitting there--waiting for him to come out--it was like they were a couple. He brought back two steaming cups. She picked up one and felt the styrofoam warming her hands; the lemony tea and Paul's kindness also added to her cared for feeling as he folded his height down, sitting across from her.

"Holly, you can't just hit the gas and run away from your problems. It doesn't work in the long run."

Running. That's what she always did.

He was still talking, "I know you're angry at your brothers, but although it hurts, sometimes you have to let go of the past, or you can't move on."

"I've waited seventeen years for the three of us to be together if they sell the mansion we'll all go our s-s-s-separate ways again."

"They've said that?"

"No. But it'll happen. The last time we talked about it, Frost was thinking about moving in with a guy he works with and Noel's been looking into prices for a room in the YMCA."

"Sounds like with their jobs, they'll be staying in the area." He took a drink of his cup, then said, "Maybe you could stay around here too?"

"On part-time wages, I can't rent an apartment around here."

"People get two jobs. Full-time jobs. What are you trained for?"

"You mean college? Liberal Arts and I flunked out."

That soft rosy aura of his that had been reaching out to her was suddenly drawing back. Apparently 'no college' to him was a deal breaker. "Why liberal arts?" His voice had a touch of disapproval. "What kind of job did you plan to get with that?"

She looked down at her still steaming tea. "I'm not so great at planning. I liked to draw and paint. My aunt thought I'd wasn't getting anywhere when I just went to work and came home, so she thought I should go to college to meet someone who'd marry me."

"Did you?" He really looked interested.

How did she explain to him that although many, many guys were attracted to her, she read them. They were all planning to just get laid and move on, the lies she read in their auras and vibrations repelled her. The disgusting way their thoughts possessed her made Holly feel dirty. The nasty things they said when she kept turning them down hurt, but to Paul she only said, "College was a total failure."

"Guys in California are blind." He took another drink of his tea. "You seem intelligent."

She wrinkled her nose in distaste. "It's the old style glasses."

He only smiled at that. "You could always go back to college. This time with a plan to go for something that will get you a better job."

She didn't want to discuss this. "Did you need a degree to become a policeman?"

"Associate degree. After high school, I went into the Marines, and they paid for my two-year degree. Since I've got this job, I've been taking night courses in Police Science. Got my four-year degree. And I'm going for a masters, but just taking night courses, it takes a long time."

She envied someone having such a firm plan for his life. "Right now finances are tight."

"The property that you own with your brothers, that's got some acreage?"

"Frost says a little over ten. The North property line follows a stream."

"If you sold some of the land, that would give you money. It'll melt away fast unless you come up with a doable strategy." He was studying her face. "Also, that house might not sell for a while, because a lot of stuff around here has been sitting on the market. You might have some time to work up a plan." He looked at his wristwatch then was getting up. "Got to be going. You promise not to take any more mad drives?"

She nodded, being with him let her smile a little. "I'll be going back home to talk to my brothers. Thank you for the tea."

He smiled as he left, and she was surprised that a virtual stranger leaving could make her feel so suddenly abandoned?

Chapter 21

At breakfast, she and her brothers were at least talking again. But on a barely polite, '*Pass the milk*' or '*Anybody wants the last apple*?' level.

Both guys were going in early to work. After she dropped them off, she still had hours before her job started at the Rainbow Realm. Holly decided to go back and clean the mansion for a while. It didn't help that when she was walking back to the mansion, she found another of those little red flannel bags nearer the porch. She needed to tell Frost and Noel about these curse things; maybe Frost knew someone around here who hated him? Should she call the police? Call Paul? Like he'd care about some stupid red bags? Or her? Holly felt tired and drained.

Thor needed a walk, and she needed a run, a lot more than he did. She pulled out that blasted leash, but she wasn't going to take that damned cruel collar. Holly searched around. The clothesline outside had an extra length twisted up. She unwrapped it and cut off enough to knot around Thor's neck.

"There. You're quite handsome, sir." Thor barked, eager to be off and Holly decided she might go see if the Hoyts had any pumpkins in their fields. While they ran on the main road with houses, she kept him on the leash, but when they turned right again, they were back along woods and fields, so Holly figured she could let him loose.

The canopy of trees gave way to well-maintained farm fields. Here the frost brought rocks up every spring that was called 'New England potatoes.' Thrifty Yankee farmers cleared their land of stones by using them to build a mortarless dry rock wall to mark off their property. On the Hoyt land, those stone walls still enclosed fields for grazing and planting. This summer they had huge fields of corn planted, now Holly saw a man on a tractor, plowing picked stalks under. Relative of the Hoyts? Hired hand? Or were they leasing out the fields? Was this still their land?

The Rottweiler ranged ahead, flushing a golden-brown pheasant with an explosive whirl of wings. "Thor!" She called him over, clipping on the leash back on since they might run into that baby carriage again. Beside the road was a stone wall enclosure with tall pine trees inside it. She hadn't noticed it from the road before. A glossy, black painted ornamental iron railing surrounding a family graveyard, with about two dozen headstones. No grass, just red-matted pine needles, and spongy moss. Probably in the spring lilies of the valley carpeted it, because Holly seemed to remember coming here with her mother and smelling the sweet little white bells.

Raising the latch, Holly swung the oiled gate open and let herself and Thor in. The stones in the front were the newer. She stopped by two substantial, square granite monuments from the 1930's, *Richard Hoyt 1847-1931* and *Evangeline Le Fleur Hoyt 1857 -1931.* Most of the stones were Hoyts. Some of the wives' maiden names were Scofield, Water or Fuller. The Fullers came over on the Mayflower, Holly remembered.

The mid-rows were curved or flat-topped, white marble spotted with black fungus and seemed to date from the 1800's. Farther in the back, worn, dark gray slate slabs, with lifespans predating the Revolutionary War. She stopped at a 1700's stone: *wife of Giles Hoyt, Sylvia Farrington.* Farrington was her mother's maiden name. Were they related to the Hoyts? That'd be logical; it was a small area with generations of the same families meeting and intermarrying.

As usual, Holly didn't hear the spirits in a graveyard, but always loved to study them: read the inscriptions on old cemetery stones, '*Where I lie soon will you*'; feel pain at the sad little marble lambs for the babies; Enjoy names like *Freelove* and *Charity*, *Jeremiah* and *Hoglan*. A white marble one in the back said, '*Goldenrod, Indian Princess, wife of*

Walter Hoyt.' Someone must maintain this little graveyard and see that no rambles overgrew. Must be the Hoyt sisters. As she headed back out a soldier from the War of 1812 had a small, faded American flag waving from his black iron star.

This was where the Hoyts buried their dead. Was this where Sarah and Abby would lie? Holly didn't see any burials after Richard and Evangeline. Did the state still allow people to be buried with their families on their land anymore? The sisters should be buried here, after all, they had roots that went back generation after generation in this soil.

And what of her roots? Where would she be buried? Where the hell would she be living in two months? Thor was pulling at the long leash. She let them both out of the gate, but before she could close it, a black and white Chevy Tahoe car pulled up. Plate number 609.

Holly was surprised at how happy she was to see Paul pulling up. Usually she was always a little afraid of policemen and as she walked to his car, Thor was already starting with his thunderous barks. Paul got out as Holly tried to pull back on Thor's newly made rope collar, but she couldn't.

He frowned at that. "As I mentioned before, they have special choker collars to control large dogs."

"Noel bought one," Holly admitted.

Paul sounded very cop-like as he asked. "Why isn't he wearing it?"

"I don't want him wearing that cruel thing! He's not a bad dog. I can control him." Thor sat, and she petted his soft head. "We haven't been able to get a dog license yet, but we got him a rabies shot."

Paul knelt down and ran his hand over Thor's head. The dog opened his mouth to pant, showing his formidable set of ivory teeth. "Glad I wasn't that veterinarian."

"Noel–N.C.-- took him. He obeys N.C. absolutely."

"Department's records show Frost's has gotten his

learner's permit." She had a brief moment of happiness that Paul had cared enough to check, then he asked, "How are you guys doing with the house?"

Her happy sunny feeling clouded. "There's still paperwork from the estate that has to be closed out. And we have to fix some things up, but then it goes on the market."

"So you've got time. Probably not much, but when it sells, you might have some money and can do some planning."

He was walking back to his patrol car. Soon he'd be driving off. She had so hoped he'd ask her out on a date–even if she was a non-college degreed lady. He didn't.

She looked down at her faded jeans. At least they hugged her curves, but her hands looked beat up from rough work. Holly had shapely hands, but the nails needed work. Maybe get some polish. She'd seen heavy duty rubber gloves on sale at Goodman's Deli; maybe she should go buy some if she was going to keep sticking her hands in strong cleaning fluids.

Before getting in his car, he turned toward her. For a second, she thought he might be about to ask her out, but instead, he said, "Holly if that dog ever decides to take off in front of a truck, let go of that leash. Aaup?" Then he was gone.

Being with him gave her feelings that she couldn't quite damp down. Longings. Making her want things she knew wasn't going to happen. She pictured them as dating, walking beside that tall man, holding his big hand, being his. But he only saw her as a potential lawbreaker.

Could she push him her way a little bit? Aunt Maureen said her mother and father were into that '*witchcraft nonsense,*' that's what destroyed them. Could she do something that would be harmless but make him notice her? Make him think she was more attractive than she was? Was it wrong for her to wish for him to want her? Light a candle–that wouldn't really be wrong. He'd only come to her if he wanted to. She was only trying to hasten things a little. Would they have something in The Rainbow Realm she could use? Not to hex him because that would be wrong, but just to get him to notice her a little more?

Pumpkins forgotten, with Thor alongside her, Holly ran almost all of the way home. The hard exercise helped with her body's yearning. She was too tired to climb two flights up and fill her tub. Instead, she used the shower in Frost's small bathroom in the kitchen wing. She thought it would help, but as she sponged her body off, she found herself imagining Paul's big hands rubbing up her hips to her breasts. She had to do something!

There were books all over the mansion. She decided to start in the old library wing, and as she settled herself on the floor before the bookcase wall alongside the fireplace, Holly smelled the brief scent of honeysuckle again. It seemed to come and go in this mansion. She looked at the books on the bottom shelves, some worn leather bound, some narrow paper pamphlets and other pocketbooks. She started looking through them: herbal usage accounts of paranormal craft, colonial histories, and treaties on Indian medicine.

Holly reached out for a small, thick volume. Only five inches high with a black pebbled cover; she pulled it out and found it was only eight inches long. Not a book–a photo album. She started thumbing through the thick, black pages. Some black and white photos of an older woman and man that she had thought she'd seen before. From other pictures hanging on the walls in this house, it was her father's parents, her grandparents; reverently Holly kept turning pages.

Color pictures are now showing groups of younger people together. Most of these pictures were strange squares, with wide white margins, thicker at the bottom. Holly studied a dark-haired man, his arm loving around a smiling blonde woman. Holly realized suddenly this woman looked like her;

this was her mother, Hester. Holly stared at her parents for a moment, they looked so happy and in love.

The next page her mother was in bed holding three tiny babes nestled into her arms. Then there were pictures of the three of them walking. And all on the back of one pony at what, five? A tiny flower of lavender had been taped near that picture, to decorate the book? Or for protection? Holly rested a fingertip on the yellow tape feeling for vibrations. Her mother hadn't done this. Maybe her grandmother?

What was in the rest of this book? A big group picture. A handsome man in the center, holding his body in a command stance, a lot like Noel. This was the man she thought was her father, surrounded by young women. Holly had to look carefully until she finally did see her mother, off to the end on the left. Not smiling like the others, but not looking angry. Holly gently put a hand over the photograph, but she felt nothing. She studied it again and suddenly realized there was another woman in that photo she recognized.

It was hard as the girl was obviously in her late teens. Still, Holly knew the wide cheeks and large eyes. Her hair appeared darker, more black than the bronze-red it was today, but she had still been outlining her eyes with kohl, even in those days. Skye Rainbow was standing alongside her father; his arm was around her shoulders. Skye Rainbow knew her father more than just having heard of him. From this picture, she knew him well! Why had she lied about it?

Gault Corey's other arm was on the shoulder of another woman Holly didn't recognize. There were twelve women in that photo. Her grandmother wasn't there, but as Holly scanned the group more closely, she realized there were two other women she did recognize. Two women in their early forties are standing to the edge of the group on the right. Both familiar, one with reddish blonde hair and the other dark brown, both smiling widely like the rest. Sarah and Abigail

Hoyt were obviously two women who also knew a lot more about her parents than they let on.

She continued to study that picture. Something was wrong. Something didn't fit. From the photos placement in the book, that brightly colored, horizontal group with Sarah and Abigail Hoyt was at least seventeen years old. Maybe twenty-two, judging from the photos on the next page of Holly and her brothers as toddlers. Yet in that group picture of her father and his friends what was wrong? It took a moment for Holly to figure it out: Sarah and Abby looked exactly the same age then as they did today!

Chapter 22

The next day at work, Holly found Skye very friendly as she cheerily asked again, "Find your mother's Book of Shadows?"

"N-not yet," Holly added small bottles of essences to the display in the oils section. "I did find an old photograph book with pictures of my family. It also had friends of my parents."

"Did it?" Skye asked absentmindedly as she was busy marking down reorders from the incense catalog.

"It had pictures of the Hoyt sisters."

"Sarah and Abigail?" At last, Holly seemed to have gotten Skye's attention.

So Holly continued. "They really haven't changed too much over the years."

"Abigail and Sarah? They live by you, don't they?" Skye paused, but then turned back to her catalog. "I'd stay away from the Hoyt sisters."

"Why?"

"People who emanate negative energy weight you down."

Holly thought about it. "I don't really find the Hoyt sisters negative."

"Can you read them?" Skye asked what sounded like an idle question.

"No." Holly half thought about mentioning she couldn't read Skye either, but she didn't. Instead she started to probe on another point. "Sarah and Abby knew my parents."

"Well, your parents lived nearby, but Sarah and Abigail weren't really in the younger peoples' social set."

"But you were?"

Suddenly Skye had become interested in rearranging Saint candles. "What makes you say that?"

"I found some photographs at the house, of my father and a group of women. You were in Gault's coven weren't you?"

She didn't say anything, so Holly just waited. Finally, Skye began speaking softly, "I was only seventeen then, and your father was a magnetic man. Commanding." Her voice softened. "Gault's eyes were positively mesmerizing."

"Were you his lover?"

Skye looked at her and then spoke quite casually. "One of them. I wasn't a significant coven member, and we weren't lovers per se. We were renewing the earth with fertility rites in the moonlight by the mill pond. It was quite romantic." Skye's face took on a dreamy expression. "Together we raised tremendous energy. Your father was the high priest and, Gault always lead, sometimes with your mother, sometimes with one of the others, sometimes with me."

Pain flooded Holly, "Because my father was unfaithful–is that why my mother killed herself?"

"Oh, no. Your parents had an open marriage. They were very adult about these things. Understanding that physical and mental relationships should be for the expansion of our conscious, not for the limiting of it."

Holly couldn't believe they were talking about this so matter-of-factly. "But my mother killed herself?"

"Not over me or anyone else who was with your father," Skye stated firmly, "She had a very open attitude, and I was away at school when that happened. And who said it was suicide? It could have just been an accident? We always practiced with sacred fires." She seemed quite casual as she continued. "We lit them, then performed the rituals with the athames. As a coven, we worshiped in the fields on moonlit nights, and when rained, we went indoors to the old mill building. Perhaps your mother was practicing a ritual. Yes, I sure your mother's death was an accident."

Since Holly could not read Skye, she didn't know if the woman was telling the truth or not.

Chapter 23

In the kitchen, Holly opened two large cans of beef stew and poured them into the pot for supper. "Frost, that painting I have upstairs..."

"The one you brought back to the mansion?"

"Yes. I think it might be a Warren John Thomas. It looks like his style."

"Could be or could be one of his students. It came from here originally didn't it?"

"Yes, " Holly said softly. "After Noel was driven away when Aunt Maureen was packing the car to take me away from you too, I started crying. Begging for the painting, like if I had it, I still lived here a little. Uncle Benjamin thought it was ridiculous, but Grandmother gave it to me. Now that we're back together again, I don't need it as much." Frost was helping by pulling her smoking tray of biscuits out of the oven. She never could seem to get everything in a meal coming done at the same time. "If it is an original Thomas it would be valuable, right?"

"Should be," he said, his mind obviously elsewhere.

"Would the seaport museum want it?"

"Sure. If you were willing to donate it."

The growing, soaring hope suddenly felt flat. "They wouldn't pay for it?"

"Not unless you could line up a wealthy donor to buy it for them. How about that woman you work for, Skye?"

"Not too many people have been buying in the store lately."

He looked surprised at that. "Her Rainbow Realm is still donating to the seaport museum."

Noel came back from walking Thor, and he was holding one of those tiny, red flannel bags between his fingers. "Found another one."

"Where was this one?" Frost asked.

"In the rhododendron bushes, close to the back steps."

"They're getting closer..." said Holly in a muted voice.

"Someone's cursing us?" asked Frost. "Why?"

Holly studied the bag more closely, opening it and looking in. It was carefully made, turned neatly inside out to hide the hand sewed seams. A careful evenly stitched turnover for the black drawstring and she noted the stitches were of equal size and equal spacing, done by a very expert sewer. Taking a mailing ad and turning it on its white, blank side, Holly poured out an assortment of dried leaves and berries. Less than half an ounce. And...she looked more carefully, spreading the contents with a shapely fingernail–there was a tiny bone in it. "Someone's taking an awful lot of time on this. I wonder if its connected to finding Rolf's body in our backyard?" Absentmindedly she poured the contents back into its bag.

"Is it safe to keep it in the house?" Noel frowned to Frost. "I mean–don't you know more about this witchcraft stuff than we do?"

Holly closed her fingers around the small, soft bag to feel its vibrations and then she shrugged. "It doesn't feel harmful."

Frost took the bag from Holly and smelled it. "Herby."

"The question is–who is putting them out there and why?" Noel pointed out.

"What we need is one of those motion activated, night-sight cameras that could catch our mad-bag-placer in the act," Frost said.

"We've got them at the Aquarium," said Noel. "We lend out have-a-heart cages and cameras to people with wildlife problems. I'll ask Dr. Morjessky if I can borrow one."

Holly was stirring the stew when she saw Frost give

a high sign to Noel, who walked over. "Holly, I was speaking with Laura. She's setting a date for putting the house on the market."

Holly reacted with panic. "We aren't going to finish cleaning it up? I thought we were going to replace those broken floor boards. Paint the house–surely we'd get a better price. You want the best price don't you?"

"We can't afford the paint, much less painters," finished Noel regretfully.

"What about my idea of opening it as a Bed and Breakfast again?" She was begging. "They're popular in tourist spots. I could run it. We could all live here, and the mansion would pay for itself?"

From behind, Frost put his hands on her shoulders, and Holly felt his brotherly love and his raw pain at having to hurt her, but he said, "Holly, the place needs more than painting. The plumbing needs to be replaced in the guest rooms, this mansion has forty amp electrical fuses, and there's no cable TV, no Internet. Whose going to pay to stay here? Cavemen?"

"We could fix it up..." she pleaded.

"Even if we could do the work–paint, pipes, wood, all of that costs money that we don't have," Noel said.

"Another month. Don't sell it for another month! Please– so that we can get to know each other?" Holly begged.

"We can't," said Noel, avoiding her eyes.

Also not meeting her eyes, Frost set the table, then they sat down to Holly's dinner. The biscuits were scorched outside and underdone and doughy inside. The stew lukewarm and Holly didn't have an appetite anyway. She left Noel to clean up and headed up to the third floor for the sanctuary of her room. Her safe world–for only a short time.

Holly laid out on the four poster bed. How could they just give up so easily? How could they leave her again? And how could they not care?

Despair filled her. The waxing moon should be up; she could go up to the cupola and look out, maybe seeing the trees would calm her. Again the faint smell of honeysuckle. Wrapping her arms around her, Holly looked around this bedroom she had grown to love. Four poster bed, lady's desk, bureau and oval mirror and then she saw the painting of the seaport docks that she'd clung to all these years.

As she grew up that painting, with its faded gold-leaf frame, hanging in her bedroom. It had been a window where she could look back to a time when she, Frosty and Noel had been together. Holly never wanted to give it up, but if it could bring in enough money to keep them living here together?

She took a ball of cotton and dipped it in water. By gently dabbing years of icky yellow grime stuck to the cotton. Holly remembered this painting had once hung in the front parlor where Grandfather Frank and Uncle Ben endlessly smoking cigarettes and cigars. She started from the top down, putting off until the last moment, those smudges at the bottom where the signature should go.

Finally, she started on that last corner and could make out faint scribbles in black oil paint. A letter, a 'W,' a 'J'? And another broken, thin-thick line that could have been a Thomas signature. She was sure–maybe. There must be a gallery somewhere that could verify it and give her an estimated value!

Holly looked around her room. She needed a blanket, no, the duck-down quilt would give more protection. Yes. She wrapped the painting carefully. Tomorrow she'd put it in the back of the hearse, the guys would never look under the quilt. Tomorrow was her day off at the store, she'd look up art galleries in the phone book, and after she drove her brothers to work, she'd go sell the painting.

Chapter 24

Holly had an address, over the bridge on West street. Parking was a problem with the long hearse, and finally, she had to go back and drive down Noank road, past Paul's kiosk office. His police Tahoe wasn't there, but farther down she got parking, and then she had to haul that twenty-four inch by sixteen inches plus frame picture cocooned in its quilt. She found the Janus Gallery situated in a cocoa-brown building, with its 1893 flat roof and false front.

But inside the gallery was hung with six foot by three foot black on red abstracts canvases. A thin, mustard yellow suited man looked up from reading a book on the glass counter. "Hello, I'm Marcus Janus."

"H-how." She took a deep breath. "How do you do. My name is Holly Corey, and I think I have an original Warren John Thomas."

"Who?"

"He was a painter in the old days," she said unwrapping her treasure.

As he looked at her painting, Mr. Janus raised an unimpressed eyebrow. "Here, my dear, the old days are the 1960's. Why don't you try the Green Duck down the street. They do vintage."

Holly gave him a small smile as she carefully wrapped up her painting and noted Mr. Janus did not bother to move to open the door for her.

At the Green Duck, they seemed to specialize in folk art and painted tinware. The woman proprietor suggested Holly try the Tauten Gallery on the other side of the bridge. Their gallery's paintings were sea themed with period square riggers.

At the Tauten, a Mr. Adam pointed out the painting might very well be a Warren John Thomas, did she have any provenience?

"Provenience?"

"A chain of paperwork showed evidence of the painting's authenticity and ownership from the painter to the present owners. Or a recognized expert's opinion that the painting is genuine and the title is clear." He said that if she could get provenience, he might be able to sell it for her with a forty/sixty split.

"We'd the get sixty percent?" Holly tentatively asked.

"No, of course not." He indicated the beige clothed walled room about her. "I have expenses. Goodwill. The gallery gets the sixty percent."

"H-how much would be left?"

"Well, first you must have it researched and authenticated. I know of a researcher who will document Warren John Thomas' life for forty dollars an hour. You'll also need to display it in a more impressive, custom designed frame–that can be done here."

"How much?"

"Only $1500." Seeing Holly's face, he sighed deeply and then continued, "If you want to go inexpensive, we might be able to find one for $ 850, but that certainly would not show your painting to its greatest advantage!"

"I think we'll leave it in its present frame," Holly said.

He raised his eyebrow in disgust. "You will still have to have it cleaned."

"I dusted it already."

"No, madam, in those period oil paintings there was a protective varnish coat applied to the canvas after it dried. That varnish yellows over time. Smoke and dust bonds to it and it can only be removed by a trained conservator."

She was almost too afraid to ask. "That sounds expensive?"

He was dismissive. "We don't do that here."

This was getting hopeless. "Couldn't you just put the painting on your wall? See if it sells, and we each share fifty-

fifty?"

Mr. Adam didn't appear to think that was such a hot idea. "This painting must first be cleaned. They'll use chemical washes to remove that varnish; then they'll have to repair any surface damage, then revarnish."

"Wouldn't taking off the top layer damage the patina? That loses value with an antique doesn't it?"

His lip curled with contempt. "Did you hear that on Antique Roadshow?"

"Let me think about this."

"Certainly it's your choice, Madam, but I would suggest the cleaning first. If you wish an inexpensive repair, you might try Mr. Holmes at The Leather Bucket.

Chapter 25

Getting directions Holly wrapped up the painting, shlepped back down the road to her hearse and started off again.

She drove past The Leather Bucket three times. Only found it when she got out and walked the old tree-lined street. The words "Leather Bucket" was scrolled under two crossed firefighter nozzles on a sign outside a man's wooden garage in back of his two-story house. The sign next to the small door on the garage's side said 'ring buzzer.' Holly did.

Soon a slight, bleached-straw haired older man hurried out with a key, and as he unlocked the garage door, she noted his sun freckles. Inside the double garage, Holly saw a lot of antique firefighting equipment, hoses, fire helmets, brass calling horns, and leather buckets hanging from the wall. Most of the inventory looked dusty like not much had sold in a very long time.

But it was more an artist's workshop than an antique store. There were work tables set all around the garage walls and each neatly loaded with brushes and jars of cleaning fluids and tubes of oil paints. Several easels stood about, with paintings on them. In the center of the cement floor, there was a full sheet of 3/4 plywood set on handmade table legs, forming a table four foot by six foot that was scrupulously clean. The small, slender man looked at her quilt bundle with interest. "You have a painting for me? Let's see." He said pulling on a pair of clean, white cotton gloves.

Before she could put her burden down, he pulled a sheet of paper from a roll at the end of the table to protect painting being laid on it. As Holly put the painting down and started unwrapping it, the man pulled a cord over the table. Powerful lights went on, but not fluorescent, something that seemed to have a strong daylight spectrum.

When she had finished, he said nothing. Just looking at the painting, walking all around the table to study it from different angles, finally saying, "Looks like a Warren John Thomas? I'm Doug Holmes by the way."

Still looking at the painting, he put out a gloved hand for her to shake and she did. He had a strong grip and didn't have predator emanations. "I-I-I think this is. A T-t-thomas. I want to sell it. Do you know what it might be worth?"

"Do you have provenience?"

She shook her head.

Still looking just at the painting he said, "Actually I have several books that mention Thomas's works in the house. I might be able to find a reference or an old photo of this very painting."

"H-how much would that cost?" Holly asked miserably.

He briefly looked up at her. "To read a book? Nothing."

"That would authenticate it?" Hope was back.

"Where did you get this painting?" He was challenging.

"I've had it for years in my bedroom, but it came from the mansion, Corey House."

"Witch House?"

She blushed. "Yes. I'm H-h-holly Corey."

He finally looked up from the painting to study her. "You look like your mother."

"You knew her?" Holly asked eagerly.

"I've seen a painting of her." God, she wanted to ask him a thousand questions, but selling this painting to get money for the mansion came first. "How much do you think it could be sold for?"

He leaned back. "The market for 1800's marine landscapes isn't doing too well now."

That figured. "But you think it could be sold?"

"Maybe."

"What could it bring–at the most?"

"Five. Six figures. Maybe less. The problem is finding the right buyer."

"Do you sell paintings?"

"Sometimes. I take them on consignment." His tone was non-committal.

"Would that take long?"

He shrugged.

She needed the money now! "Another gallery said it needed cleaning. Do you do that?"

He was looking at the painting again. "It would help. Yes, I do."

"How much does that cost?"

"Under a thousand."

The rising hopes receded fast. "We need to sell it, but I'm a little short cash right now. Could you do the cleaning on speculation?"

Now he looked to be evaluating her. "Miss Corey, are you any relation to Frost Corey?"

"He's my brother. My triplet."

He nodded. "I do conservation work for Mystic Seaport Museum. I've worked with Frost at the museum, like his wood carvings a lot. Your brother's a good guy, always helping me carry stuff out to my car." He looked back down at the painting. "I could take this, clean it on speculation, on the provision that I hold the painting until it's sold or you pay the cleaning?"

"What would be the split, if you were to sell it?"

"The price of cleaning, plus fifteen percent of the sale price."

Mr. Holmes sounded too good to be true. "D-do you think it needs a new frame?"

He lifted the painting, studying the tarnished, gold-leafed frame front and back. "I think this was the original framing. I can repair those cracks, touch it up a bit with gilt, but keeping the painting in this frame might actually add to the sale price."

"Will it take long to sell?"

He shook his head and looked at it again. "Can't tell you. You need money fast?"

She nodded.

"Well, it's either gonna sell or not. There's less call for Thomas's work now, which is a shame, I've always liked his paintings. He was never a well-known artist, made most of his living by doing wall murals, but he was a very good recorder of what was there and its inherent beauty. And this is a nice view of the Mystic docks. Yes, I think it could sell."

Not too confident herself, she looked about his dim little garage workshop, with its dusty firehouse antiques and bottles of cleaning fluids. "Do you get many buyers in here?"

He smiled. "My dear, my traffic is worldwide. I'm plugged into the Internet."

"I'll leave it to be sold. C-could could I get a-a...?" Oh, she couldn't ask him.

He looked at her puzzled, then understood. "You want a receipt? I was just about to give it to you."

"I-I'm sorry," she said miserably.

"Don't be. This painting means a great deal to you doesn't it?"

Now that she was never going to see it again, Holly felt herself tearing up. "It's been with me my whole life and has been a great comfort." But what had Paul Travinsky said? *It hurts, but sometimes you have to let go of the past, or you can't move on.* "Now it's time to let it go."

Doug looked back to the painting with its blowing clouds, square-rigged sailing ships, and figures are bustling across the docks. "It's obvious this was painted here on the south shore of the harbor, probably in the 1840's, which is late mid-period for his work. Actually the height of his career." He studied the painting. "There is a limited regular market for Thomas's work, but I have two buyers that I'll start with. One--who I assume would bid the highest--lives in Australia. He has quite an interest in 1800's New England marine landscapes. But there is another, an elderly woman who lives locally, who has a very good collection that she's planning to donate to the Seaport Museum gallery upon her death. You would be taking probably five percent less in purchase price with her, but the painting would stay in Mystic?"

Holly reached out and ran her fingertips across the dry, rough surface. "I would like it to stay in the area. Maybe go to the Seaport Museum gallery so everybody can see it. Yes, please try her first."

He nodded.

She added sadly, almost to herself, "I never thought to take a picture of it."

He understood. "I'll be taking some digital ones for my website and records. I can give you a copy." Seeing her look up quickly, he added with a small smile, "for free."

Holly gave him the mansion's telephone number, saying to leave a message for her to call back if she missed him. Then it was time to go. The painting that had been with her, or she with it, since she was born. When Holly was ripped apart from her brothers, when she lost her home, her parents it had been there for her. But as Paul had said sometimes you have to do unpleasant things to keep going, but at this moment she wondered just how good it was to 'keep going'?

                    *   *   *

On loan from the Aquarium Noel had his wildlife camera, a camouflaged square of plastic about twelve inches wide by fourteen inches long and six inches thick. The three of them went outside in the backyard to find a location. They finally decided on a young oak tree, seven feet away from the back brick walkway. Here the lilacs and shrubbery had been allowed to overgrow, and most of the little red flannel bags had been found. With the step ladder from the kitchen, Noel slung the strap around the tree and hung the camera.

He pressed a test button then pulled out the small memory card, taking it inside to the kitchen, uploading it to his laptop with an adaptor from the Aquarium. They all studied the angle on the computer screen that got the brick pathway and part of the house. Taking the memory card outside, Noel inserted it back into the camera, setting a trap for their midnight visitor.

Chapter 26

Holly's first driving lesson with Frost started out not too great, but okay. The hearse's extra length and wide base made it a little hard to steer, and she was working on getting Frost to clutch earlier when stopping for red lights. But she wanted to take a chance to ask a few questions, while he was concentrating on something else.

Still, she had to remind him again. "Don't ride the clutch. It wears it out." From the back, Bernie sobbed quietly, as Holly continued, "Miranda seems lovely, but with her dressed in period garb, why does the museum allow her to have that neon green streak in her black hair?"

"She's got some fans in administration," Frost said.

"All men?"

"Meow," returned Frost, as he is concentrating on depressing the clutch.

"Why haven't you brought her home to dinner?"

"Eating stew in a kitchen isn't her thing. Miranda likes to eat out in restaurants, nice ones."

"She's always borrowing money from you for cigarettes, dry cleaning..." She is guessing at the dry cleaning, but his face confirmed it.

"No! Miranda always pays it back...usually. She just forgets sometimes," Frost said, slowing for a green light that might turn yellow. "You know, she let me take her out for lunch the other day." He sounded so happy and proud. "There's a nice Chinese wok place by the museum entrance. Inexpensive for her, but she said she wanted me to take her there." Thinking of her he wasn't paying attention his driving and not engaging the clutch in time as they approached a stop sign.

"The hearse it-it-it's stalling because..?" Holly started.

"I know! I know. Well, while we were eating, Miranda started asking me questions about finding Rolf's body. She kept asking me if I found something with him."

"Found what?"

"She wouldn't say at first, and then she admitted Rolf had taken some pictures of her. That he had an envelope that he was teasing her with. He was great photo bug, with all those fancy long lenses. Well, she thought Rolf might have had the pictures on him when he was killed at our place? She didn't want the cops to find them."

Two crossroads lay ahead. Holly wanted Frost to take a right at the second one, but she wanted to give him plenty of time to get ready. As they were passing through the first, Holly started, "T-t-turn right..." Before she could finish, Frost whipped the steering wheel hard right, cutting the intersection, crossing over into the left lane, right in front of an oncoming car.

"G-get back!" She screamed.

He swung right as the hearse rocked wildly. Then he started to brake.

"N-not here!" Holly cried, but not getting gas; the engine started to fail. "P-p-put the clutch in!" She yelled as the ghost in the back wailed out. "Bernie! Enough! Please. He's trying! F-f-frost–don't turn so hard!" The heavy hearse swayed dangerously on the road.

The sound of sirens behind them. Frost looked up in the rearview mirror and then looked over his shoulder to see who was following them.

Holly yelled again, "Keep your eyes on the cars ahead!" But she looked too; it was a black and white Tahoe bearing down on them.

Frost was smiling as he kept driving. "Maybe it's your boyfriend, Officer Travinsky?"

"Oh, God." She sank back in the car seat as the blue and red lights behind them bounced off the windshield ahead.

"What's he waving his arm for?"

Holly didn't need to look. "He wants you to pull off

the road."

Frost braked, not getting the clutch in fast enough and stalling out the engine, bring the hearse to an abrupt stop in the middle of the road.

Slamming his brakes, Paul fishtailed to a screeching stop, inches from the hearse's rear bumper. As Frost tried to restart the stalled engine, Holly could smell the white smoke of burned rubber from the Tahoe. She whispered to the ghost in the back, "Please, Bernie, don't make a sound! For me. Please!"

Finally, Frost managed to drive forward and pull the hearse onto the grass on the side of the road, as Holly told him, "Roll down the windows, don't open the door, let him do the talking."

"Been through this before," muttered Frost.

Paul-the-cop walked over to the driver's window. In an official voice he said to Frost, "Mr. Corey, did anyone tell you that a driver is not supposed to come to a sudden, dead stop in the middle of a traffic lane?"

"I didn't plan it–I stalled."

"Learner's permit and hearse registration." Then looked to her. "Ms. Corey, did you find that driver's license yet?"

"Yes." She was searching her handbag for it. "Still Ca-ca-ca..."

"Still registered in California. That's okay, you're still visiting," his voice softened just a little.

"We got Thor's dog tag from the town," she added lamely.

Still looking at Frost's learner's permit, he commented. "Good, I won't have to put the dog behind bars." Then Paul switched into heartless cop mode. "But if you are going to continue with Connecticut as your primary residence, you are required to change your hearse's registration and your license." He looked to Frost. "Wasn't your brother teaching you to drive?"

Frost tightened his jaw. "Didn't work."

Holly looked at Paul. "This all mm-my-my fault. I-I t-told Frosty to t-t-turn, but h-he..."

Bending down, Paul looked from an ashamed Frost, back to her stuttering. "Holly, this is not working! You can't teach him to drive! Not in this." He indicated the hearse.

"He needs to get his license!" she pleaded. Then looked to Frost. "You could go out with N.C. again?"

Frost was adamant. "I am not going out with Herr Hitler!"

The cop looked grim. "You three Coreys are turning into my own personal crime tsunami!" He glared at them, then said, "On my watch, this is not going to continue! First, Frost get out!"

Holly was horrified. "You're going to arrest him?"

"No, but he's not driving anymore. Holly, just slide across. You are driving this...hearse home. He's not!"

Holly's shoulders sagged as they switched places. "B-but Frost needs to learn..."

Ignoring Holly, Paul was addressing Frost as he was getting in on the passenger side. "You're off work at the Seaport when 5? 5:30?

"Around 5:20."

"That'll work. I'll be finishing my shift at the neighborhood police booth at 5:30, across the bridge. Wait for me tomorrow in the museum's parking lot; I'll pick you up and take you out myself, and then bring you back to the mansion."

Frost broke out into a wide grin. "I'm going to learn to drive in a patrol car?"

"No, in my personal truck. Which cost years of overtime for me and was just delivered to the dealer last week!" Paul glared at him. "You will not mess up my new truck!"

"He needs to learn standard..." she started.

"My truck is standard transmission," Paul said calmly passing their paperwork back to them.

"C-can, a policeman, do that? Teach a civilian?" Holly asked.

"I'll be off shift, and I'll consider it as part of my sworn duty to protect the other motorists of Connecticut from the menace of the Coreys. Now, Holly, turn this boat around carefully and slowly drive out of here!"

"Don't you need to check the r-registration?" She stammered.

He glared at her. "I've memorized it."

Blushing Holly put the car in gear. It took a lot of heavy wheel pulling, moving forward and back to turn anything as long as the hearse on this small road. Paul stayed watching, signaling an oncoming car to stop for them. As they finally did leave, Frost looked back at the police car. "Sis, we're in luck. We got a cop who likes you!"

"No." She glanced in the mirror, and he was still parked there, filing a report on his computer no doubt. "He's just doing his job. Keeping an eye on some murder suspects."

Frost smiled widely. "When he stopped us, I sensed he was sexually interested in someone. It better not be me."

She found herself blushing more. This was supposed to be a driving lesson; she could at least try to teach him. "You should indicate your turn ten-no thirty feet–well before you are going to turn."

Frost decided to change the subject. "How's the job at Rainbow Realm going?"

She had been wanting to talk about that. "Something funny happened the other day. Skye and I were decorating the outside of the shop for Halloween, putting orange and black ropes of plastic pumpkins around the display window. While we were out front, I heard the bells from the Museum's steamboat."

"It would've been Captain Gustav, taking the tourists up the river. He rings the bells and toots the steam whistle a lot. He says it's sort of a paddling advertisement for the Museum."

"Well, Skye turns to me and whispers conspiratorially. *Do you hear that*? I heard the boat and the ducks quacking in the pond, tourists were laughing, traffic noise came from the throughway, so I said, *Hear what?* She whispered back. '*The ship's bells. Bells from the Robert Fulton?*' Of course, I could hear them, so I said '*Yes.*' She giggled, then said, '*You only hear them faintly. I hear them loudly! My hearing is greatly developed, I can hear way more than a normal mortal can*'."

"What did you say to her?" Frost asked.

"Nothing."

"I think your boss better take it easy testing those medicinal herbs she's always mixing in the back."

Chapter 27

Later they were all in the kitchen as Frost flattening pizza dough for their dinner and Holly started talking about work again. "I don't know if I am going to be laid off. Skye says it's okay, but with the economy down our business is slow."

"Is it?" Frost asked. "The Rainbow Realm sponsors several underprivileged kids projects at the Museum. Skye's also paying for all the materials for us to build a Viking Karve."

"I don't see how we're not selling that much. Mostly low-end tourist items like the Wiccan mugs and incense sticks. I don't even know how she's making the store rent?"

Noel was lifting that fifty-pound bag of kibble to pour into Thor's new bowl. "She must be making money or have a wealthy family? When I've met you at work, she was wearing all linens and silk, and remember the other day, when I met you in the parking lot? She was getting into that silver car with the RainB vanity plate?"

"That's her car," said Holly. "It's small."

"Holly, that's a silver Mercedes-Benz Cl-coupe. Base price starts at over hundred thousand." Noel looked at her in exasperation. "And she's paying you next to nothing!"

"But it's a great place to work. When we're slow, I've been looking at the books on gemology and astral projection."

"So keep working there," said Frost, as he started ladling marinara sauce over the pizza dough.

"Well, I still don't think I will be working there much longer," Holly said.

"Why?" Noel asked as he sliced the pepperoni.

"It's just that she is so nice one minute and the next she's so angry and critical. And I think I just messed up the inventory."

"How?" Noel asked.

"Three large boxes of herbal oils came in with a gross

in each. I input their serial numbers in the inventory program."

"So?" Noel asked again.

"Each box had two serial numbers. I put the wrong set in–it's going to screw up the reordering inventory. "

"Can't you rekey them?" Noel asked.

"But I don't want Skye to see me."

"Does she go out for lunch?" Frost suggested.

"Usually she just sends me out to pick up something for the both of us. We eat in the storage room at Skye's desk."

Noel thought about it. "Do you have a key to open up the store yourself?"

"No. I can turn the alarm on, but I don't have the code for turning it off."

"Last Tuesday when I showed up, she was gone?" said Noel.

"Tuesday and Thursdays she leaves early to teach a yoga class at the Y," Holly confirmed.

"But the shop stays open?" Noel pursued.

"I lock up and turn on the alarm when I go."

"There's your answer," finished Noel. "Stay late and fix your problem."

A smile spread across Holly's face. "I will!"

*   *   *

On Tuesday at the Rainbow Realm, Holly was standing on the top step of a footstool, methodically wiping the dust off two dozen suncatchers hanging in the diamond panes of the window. Patiently she carefully wiped a yellow and green-winged butterfly with jewel cut eyes; although she appreciated the beauty of the stained glass, Holly considered them a pain in the butt to clean.

Using one of the mirrors on the jewelry counter, Skye was redrawing the black kohl outline around her eye. "I wanted price stickers on all those new brass candlesticks..."

She looked at the clock, sounding annoyed as she said, "I'm running late for my class, and you won't have time."

"I'll label the candlesticks before I go. I-I-I can set the alarm."

"Not tonight. You might make some mistake with the alarm, and I won't be here to fix it. Finish the candlesticks and then just lock the back door after you."

Holly took her time finding the adhesive tags and marking pen as Skye gathered up her handbag, pulling on her dun-colored, suede coat with its narrow green trimming and oversized, crescent pockets. "Remember. Don't set the alarm!"

It took just a few minutes for Holly to label the candlesticks, then close out the register. At 5:00 exactly she'd turned the front door sign to 'closed,' turned off the front lights, and went into the storage room. Paul was supposed to be giving Frost another driving lesson tonight, but as much as she wanted to be home to see him, she needed to fix that stock coding error. Back in the storeroom as the Rainbow Realm's laptop booted up, Holly gathered up piles of the boxes she incorrectly entered and set them on the counter.

Sitting down, she had to locate the right entry, and then retype the new codes over the old. It seemed to take forever, especially when she wanted so much to be home, to see Paul's broad shoulders, long legs, and tight rear end. Holly was just finishing the last of the boxes when she heard boots and a scraping sound outside the back door.

Guiltily Holly looked up. Was Skye returning? How would Holly explain still being here? She got up and pushed back the coverlets that split the storeroom. Whoever was coming in seemed to be having trouble with the lock. Trying another key? That wouldn't be Skye.

It was 6:10. All the tourists would be gone from the Olde Village shops, and even the security man would have gone home. Shit! Should she call the police? The phone was in the store itself, but the back door was opening. Holly glanced desperately about, running to Skye's desk, grabbing for the witches' knife Skye used to slit open mail.

A large man coming in with his hands full of about twenty small, brown, taped boxes. He stopped in shocked surprise.

Captain Gustav? Why would he be here?

He reacted to seeing Holly with the heavy, double-bladed athame. "Damn! Girl, don't go frightening a man so!"

"Skye isn't here."

He had stopped. She had the definite impression he didn't know what to do, but he just smoothly kept talking, "She isn't? Well, she wasn't supposed to be. Nobody was supposed to be here, that's why Skye lent me her extra key."

Holly didn't even have a key, and she worked here; she automatically moved forward to help him unload his stacks of small boxes on one of the tables.

"Holly is it? Frost's sister?"

"Yes."

"Why are you still here?"

Holly reddened. "Don't tell Skye. I made a mistake with the stock records, and I wanted to f-f-fix it..."

"Before she knew?" He nodded. "That's fine. Won't say a word."

Holly looked at the boxes. "Do you want me to open these?"

He looked at the boxes. "Better not. These are some native crafts I trade for when ships come into the harbor–actually, don't tell anybody, there's some ivory and rare parrot feathers that couldn't make it through regular customs. Skye's going to look at 'em and let me know if she wants to sell anything in the store. Yeah, better not fool with them. Skye's been so touchy. Lately, hot one moment and cold the next must be sailing herself into the change! You women and your hormone hurricanes buffer a man so! Didn't even check these boxes myself to see if anything was missing. Don't want me or you blamed if there is! In fact, young lady, you should be going home, let me walk you out, the parking lot looks as empty as the endless sea. A pretty young girl like yourself shouldn't be walking alone out of a deserted island like this village."

"But Skye might want..."

"C'mon, girl I'm running late, and I'm not leaving Frost's sister here alone!"

"I-I-I've got to input one last box and shut down the computer."

He didn't look happy, but he was white knight enough to say, "No problem. I'll wait."

She finished inputting, with a patient Gustav watching her. She smelled nicotine and strong shaving lotion on him. He wasn't saying anything, but the baseness of his aura colors made her kind of uneasy. Especially being alone in the storeroom with him.

When she finally was ready, he insisted on holding the back door open for her, but before she stepped out, Holly stopped. "The key?"

"Key?" Gustav asked.

"You borrowed Skye's key. Aren't you going to leave it here for her?"

"Aye, thank you for reminding me." He quickly fished up his key ring and unhooked it, putting the brass key down on the shelf beside the door. And then he held the door open so that she would have to brush past him to get out.

Outside the back of the store, Holly glanced down at that little gnome statuette beside the thresh hold block. It had a face that reminded her very much of Gustav's leering looks, but she had to admit, the captain acted a perfect gentlemen as he escorted her out. Only raising an eyebrow when he saw the hearse, but saying nothing.

As she drove away, Holly wondered where his car

was? He must have parked it in the North lot or walked over from the Seaport Museum. She didn't spend much time thinking about it; Holly was anxious to get home. "Oh, Bernie, I hope I haven't missed Paul!" She put her foot down hard on the gas, then remembering her policeman might be on the road, so she eased off.

N.C. was making dinner for them tonight; maybe when Paul and Frost came back from the driving lesson, she could smoothly invite Paul to stay for dinner. There'd be enough lasagna if she didn't eat much. Reaching home, Holly passed the screening fir trees before the crescent driveway in front. She kept left, driving into the back parking lot and her heart leaped up as she saw Paul's tall figure next to her brothers.

And then Holly saw Paul's shiny new king cab truck–with its broken tailgate, bent in rear bumper and one tail light smashed out.

Chapter 28

Staring forlornly, Paul, N.C. and Frost were standing at the front of the blue truck as Holly joined them. Here the damage wasn't as bad, but Paul had his shiny new toy what less than two weeks? Now it was a total wreck because of the Coreys. He would hate Frost and her and N.C. and Witch House. Holly wanted to cry–she was getting a really bad headache, but she had to ask, "You had an accident?"

"Aaup," said Paul grimly.

They were all silent; then she looked to Frost. "Did you get hurt?"

"No. I made him put his seatbelt on," Paul finished grimly. "And since you didn't think to ask, yes, I'm fine too."

Holly stated the obvious, "Your new truck's a mess."

As always Frost tried for funny. "As a trained police investigator, I think he's noticed."

Paul was saying nothing as he kept surveying the damage, his aura radiating sad, drab colors.

"I-I-I'm so sorry," Holly blathered. "I should never have let you teach Frosty. If we try again, we'll go out of your jur-jurisdiction...where does your jur–jur.. end?"

"Not far enough away from you guys," Paul finished glumly.

"Did Frost get a ticket?"

"No," Paul said. He spoke deliberately with control; but Holly intuited so much free-floating, flaring anger, she couldn't read his deeper emotions and know who exactly he was angry at. Frost or herself?

"Did you get a ticket because you were the driver in charge?"

"No."

"You did a hit and run?" she asked shocked.

Paul shook his head to her and even smiled a bit tightly. "This accident was not your brother's fault or mine.

Frost was stopped correctly for a light, behind an Explorer filled with wedding cakes. Some idiot kid with a Cadillac Escalade and an open bottle of tequila on the front seat rammed us from behind. His momentum knocked my truck into the car ahead of us. The kid had a suspended license, but the car was insured in his father's name. A buddy of mine came and wrote it all up. Had a great laugh at my expense, and Henry did a Breathalyzer on the kid that lit up the road!"

"Smashed wedding cakes were all over the back of the Explorer," added Frost.

Paul continued, "We arrested the drunken driver, and Henry is filling out the paperwork, and I'm going to have to get a lawyer, but I'm going to have a new truck when this is done!"

Holly's head was lowered in shame as she suggested, "I could drive you to work while your truck is being fixed?"

Paul smiled ruefully at her. "I'll get a rental while this is being fixed. His insurance will pay!"

"Then Frost's lessons are over," she said sadly.

"No," said Paul, "when you two aren't yelling at him, Frost calms down quite a bit. In a couple of weeks, I think your brother might be ready to pass a driving test. Unfortunately."

"U-u-unfortunately?" Holly asked.

"Yeah, for me." He turned away from the truck that caused him such pain to look at, to turn those bright blue eyes on her. "Then I'll have to think of another reason just to drop by and visit you guys."

Noel looked up. "Wouldn't it be simpler to just ask for a date?"

Paul nodded his head. "That's not a bad idea. How about going with me to a real restaurant Friday night at six thirty?"

"Oh, I'd love to," teased a deadpanning Frost. "N.C., whatever will I wear?"

"Fool, he means just Holly!" said Noel.

Holly nodded yes and then felt herself blushing deeply. "Y-Y-You want to have d-dinner with us tonight?" she asked Paul softly.

Before he could answer, Frost asked, "Who's cooking tonight. You or N.C.?"

"Me," said Noel.

Frost turned back to Paul. "Then it's okay. If it's not my sister, the food should be edible."

Holly just punched his shoulder, and Frost yelped, grabbing his arm, writhing as if in agonizing pain. "You saw that! She assaulted me!"

"I'll take her into custody," said Paul smiling, as he took Holly's arm and they headed for the mansion. That night, after home-made lasagna it was all of them talking in the parlor, going on one topic after another. It was obvious Paul seemed impressed with N.C. and his master's degree knowledge, but Frost kept up his end, arguing points on International fishing rights, modern jazz, and colonial construction techniques. Holly talked a little, but mostly she just listened, watching Paul. It was after ten when he got up to leave, and mercifully her brothers disappeared to '*clean up*' the kitchen.

Holly walked with Paul to the front entrance so they could have just a little more time together, as they walked around to the back parking. In the darkness, his new truck didn't look as damaged. "My brothers like you."

"They're fun guys to talk to." Stopping he looked down at her. " All you Coreys seem to know quite a lot about a wide range of topics, but I'm rather glad it's going to be just us on Friday."

She smiled. "I like that too." She reached up on tiptoes as he was reaching down to kiss her.

He took her in warm, strong arms, just a gentle, firm kiss, then he set her back on her heels. "Morning comes early."

Long after she saw his single tail light pulling away, Holly stood there reliving the feel of being in his arms. Of his wonderful kiss.

It was dark now with no wind. The moon hadn't risen yet, but hard diamond chips twinkled in the black, cold sky above her. She was home, Paul had just kissed her, and she could hear her brothers laughing as they cleaned up the kitchen inside. All was good unless some weirdo was sneaking on the property right now. Skulking around and leaving those little red flannel curse bags hanging from the shrubbery. Why would anyone want to hurt them? Again Holly thought of Miranda. Could they get a picture of her sneaking around on the property, looking for Rolf's photographs, but why signal that with some creepy red bags?

And why was Rolf Van Hom on their property in the first place? Couldn't he have gotten himself murdered somewhere else? He had photos of Miranda that she considered incriminating. Had he brought them here? Why? To show Frost, he was sleeping with Miranda? Taunt him? Or to ask for blackmail money? Could the photos still be here, hidden on the property? It was way too dark to search now, but tomorrow she would look in the overgrowth of the lilacs near where his body was found.

Or could Frost have found photos so incriminating to Miranda that he burned them?

For just a brief second Holly had a sickening suspicion–Frost was so crazy in love with Miranda that Rolf's taunting drove her brother into a murderous rage? Killed his rival? Lately, she had seen Frost and Noel going nose-to-nose over those silly driving lessons, and it frightened her, to see the two males in her life near physical combat. Both of her brothers were normally gentlemen, but they were both strong, and they weren't even fighting over a woman!

Would Frost have shot Rolf? One of them would have

had to bring the gun, could Frosty have cold-bloodedly planned to murder his rival? She knew he couldn't have carried Ben's revolver out here, shot his rival, and then calmly put on his blue tour guide shirt to go meet her and Noel? Would Frosty have brought her back here to 'discover' his victim as an alibi for himself? She hated herself for even thinking it.

Feeling chilled, she walked back into the kitchen. It has been over a week and no word about the painting from the art garage guy, but she'd have to wait until her brothers were back in their rooms for the night before she checked the phone messages. If she could only sell that painting, they could pay off the taxes, redo the plumbing and electrical, and open Witch House as the Corey Bed and Breakfast. Finally living here as a family again.

Chapter 29

Next day, Holly didn't find any photos in the backyard and when she got to work the back door of the Rainbow Realm was locked. Holly knocked, and Skye opened it looking angry. "You were here when Captain Gustav came last night? Why?"

"I-I-I dropped some beads. I stayed after to pick them all up."

Her boss held up the brass key. "But he left this–he shouldn't have done that!" Skye glared at Holly. "I want him to bring more cargo in! It sells well." As Holly walked away, she asked sharply. "Did you open any of the boxes?"

Skye's anger frightened Holly. "N-n-no. Gustav said that you would enjoy doing that yourself."

"Yes, I do." Then anger was instantly gone, replaced by a sunny smile as Skye said happily, "Yes. Each new package is like an unopened birthday gift. I always get a thrill at being the first to open and unwrap each figurine or necklace." On the work table, there were new parrot feather earrings, coconut sculptures, and turtle shell bracelets spread out.

"Do you want me to help you put them on display?"

"No," Skye said more evenly. "He's got some one-of-a-kind stuff. I think I may try auctioning them on the Internet first." She smiled her radiant best. "I can't have the merchandise selling if I'm advertising it on e-bay."

*   *   *

Thursday night Holly pulled out every pathetic item of clothing she had and spread them out on her bed. Only one dress–too summery, one skirt–too old maid secretary, all her polyester suit pants had pulls from wear, and the red cotton capri pants had stains on the back she couldn't get out. Finally, Holly narrowed if down to three outfits for tomorrow's date, none that she really liked, but they were the best she had. And she couldn't afford to buy anything else. She wore a pair of purple pants and carried the other two outfits down to show Frost and Noel.

Her brothers were in the kitchen arguing over whether to put sausage or meatballs in the spaghetti sauce. Holly twirled in her Bermuda pants paired with a mauve wool, long-sleeved top.

"Isn't that two different seasons," said Noel shaking his head.

Frost looked at the stuff in her hands. "You know if you took that bubble-gum pink top with the sparkles and paired them with your black jeans?"

"My black jeans are tight," said Holly.

"That's a reason to wear them, Sis," Frost suggested.

Noel finished. "Holly, you've got great curves, especially from the rear. Accentuate the positive!"

She blushed. "But jeans for a nice place?"

Frost urged, "With that pink, spangled top that makes it sort of casual-formal."

"He'll like it," Nodded Noel.

They had a good meatball-sausage sauce dinner, and at least tonight didn't wind up fighting over the sale of the mansion.

Chapter 30

Friday night her last next big decision was whether to wear her stupid red eyeglass frames or not. Holly wished she could afford contact lenses, maybe in some sultry, amethyst color. Men like a woman without glasses, but then without glasses she wouldn't see much of the town or the restaurant or even Paul. She might not even be able to even read the menu; she'd have to wear her only pair of glasses.

And what if Paul was taking her out just to question her about his murder case? He was an ambitious man–it might be worth an expensive dinner to rack up points with the department by questioning a suspect? The closer a person got to Holly, especially a man she really wanted, the less she could rely on her ability to read that person's intentions. Yes, this date might just be an attempt to nail her brother with a murder charge, but Holly tried to push that thought from her mind.

Soon she was delighted to be sitting high in Paul's new Ford 150 King Cab. Not going formal, he had worn dark slacks and a blue golf shirt and leather jacket. In the seaport, they drove across the drawbridge that spanned the river as it entered the harbor and then turned left. Paul pointed out a little, one-story brick '*Community Policing*' station. "It's a glorified phone booth, and I'm spending most of my time there now, catching up with administrative work."

"You like that?"

He didn't appear thrilled. "It's a step up the ladder, but I miss patrolling."

Getting ahead was always so important to him and so impossible for her. On her left, she saw Victorian houses, boatyards and moored sailboats and beyond them, Holly glimpsed the river, well now it had become Mystic harbor. Ahead on her right was a three-story almost barn-like building, with a side wing of balconied rooms which was identified by the gold tracing of the '*Captain Daniel Packer Inne*' signboard. Paul pulled up into the parking lot on a small hill, behind the dark gray stained building built into the hillside. "How hungry are you? There is a walk-in basement from the roadside with their bar and a small area for dancing. We could get drinks before we eat? The second and third floors are for dining."

Drinks would just add to his bill. "I'd like to eat now."

They entered from the back parking lot to the second-floor dining room, an expanse of wide maple wood floor-boards and post beams. Just inside was a small school master's desk for reservations and a Quaker bench. While they waited for a table, Paul showed her photographs on the wall of the property under reconstruction. "This was originally built as an Inn in 1756 by a former square rigger captain, who also ran the rope ferry where the bridge now sits. The building stayed in one family's ownership until the 1970's." He pointed to another photo. "There it's almost totally gutted, it's a wonder it wasn't torn down. Then, fortunately, the couple who bought it wanted to restore it as a restaurant and a bed and breakfast."

"Do they have a lot of bed and breakfasts around here?"

"Aaup. Usually, all booked up in the summer and fall. B&B's are very popular with the history loving crowd that visits mystic." He pointed to one of the original fireplaces in the room. "The owners had this all rebuilt, using methods of construction that date back to the 1700's." His finger traced a heavy beam. "Look at that. It's a replacement, but it's been shaped with an adze." He pointed to the beamed ceiling and plaster walls. "The work those guys put into this is amazing."

They were soon seated and served jumbo shrimp cocktails for appetizers. He ordered a blackjack sirloin, and Holly selected the lobster and shrimp ravioli. A three-year-old started crying at a table near them. Some guy in a camel sports coat was yelling at his wife to '*shut your son up*' and for the waiter to bring him another martini. The guy had two kids and a big thirst, downing martinis throughout their meal.

Holly found herself watching Paul watch them; then she started to focus on her own problems. This meal was going to cost him quite a bit, what would he expect? Sex? Where? Not back at the mansion, with Frost and Noel. Especially since it might not go well. His place? Did he have one by himself or did he have roommates? Would he have protection? Would he guess she was a virgin? Should she tell him? She wanted him, but how did she go about doing this–as her panic grew the delicious lobster ravioli started tasting not too hot.

They were finishing their entrees when the loud family started leaving. The sports coat guy started walking out, leaving the wife to get the two kids out of their high chairs and into their little jackets, but she seemed used to this. Uncoordinated, he stumbled near Holly's table, kicking a vacant chair out of his way, cursing. Trailing with the kids, his wife hurried up to reach out and to steady him, but he just shoved her hand away.

Paul watched with his lips tightening as the mother stopped to zip up the little boy's jacket. The husband didn't even wait for her, opening the back door and closing it behind himself, before she could catch up with the kids. After the woman with the kids in tow left, Paul just sat there watching the door. Then angrily, he threw down his napkin. Saying, "Excuse me," he got up and left.

Paul had walked out the restaurant's back door, and he was gone.

Seeing him go, the waiter came over. "Madam, do you wish dessert?"

She didn't know what to say. "M-m-maybe. Maybe later."

The waiter made a show of clearing the table of their

dinner dishes and looking out at the door that led to the parking lot. Embarrassed Holly just sat there. Waiting at the empty table. Had Paul just left, sticking her with the bill? Was this some sort of a cruel joke? Did he leave because he was sick? Should she go outside to help him? But they hadn't paid the bill yet so she couldn't leave. Did she have enough money to pay the bill? If she left her handbag as security with the waiter, could she go outside to see if Paul was okay? The waiter was looking over at her. Probably thinking she too might try to sneak out without paying.

Mortified Holly just sat there.

Then to her relief, the back door opened, and Paul was coming back. When he got back to their table, he said, "I'm sorry, Holly." He sat down. "Do you want dessert?"

"W-what happened?"

"That idiot was getting into the driver's side. He's got a wife strapping two babies in infant seats, and he's gonna drive when he can't even walk straight! Showed him my badge, and told him he wasn't driving. Then he started to give me an argument."

"Shouldn't you have called for b-back up? What if he hurt you?"

"Holly, in his condition it would have been a two punch fight. I just told him if he drove off I'd call in his plate and he'd be met by a patrol car and charged with DWI before he hit the main road. I asked to see the wife's license. While the damn fool was mouthing off in front of his kids, she showed me a valid one. In the end, he got in the passenger seat, and she drove off." Paul shook his head in puzzlement. "Why would a guy who has a nice wife and two kids act like that? Why would a woman put up with a guy like that? I'll never understand."

"Are you on duty all the time?" she was curious.

He looked tired. "I could've looked the other way, but with kids involved..." He shook his head. "I am sorry if I embarrassed you."

"No. Not at all!" Holly reached over and put her hand over his large one, as she was filled with pride for her man. She did order dessert, well, she wanted the chocolate torte drizzled with raspberries, but much more she wanted to just keep this magical dinner going. No pressure, just happiness as she listened to him talk about his tournament shooting, going deer hunting, and growing up in Boston.

He asked her if she wanted to go to a bar with dancing, but explained they couldn't stay too late as he had an early call tomorrow. She didn't want to dance, but she did want to the see water with him. They parked near a dock he knew and walked a bit, hand in hand.

They kissed. A little more aggressively this time, his hands on her arms, his lips pressing hard against her. Maybe he wanted only a college educated wife, maybe he wasn't going to be '*the one,*' but she wanted him. In bed. Tonight. But in the end, he just drove her home and walked her to the back door of the mansion. Maybe he too was still working this out for himself.

"Thank you. It was lovely," Holly whispered.

He reached down and kissed her. "Next Friday?"

"Yes," she said happily.

Chapter 31

The next Friday, he offered a nice steakhouse, but Holly asked to go to that cheaper Chinese Wok place that Frost had mentioned.

The place was a take-out with only four tables in the storefront window, but the shrimp, noddles, and conversation was great. She'd gotten past the *'don't say anything that might offend him'* and found they were having fun arguing educational methods, the best way to eat clams, and what happened to the famed Oak Island's treasure?

"Where do you want to go next Friday?" Paul asked. "There's a lobster place up the coast that's really good."

She colored a bit. "If we eat in my house, it'll be better and cheaper." And maybe she could ask Noel and Frosty to go out that night.

He flushed a little bit himself. "But kinda crowded there with the four of us." He seemed to be trying to speak causally, "You know, I could cook you a dinner at my apartment?"

"You cook?"

"Sure. I eat, I cook."

Why was it that everybody in the world could cook a decent meal but her? And what did she answer because it wasn't just dinner he was proposing. Holly studied his aura: strong scarlet red predominating from the base chakra at his thighs, the baser needs, the mating color; but colors blending to pink, then green higher up in the throat and crown, the color of affection, love. His intentions were abundantly clear, but she also sensed he wanted pleasure for her as much as he wanted it for himself.

She would agree to have dinner at his apartment with all it entailed. "I would like that very much," she answered firmly. A little afraid, but so excited at the prospect.

Chapter 32

On Friday, two or three people were browsing as the bell over the Rainbow Realm door jangled. Skye was at the back counter ringing up customers, as Holly refilled a front table with sparkle dusted elf figurines. Hearing the bell, she looked up and then looked higher, delighted to see a smiling Paul was coming in. He was off duty, in a bowling jacket and jeans, saying, "Holly, this afternoon, I have to do a favor for a buddy and drive his wife to a specialist in Hartford. That may make me a little late to pick you up? Or did you want to postpone?"

Seeing him made her day so radiant, her happiness bubbled within. "No, I'll be waiting at my house." He didn't kiss her, but their aura's touched melded together and lighted hers up to match his greens and golds. Then with that same lopsided smile, he was gone.

Pretending to need to straighten something in the window, Holly watched through the diamond panes as he walked away down the village lanes. Longing so much to be walking by his side and holding his hand.

"Holly!" Skye's aura was unreadable, but her face wasn't. She looked upset. "Do you know who that man is?"

"P-p-paul. Paul Travinsky."

"He's a town patrolman."

"He's a sergeant."

"Why isn't he wearing a uniform?"

"Paul's off duty today."

"Why was he here?"

"He had to tell me he would be late to pick me up tonight." Why was Skye making such a thing of this?

"He's your boyfriend?" Skye said it like she was shocked that Holly had a boyfriend.

"Not a b-b-boyfriend. He's a man I happen to be going out to dinner with," Holly corrected.

Skye stood there looking out the window, then finally she said, "Your brother is under suspicion for the murder of Rolf Van Hom. Don't you think it's a little too coincidental that a cop suddenly wants to talk to you? Date you?"

"We just met when he investigated the m-m-murder, but..."

"Is he asking you questions? About your brother? About you working here?"

"N-no. We just talk."

"About what?"

A heavyset woman carried a knitted, black silk bodice over to them. "Do you have this in goddess size?"

"We might have it in the back." Holly started for the storeroom, as several elderly women were walking in the door, it was senior bus tour time.

"No! I'll check the back!" ordered Skye curtly. "You go to the jewelry counter and ring up that woman's candles!"

As Holly hurried to the jewelry counter, more elderly women were pouring in. Soon she was ringing up incense sticks and musk oils.

"Miss, could I try that garnet necklace on?" A platinum blonde asked.

She had to unlock the cabinet, where the good jewelry was kept. Taking the expensive necklace off its black velvet stand, Holly handed it to her and then watched as the woman struggled with the clasp.

"May I see that opal ring." A short, improbably dark brunet asked, as another said, "That star pin. How much is it?"

All the ladies knew if they weren't back in time the bus might leave without them, so all wanted to get waited on first and were crowding the counter. Rapidly Holly found herself putting away the opal ring, taking out gold pendants and silver pins. Ringing up jewelry, scarves, books and sensual chocolate by herself. Where was Skye? Busy in the books section, advising women on yoga poses.

Finally, the tide turned, and it was time for them all to get back on their buses, as most of the women hurried out. With only two younger women browsing, Holly glanced down beside the register and saw Hazel Donald's Visa card was still there. She grabbed it up and raced out of the shop, looked quickly down the brick pathways, and took off after the first receding seniors' group. Catching up to the women in front of the bakery, Holly called out. "Hazel?"

A bright-eyed, white-haired woman turned to her. "Yes?"

"Hazel Donald?"

"Yes?"

"You left your card."

"Oh, thank you, dear." The elderly woman started fumbling with her handbag, "You should have a reward..."

"No. No, thank you." Smiling, Holly turned and ran back to the Rainbow Realm.

All the customers were gone when she got back in, but an annoyed looking Skye stood at the counter glaring at her. "You just ran off–where did you go?"

"A lady left her credit card."

"And you forgot to give it back to her? Now we'll have to report it!"

"No, I found her."

"You gave the card back? Did she show you her driver's license?"

"Her license? Why?"

"To prove who she was?"

"I just called out her name."

"You didn't check her license to see if you were giving a customer's credit card to the right person?" Skye sounded furious.

Holly felt herself blushing. "No, b-but..."

Skye was looking down at the glass case. "Where is

that garnet necklace?"

Suddenly terrified, Holly moved to the counter. The black velvet holder was empty. "It was right here. I had it out to show a customer."

"Do you see it here?" Skye was yelling at her.

"Well, you were right over there..." Holly started.

"You're blaming me for your carelessness?"

"I-I know which woman tried it on. I'll go look for her..."

"And then what? Accuse a customer of stealing my necklace? Do you think she's going to admit it? Are you going to have your cop boyfriend strip search every tourist out there on the pathways?

Holly desperately looked the length of the cabinet. "I'm so s-s-sorry!"

"You should have been watching!"

"I'll pay for the necklace!" said Holly miserably.

"With what? You won't be working for me anymore! You're fired!"

Chapter 33

Feeling horrible, Holly went into the storage room, grabbed up her jacket, handbag and looked about, was anything else hers? Yhep. The tea mug with the ship's masts on it that Frost had given her, and the blue, insulated lunch bag that Noel had gotten Holly to celebrate this job. Sick, she couldn't face going out the front way and seeing Skye. What if she apologized again and begged for her job? No, Holly intuited Skye wanted her out and wouldn't budge. She just grabbed her things and headed out the back door. Outside a clean wind blew from the land and there was the earthy smell of the marigolds planted around the back of the building. It helped.

Wanting not to cry, she just started walking. Frost had said today he and Tarus were taking the launch down to a boatyard in Stratford to pick up some donated engine part and it would be hours before they were back. She couldn't bear to just go home and be in that big mansion all alone. A house that she loved, but could never pay for, so she was losing it, as she would lose her brothers again when they all moved off. Everything was her fault!

Without planning it, she had walked to the Aquarium. Just walking seemed to help. At the Admission kiosk, she thought about asking the ticket taker if Noel could come out and talk with her, but Holly didn't want to get him in trouble and have him lose his job too. She paid the admission to go inside. She lost her job and yet she was paying fifteen bucks for the comfort of maybe seeing her brother at a distance.

Inside the cobblestoned entrance courtyard, she walked down to the windows in front of the beluga tank. White shapes were swimming and thrilling the crowd, as someone threw them fish. It was a redshirted woman, not Noel. Holly walked inside the main Aquarium building, past the tropical forest tanks, with their red, yellow and bright blue poison frogs. Ahead was a twelve-foot high plexiglass cylinder with its crowding of translucent, pulsating jellyfishes. Noel said a flock of jellyfishes was called a 'smack,' 'bloom,' or 'swarm.' Their half moon bodies, dangling curling tentacles and their bouncing, floating movements reminded Holly of the graceful white-tulled dancers in swan lake. Watching them gently float up and down for awhile calmed and centered her.

"Holly?"

She turned finding Noel was there, awkwardly balancing a heavy, three foot long, white plastic ice chest.

"Why aren't you at work?"

"I g-g-got f-fired," she said miserably.

He looked down at the cooler. "There is going to be a show in the Marine theater in five minutes, I'm carrying fish for the principles–but I felt...that I should come here?" He looked around the area, then looked at her strangely. "Look, go in and watch the show. When it's done, I can take a break. We'll talk, okay, Sis?" She started to follow him. "No, Holly, I'm going in the staff entrance. You go in the public entrance over there. Don't sit in the first six rows!"

She followed the crowds inside a giant amphitheater, many of the steep upper tier seats were already taken in front of a raised, huge crystal clear pool with windows built into its front. Tired she just sat down in the first open seat in the third row, watching as Noel and a young woman in their red shirts set up rings and platforms on the deck above the pool.

Finally, wearing a head microphone the woman lectured the crowd, explaining they had three interlocking tanks. If an animal didn't want to perform that day, they could stay in their home tank, but when the show began eager dolphins racing across the pool, standing almost upright on their tails; diving in streaks of bubbles in front of the tank windows; then leaping high to jump through hoops lowered from the ceiling.

As the woman explained each trick, Noel tossed the actors rewards of fish. Seals and sea lions performed by jumping up on to the deck, balancing balls and diving after thrown barbells. Soon Holly remembered what Noel had said about not sitting in the seat rows closest to the tank, as ice cold water splashed over her.

Wet, but was feeling much better, Holly waited until Noel could join her after the show. "That's a-a-amazing! Do you do that every day?"

"Nope. I'm usually with the belugas. The regular seal trainer was out sick, and Dr. Morjessky told me she wanted me to learn as many of the jobs around here as I can."

"You're doing great!" said Holly enthusiastically.

"I haven't got a doctorate program set up yet."

"You will!"

"I've got to pay down some of my loans first." He frowned. "How did you get in here?"

"I-I bought a ticket."

"Why?" he sounded unhappy.

"I wanted to talk with you."

"You could've had them call me to the admission desk! That's fifteen bucks gone we could've used." He looked around. "Well, it's done. Let's go to the café. We can talk–but only if you keep your voice down!" he warned.

In the Aquarium's cafeteria, Noel bought them two teas and a paper plate of her favorite peanut butter cookies. "What happened?"

Holly related the saga of the credit card and necklace, and it all seemed sad, but not as terrible as before. "I-I-I was so stupid!"

"You should have stayed serving just one customer until that necklace was returned to the case, but then those other bus people wouldn't have enough time to buy anything."

"I'm going to pay for that necklace; it was two

hundred and eighty."

"No, you're not!" he said firmly.

"But..."

"Did you steal it?"

"N-no!"

"You and your boss both were in the store. Both of you should have been on the register counter. She shouldn't have been over discussing yoga theory when you're swamped checking out a load of tourists running to catch a bus! If your boss wanted a dedicated security person she should have hired one, and you did just fine with the credit card! That Ms. Rainbow has been underpaying you and overworking you! Holly, you'll get another job, a better one! Maybe we can get something for you at the souvenir shop here."

Holly looked down in shame. "Not with a reputation of losing valuable necklaces."

Noel looked at her, his voice hard. "If Skye talks that around, we'll sue her for defamation!"

After he went back to work, she spent the rest of the afternoon walking around that amazing Aquarium. Still, she was depressed when they drove to pick up their brother at the Seaport Museum. Soon, with even more of an effervescent aura than usual, Frost hopped in the hearse announcing, "I've got jobs for the both of you!"

Chapter 34

"I got a job," answered Noel, "but Holly just lost hers today."

"A shame," said Frost, not seeming to care as Holly pulled the hearse out onto the main road. "Time coming up for the 'Haunted Seaport.'"

"What's that?" Holly asked.

"I forget you guys don't know. It's a big thing around here," explained Frost. "You know all these amusement parks and zoos that raise extra money by decorating themselves for holiday visitors?"

"Yeah," said Noel.

"The Mystic Museum Village becomes the Haunted Seaport for three weeks before Halloween, and with last year's roof leak, we lost a lot of signs and decorating props to water damage, so the museum's going to be hiring people to paint and decorate–that's you, Holly. Then for the weeks of the Haunted Seaport, they'll pay for people to dress up in zombie suits and pirate costumes to scare the paying customers."

"For how much?" asked Noel.

Frost shrugged. "Minimum wage. But you don't have to be there the whole day. They want more staff for the night crowd, so that you can do it too, N.C."

Noel didn't look too happy, but Holly coaxed, "It'll be fun!"

Frost was continuing, "Holly, I've talked to my boss. They want your hearse parked in the museum village when the Haunted Seaport is open. You'll drive it in the morning and leave parked on their 'village green' until they close at nine."

"They're paying for that?" asked Noel. "That'll mean she can't drive it during all those hours?"

"I tried for money, but the museum's budget is stretched with the lost props. The best I could get was that if

Holly will park her hearse there for the whole show, we'll each get a year's free family pass, which means we can take dates in and get free tea and cookies at the membership house. Holly, you can take Paul!"

"Big deal," commented Noel acerbically.

"But what if Bernie yells?" asked Holly.

Frost thought about it, "We'll say the hearse comes with sound effects."

"Halloween is always fun," she said dreamily picturing Paul in a pirate costume, with his handsome, muscled chest bared.

The next day Holly went into the Seaport Administration office to sign up. She got her working packet, schedule and was immediately assigned to next week's decorating crew, without even showing them a portfolio of her drawings. Outside she decided to take a detour and go see Frost before she left. She walked past the moored whaler and ropewalk building, past the lighthouse, then she stood near the darkness of the boat building barn.

No Frost. And from the weak residue of his thought emissions, he hadn't been here for some time.

From here she looked down the side of the building to the docks. She could see a launch taking off, with Captain Gustav at the helm. He was angling up river, and Holly found herself feeling drawn to watch him, for a reason she couldn't fathom, but when she started to move forward, a sing-songy voice stopped her. "Little Sister, Frost is not here." It came from the cavernous, shaded interior of the boat building shed.

She turned to see a cigarette tip glowing in the darkness and realized that the man standing there must have been silently watching her. And she hadn't sensed it! Tarus walked into the sunlight. These days were cool for a Connecticut Fall, with temperatures below fifty degrees, yet Tarus still worked in the shop barechested, with open sandals on his feet. For clothing, he wore only a pair of khaki Bermuda shorts, which on his short legs came down below his knees. With one hand he smoked, while with the other he carried a wooden beam on his shoulder that was at least eight inches thick and about five foot long. That thing must weight almost what she did, yet that wrinkled, little man carried it as easily as she would carry a shovel on her shoulder.

"Where is Frost?"

Tarus spoke softly, "Policeman come to take him to talk."

Fear gripped her. "Again? Tarus, he didn't kill anyone."

"Frost good boy." Tarus lowered his beam burden, dropping it the last two feet on to the wood planking, choking dust rose as it landed heavily.

"You knew Rolf Van Hom?" Holly asked.

"Does that matter?"

"Yes."

"Little sister, why do you question?"

"My brother is in trouble."

"You fish in waters you do not know, that is not wise, little one. The currents that buffet Frost are stronger and deeper than you think."

A feeling still nagged at her. "Captain Gustav took out his launch from the museum's dock? Where do you think he's going?"

Tarus shrugged as he glanced once toward the empty dock, then he turned back to his boatbuilding shed. He was another of the people she couldn't read lately, and that bothered her because Holly was sure that Tarus could tell her something if he chose to.

When she left the seaport, it was too early to pick up Noel. Well, since she was fired from the Rainbow Realm, she had time to shop now, but no money. And no word from Mr. Douglas. If he couldn't sell the Warren John Thomas, she had agreed to pay for that cleaning or forfeit the painting. It looked like she'd lost her painting and would be getting nothing out of the bungled deal. She had to do something besides just worry. With all the time in the world, she could use it do something positive, that might help Frost. Holly parked the hearse in the Mystic Motel lot.

When she walked into the lobby, Alice looked up with a friendly smile. "Holly, I thought you would be working now?"

"I've left the Rainbow Realm. I'm going to be painting signs at the Seaport Museum for their Haunted Seaport."

To Holly's relief, Alice was interested in another topic. "I hear you went out with Paul to the Captain Daniel Packer Inne?" Not a question, just a statement, but Alice obviously wanted to hear more.

Holly found herself blushing. "Y-y-yes."

"Those Boston boys are a thrifty lot. A fancy place like that–he must really be interested in you?"

Or interested in proving her brother was a murderer and advancing to detective Holly thought as she blushed deeper. "It-it was nice."

"Paul's a good guy." Alice was looking back to her booking screen.

"Actually, Alice, I was c-c-curious about something. Have the police released Rolf's Van Hom's room yet?"

"Finally," she said with disgust. "Dorrie just cleaned out all that yellow crime scene tape this morning."

"What happened to his things?"

"The police took away a bunch of boxes, and I think they found some drugs, but wouldn't tell me."

"Could I see his room?"

"Nothing of his is left."

"I-I-I'd still like to look at it?"

Chapter 35

Alice looked at her strangely. "Well, it's not rented yet." The manager seemed to think about it and then said, "No harm." She looked at her sign-in desk and handed Holly one of the maid's pass-key cards. "216."

Rolf Van Hom had been staying on the second floor, the end room overlooking the trees about the river. Up here Holly could smell the salty incoming tide water. She hesitated before slipping the key card in, then she took a deep, centering breath and walked in.

The front picture window's curtains were closed, darkening the room, so she flipped on the light switch: two queen beds, now neatly made with brown and orange quilted bedspreads; more framed prints of America Class sailboats. No residual feeling of a murdered victim here. Well, Rolf died behind her house, but one could think there would have been something left? Holly rested her hand on the desk. It smelled of wood polish and disinfectant and not even the feeling of the police forensic experts was left here, Dorrie had done a thorough job of wiping this room clean.

Holly walked into the bathroom, resting her hands on the air vents she could reach. The cream-colored paint was scratched off the vent screws heads; cops must have opened them and checked. Nothing hidden here, nothing left, pretty much like Rolf Van Hom's life, ended abruptly, with nothing remaining. Despair was washing over her; this room wasn't going to help Holly prove her brother wasn't a murderer!

She turned off the lights and closed the door, feeling depressed as she walked out to the balcony railing, overlooking the parking lot. To her right behind the trees the river ran down to the sea and to her left was the main road that ran past the seaport museum and then to the drawbridge that crossed town. Just ahead of her was the Mystic cemetery, where Frosty might lie if convicted of murder. Holly started to shiver from the fall air and pulled her sweater tighter about her shoulders. Standing there, she focused on the sugar maple across from her; it had a thick halo of bright yellow leaves, the endless beauty of nature always calmed her, so that she could think clearly.

Rolf lived here in this motel for months, nearly a year. It wasn't overly expensive, but he could have rented a one bedroom apartment for a lot less money. Alice said he had a lot of visitors, with strangers constantly coming in and out, a motel was a good place to cover drug dealing. Rolf was doing something that got him murdered; maybe the police found the drugs he was selling? But most addicts don't kill their suppliers, and why kill Van Hom in Frost's backyard?

The police had looked through and taken all his belongings, and Dorrie cleaned that room. Yet Holly felt she should still be looking here for something else–for what? Holly watched a seagull fly high and drop a mussel shell, to crack it on the parking asphalt, and then the bird swooped down to eat his prize. If Rolf had anything he wanted to hide, leaving it in a room that was daily accessed by a motel maid seemed to be a poor way to go.

Frost said the police searched Rolf's locker at the Seaport Museum and they towed his car away. She wished she could have touched that car for vibrations, but Frost said it was a rental. A Lexus, a rather expensive rental. Could Paul get her into the police car impound? No, she couldn't ask him. Did Rolf have a post office box? Or bank deposit box? The police must have checked those out too.

Holly started to walk back to the stairs, passing green door after green door. All rooms, all alike and all empty. A rumbling noise made her stop; then she realized it was only ice falling in the machine. Here a central corridor divided the room blocks on both floors, where the maid's closets were, a Soda and candy machines were tucked into small alcoves on each side of the interior hallway.

She walked past. Then stopped. There was a nagging feeling. Over the years, when she had been looking for something lost Holly had learned to pay attention to that tiny urging. She walked back to the central corridor, to the soda machine. Lightly running her hand along the pay slots and the selection buttons she felt much faint human residue, but she didn't even know what Rolf's life force felt like since she had only seen him dead, with his spirit gone. So how could she determine if any lingering sensations were from him?

Stepping back, closing her eyes and concentrating, Holly felt something. Something out of place. Alien. Not the soda or candy machines, no it seemed centered on the ice machine. She walked in front of the tall, gray metal rectangle with its square opening. Stood there, breathing deeply, allowing random sensations to wash over her.

It was like that kids' game–*getting warmer, warmer, now colder*. In front of the ice machine, she was *colder*. Holly stepped to the side, *slightly warmer*. She stepped closer to the machine's side, *much warmer*. She ran her hand across the side feeling smooth steel. When she ran her hand forward toward the front of the machine, her hand was leaving *'it,'* getting *colde*r. When she ran her hand to the rear of the machine, she was getting *warmer*!

Walking to the back of the machine, she smelled oil and dust and heard the motor's humming. Slipping her hand behind the machine, she felt along its back which had an unpleasant greasy-dirty feel. Then something plastic. Textured plastic, evenly edged, three inches wide like tape, duct tape. Holly tried to push the machine forward a bit but couldn't; it was way too heavy. She ran her hand back along the tape; it was holding something stiff, paper? Was it an envelope? Digging with her nails, Holly picked at the resisting, sticky duck tape. How had Rolf taped it here–she knew it was Rolf. It must've been him! She tried to angle her nails under the stiff envelope and claw at the tape. Finally, something fell to the floor behind the ice machine, and on her knees, she frantically felt through the dust bunnies until she could pull the mess out.

The gray tape covered manilla envelope was nine inches by twelve, closed with just a bendable metal clasp. Inside were papers, a quarter of an inch thick, which she pulled out, photos, digital photos run off on a computer printer on regular typing paper. Some fuzzy, some sharply focused: some large ocean-going yachts and broken down fishing boats in focus. A few close-ups of the bottom of a gray wood siding door with yellow flowers, a worn stoop stone, and nearby a small garden statue.

These off-center photos couldn't even be considered remotely artistic, yet they had been worth hiding. From the police? Or from Rolf's killer? Or both? She looked at more of the photos. A naked woman, taken from above, her face cloyingly hidden. She was in a number of the photos, all in provocative poses, her face unseen. In some poses, the woman offered a smoking bong, and in others, portions of her naked body rested near small empty glass vials. Dark, long hair is tumbling forward. Finally a face! Miranda, looking up at the camera lasciviously, teasingly holding up a filled hypodermic needle.

Another series of pictures with a tall, stocky man dressed in a pea coat jacket, looking away from the camera, probably not even aware he was being photographed. The flattened perspective picture had the feel of a long distance lens. The next had a better angle, and now she saw who the man was, Captain Herald Gustav. In one he was talking with another man, aboard a large ship's deck. Another picture of the same men zoomed back on a ship's bow that was labeled the Argus. Several more pictures are showing registration numbers on the sterns of several large craft and pictures of Gustav walking down gangplanks. Another closer picture, with head chopped off, centered on a man's hands holding a small, flat package, he was slipping under his jacket.

Why hide these photographs, unless they were important? Gustav is picking something off a ship. Smuggling? Well, she had found out he did get illegal ivory for Skye's shop, but smuggling banned parrot feathers, or crocodile skins was not a capital crime, just confiscation of the endangered animal product and a fine if he was caught. Certainly not a reason to kill someone for blackmailing him? Was Gustav smuggling more? Was Rolf an uncover policeman? Unlikely.

What if these weren't even Rolf's photos? Somebody else could be stashing their stuff here, in a shielded but open corridor. But somebody who was doing drugs and sleeping with Miranda Talmadge? Even if she couldn't prove it, Holly was sure it was Rolf.

There was something else at the bottom of the envelope. Light, small, three somethings, Holly fished one out. Thin. Less than an inch of black plastic with a red and white label, a rectangle with metal contacts on the back, probably something with computers, Holly dropped it back into the packet. These photographs might have Rolf's fingerprints on it. Should she turn them into the police? Turn it into Paul? How would she explain finding it? *I'm a compulsive cleaner who goes to public places to wipe down the back of vending machines? The ice machine started making a funny noise, so I was examining it for a fire hazard?*

And those naked pictures of Miranda with the drug paraphernalia, that reinforced an intimate sexual relationship between her and Rolf Van Holm. A relationship that cut Frost out, and may have given her brother even more of a motive for killing his rival over Miranda?

She wanted to help her brother, not hurt him. Should she just put the envelope back–say nothing? Paul was coming tonight, they were dating, and he liked her, could she trust him to tell her what was the best thing to do? Or was he just an ambitious cop trying to get advancement by dating the sister to spy on a murder suspect? Not wanting Alice to see the package Holly hid it in the hearse before she returned the maid's pass card at the lobby desk.

As she drove off, she pictured the photos: Miranda; the ships; and Gustav. She thought of the photo with the bottom of the gray door with the small, yellow flowers beside it and the strange stone statue. Where had she seen that before?

Chapter 36

When they all got home, she called a family meeting at the kitchen table. Noel moved to wash the breakfast dishes as he listened, but Frost sat down with her as Holly explained, "I found this taped to the back of the second-floor ice machine at the Mystic motel."

"Why were you there?" demanded Noel.

"I was looking through Rolf's room."

"Holly!" Noel started...

But Frost was taking photo printouts from the envelope. "Do you think it's Rolf's?"

"Yes," she said.

As Frost looked each photo, Holly felt pain for him when he came to the naked pictures of Miranda. "I-I-I'm sorry you have to see that."

Frost just shrugged. "I've seen the real thing."

Rinsing soapy water off his hands and drying them, Noel came over. "Are you touching those with your bare hands? You'll leave fingerprints all over them!" From a kitchen drawer he took out Holly's rubber dishwashing gloves, then Noel started to go through the photos. "Good camera, great telephoto lenses, but lousy photographer. Nothing's famed well..."

"They don't have to be perfect. They're blackmail pictures," objected Holly.

"For what?" asked Frost. "I love Miranda, but, trust me, she doesn't spend much time worrying about the purity of her reputation. If these are Rolf's photos, I can't see why she wanted the pictures back; she's got a lot hotter ones than these in her apartment."

Noel took a long look at the Miranda-with-needle one. "It's this guy's personal porno. Maybe it's Rolf, maybe not or maybe it's some married guy? Or a teenager who has to hide his stuff in the corridor?"

"What about the ones of Gustav and the ships?" Holly reasoned. " I already know he brings in ivory rings for Skye. He must be smuggling something else? "

"Everybody does," said Frost. "Best place to get tax free cigarettes is on the docks."

What was the matter with her dumb brothers? "Rolf Van Hom wasn't killed because someone was smuggling cigarettes. It must be something more, drugs, stolen diamonds? Something he could blackmail Captain Gustav with?"

"Why do you think it's him?" said Noel.

"The pictures of him boarded the ships." Holly shook the empty envelope and dropped out the rest of its contents. "There's also these little squares."

Noel used his rubber-gloved hands to pick one up. "Memory cards from a digital camera. With these out, he could have erased the camera and computer's memories, so there is no tie to these photographs." Noel looked up at her. "What are you going to do with them? How are you going to explain how you even found them?"

"Yeah," said Frost. "We should take the ones of Miranda out..."

"No," said Noel. "You can't unless you erase what is obviously on those memory cards. That stuff will be sequentially numbered." Noel put everything back into the envelope. "Look, Rolf might have taken them or he might not have. I don't know what you are going to do with these pictures, Holly, but don't touch them again without gloves! Now, what are we making for dinner?"

Holly turned to Frost, but he put on a happy face saying, "Maybe we should splurge tonight? Cook those three steaks we were saving for some time?"

"N–n-o. I'm eating out." Holly started to redden.

"Again?" asked Frost. "Where?"

Noel cocked his head. "The question is not where, but

with whom?"

"I know that already," said Frost. "I intuit a tall man in a dark blue uniform. Paul Travinsky."

"Where are you going?" continued Noel.

She averted her eyes. "Nowhere."

"We could cut up the steaks for four," said practical Noel. "Save Paul the cost of a restaurant?"

Holly shook her head. "N-n-no! We-we're going to Paul's apartment."

"His apartment? Wow." Frost looked at her carefully. "Holly, what's the matter? Something's wrong. You can't lie to us; we can read auras too."

She stiffened, trying to blank her mind, block them, but it was too late, and she was aware of the heat in her face, that she was blushing redder. "He's cooking me dinner at his apartment. N-nothing wrong with that."

Frost gave a high sign to a frowning Noel, and in a sing-song voice, he chanted. "Sounds like it's gonna be more than dinner!"

"That's-that's my business!" said Holly.

"Sister Holly's gonna get laid!" Happily chanted Frost.

But Noel's blue-green eyes, mirrors of hers, searched her face. "What's wrong? You're not happy. You're afraid. Don't go if you're not ready."

"Then he'll drop me."

"I don't think Paul's that way," reasoned Noel. "He's got sisters back in Boston. He's not going to push a girl faster than she can handle."

But Frost could read her stronger. "Holly, you've never been with a man!"

"Of course I have!" She could feel her face was now bright red.

"Oh...boy," said Frost. "She's lying. She's a virgin."

Noel closed his eyes in pain. "Did you tell Paul this?"

"**No!**" Holly yelled. Her brothers looked from one to another, as Holly finished plaintively, "I thought men wanted virgins?"

"When they're seventeen. He's what, twenty-eight?" said Frost.

"Holly, most guys like to ride a subway, not build one," quoted Noel.

"H-he won't know," she stammered.

"I think he'll figure it out," said Noel sounding concerned. "And he might not be too happy."

"Around the seaport I've heard Paul has dated a number of women," Frost cautioned, "but not for long, he's really into the career thing."

"I'm going to his apartment at six for dinner, and that's it!" Holly felt like she was going to throw up.

But six p.m. came and went, six thirty, and then seven. Holly sat in the kitchen, looking dejected, while Frost wiped soap water off the tin plates from dinner.

A seven fifteen, Thor let out a thunderous growling-barking at the back door. From outside they heard Paul's voice, "I surrender."

Noel moved to grab Thor and drag him to Frost's bedroom, while Frost opened the door. Paul came in dressed in the same bowling jacket and black jeans. "That doctor's appointment ran long. I'm sorry I'm late." He looked at the plates. "You already had dinner?"

"No, my brothers did," said Holly. "Let's go." She gave a warning look at her brothers. "Don't wait up."

Noel had come over, and he was looking to Frost with a worried expression. Seeing something between them, Paul asked quietly, "Is there a problem?"

Frost said, "No."

Noel also answered, "Not really."

As Holly grabbed her jacket, Paul still stared at her obviously unhappy brothers.

"No problem, but if you plan anything tonight..." Noel started.

"**N.C.!**" Holly warned.

Frost finished, "You should know it will be my sister's first time."

A dumfounded Paul looked from him to Holly. In the silence, she wet her lips and asked. "Is dinner off?"

Paul shook his head. "No. Dinner still on, but dessert just got flushed down the toilet! Holly, why didn't you say something?"

She felt like crying. "We can buy protection on the way."

"That's not the problem!" He looked from her to her two brothers. "This conversation should be private. C'mon."

Holly glared at her brothers. "I'm never going to talk to either of you two traitors again!"

Chapter 37

She climbed up into his truck. They didn't talk as he drove downtown and across the counter-weighted bridge. He turned left on Nonark, passing the community police station, following the shoreline. Then he parked alongside a three-story; mansard-roofed Victorian mansion that was painted a light aqua with maroon trim. Paul unlocked the door to the front hall, and Holly saw the mansion had been subdivided into apartments.

"It's a walk up," he said regretfully, and Holly followed to the second floor.

His apartment's neat living room had a high ceiling with two tall windows overlooking the river. Looking about fast she saw old beige walls that were being spackled for repainting, and a large gun safe, two bookcases full of textbooks and paperbacks. In one part, she saw a clean-lined, blue futon couch with a WWII Marine footlocker for a coffee table, two armless, green chairs, and a big, big flat panel t-v. After moving in, she took her glasses off and stuffed them into her handbag. *Men don't make passes at girl's who wear glasses.*

She waited eagerly as he closed the door behind them and then she rushed into his arms. On tiptoes, she reached up passionately, but he gave her a sisterly kiss as she brushed against the beard stubble on his cheeks.

Disappointed she settled back down. "Because of what my brothers said, we aren't go-going to do anything!"

He drew back. "We're going to have dinner."

"Paul..."

"Look, Holly." He stopped, then started again, "I signed on for cleaning my apartment, cooking dinner and," he shrugged, "if you were willing, some fun for the both us. That's all I wanted tonight."

"We can do that..."

"I wasn't planning to take on the responsibility of possibly ruining a woman's sexual responses for the rest of her life!"

"I–I take my own res-responsibility!"

"Holly, I'm still taking college courses. I'm going to be a detective someday; then I'll be in a position to buy a house on a lake, have long-term relationships, a family, maybe–but not now!"

"All I want is one night."

"I know you might want to be made a woman..."

"**Made a woman?**" Holly bristled. "I am a woman! No woman needs a man's input to be '*made a woman*'!"

Paul cut in, "That was stupid! I'm sorry. Look, honey, I've got two younger sisters. A girl's first time shouldn't be in a half-painted apartment, with a bowl of stale pretzels. It should be special, with candles, flowers, and wine."

"Those are wine b-b-bottles over there."

"Those are beer. Holly, God." He looked at her in horror. "Have you ever had an alcoholic drink before?"

"Of course I have! That's stupid."

"You haven't ordered anything when we went out?"

"I didn't want to waste your money."

"When N.C. made pizzas at your house, your brothers and I had beers, but you drank only water."

"That was because we only had three beers in the house."

"God, I drank your last beer? You guys shouldn't have done that!"

"We wanted to! It's basic hospitably. Paul, all I care about is being with you–tonight." But he looked so bereft; she had to sadly say, "Do you want to just take me home?"

"Nope. I've already defrosted the steaks."

Only he could fit in the tiny galley kitchen, so restless she walked about his living room. The paperbacks were all Science Fiction. The magazines on the locker table were about hunting. She heard voices behind a closed door. Must be coming from the bedroom; Holly listened carefully and then realized he had a police scanner playing in there. In a bedroom, she wasn't going to get in. Sighing, she looked about. Painted to the tired beige wall were scarlet red and orange samples. "You're painting. Is this your building?'

He laughed bringing out glasses with two cold beers and a bowl of pretzels. "No. But the walls need work, and my landlord will give me credit on my rent for painting it whatever color I want."

The huge flat panel T-V dominated one wall. Under it, a shelf, no several shelves with shooting trophies on them. Framed pictures of Paul and other shooters, another one of Paul, bare-chested in shorts, kneeling next to a pole and huge fish. God, that perfect, muscular chest, she wanted to run her hands along it, and now because of her two big mouthed brothers, she was getting nothing!

Card table by the kitchen, with two chairs, must be his dining room table, definitely, he needed a decorator, and she could do that. Holly walked over to the pocket door to the small kitchen. "Those color samples are awfully bright. When you do a full wall, it's g-going to be too strong."

He stepped out of the kitchen, stirring boxed mashed potatoes in a pot, as he studied the paint smears critically. "What would you do?"

"Staying with the blue and a sage green will tone down the intensity of your colors and make a soothing room for when you come home."

He nodded in agreement.

After a decent steak dinner he turned on the t-v to the Antique Road Show, and they cuddled on his coach. "This is just as much fun, right?" she asked hopefully.

He smiled lopsidedly. "Sure."

Snuggling deeper, she smiled contentedly. Now she knew what her man's '*lying aura*' colors were.

And the way things were going all she had to do was work on him a little more, and she'd have her '*dinner plus.*'

Chapter 38

Frowning, Paul looked at the duty board in police headquarters. Eric and Henry were walking over, Eric complaining, "610 is in repair, the transmission is slipping. They said they probably couldn't even look at it today."

"Great." Paul looked down the list. "Third car being worked on, Rick's still in Washington training, and two more patrolmen are out with the flu. Why don't we just close up shop and all of us go on vacation?" He studied the board again. "Eric, pick up the extra keys for Rick's 602 from Mary. Its parked in his driveway. I'll take you over there; then I can check in on Daphne. Don't want her going into labor because she looks out the window and thinks she's lost her husband's patrol car."

"Paul," Mary called from behind the desk. The chief dispatcher's short, silver hair was as neat as her uniform. Now she looked over her half-glasses saying uncharacteristically businesslike. "The Chief would like to see you at 9:15."

Paul looked at the clock on the wall, 8:40. "I was just going out. Could I just run in his office now? Or catch him after lunch?"

She continued that unaccustomed firmness. "He's given you an appointment at 9:15."

Henry shot him a questioning look.

"Appointment?" Paul asked. "That's a bit formal, isn't it?"

"9:15."

Paul tried for humor. "This going in my personal file?"

"You can wait over there." She indicated the bench along the wall and walked back to her desk.

Henry came over closer, saying in an undertone. "The bad kids have to sit outside the principal's office and wait to catch it. What'd you do?"

Paul shrugged, then said also in an undertone. "You know anything?"

"Nope."

That made two of them with no idea what this was about. Well, it was time to roll out. Paul changed the plans. "I want Eric on patrol. You drive him over to pick up Rick's car. I'll call Daphne from here, to let her know you're coming. Knock on the door. See what she looks like and if she needs me to pick up anything for her, aaup?"

Henry nodded as the morning shift started filing out.

Paul made his call to Daphne, then sat down on the visitor's bench and noticed Mary Ryan was working at not making eye contact.

Chief Lewis had white hair on top of a square, Irish Polish face. Today, at 9:15, the Irish eyes were not smiling. The chief's office was like himself, plain, no-nonsense. It had an old style desk, file cabinets and a wall of photos of Lewis' hunting and the departmental shooting trophies. As the chief marksman on the department's shooting team, Paul was in a few of those photos. No computer here, but a filled candy dish on the desktop and--for the chosen--a box of cigars in the bottom right-hand drawer. Paul was used to just dropping in, getting his orders and talking a bit. He started to walk to one of the two brown leather chairs in front of the chief's desk, when Lewis said, "Don't bother to make yourself comfortable. You won't be staying that long."

Aaup. Just stand at attention and take it. He was in trouble, but for what? "Sir."

"How's the college coming?"

That was unexpected. "It's little hard keeping up, with all the overtime I've been getting. Is that problem? They're complaining I've been taking too much overtime pay?"

"No. We appreciate the amount of time you're willing to put in. In fact, you have had an excellent record with this department. I've assumed you would be rising further up the ranks. Perhaps taking my job one day."

"That's something I'm working for," responded Paul carefully.

"You were in a car accident the other day. Your new truck?"

"Yes, sir. The accident report should have been clear. I was training a student driver. He correctly stopped for a red light, and we were rammed from behind by a driver, who I believe will be prosecuted for DWI."

Chief Lewis picked up his reading glasses and lifted up the report in front of him. "The student driver you were training was one Frost C. Corey?"

"Yes, sir." It just hit the fan.

"The same Frost C. Corey involved in the Rolf Van Hom murder case?"

"Tangentially, sir. Yes."

"That case is still open."

"Frost only found the body, with his brother and sister."

"On his property. And I believe there was some involvement with him, Van Hom, and a woman? A Miss Miranda Talmadge?"

"They all worked at the Seaport Museum Village."

"And both Mr. Corey and Mr. Van Hom dated Miss Talmadge?"

"She seems to have dated everybody with pants, sir."

The chief took off his glasses and looked directly at him. "Let's talk about your dating choices. You have been seen with Mr. Corey's sister, one Holly Corey?"

"I wasn't aware I'd done anything to place me under surveillance?" Paul said with a touch of anger.

His chief ignored that. "Answer the question."

Paul felt himself reddening. "Yes, sir. I have gone to dinner with Miss Corey." Did Lewis know about tea at the deli, after a traffic stop?

"Anything serious?"

"Respectfully, sir, I do not think that is any of the department's business."

"Her brother and herself are suspects in an unsolved murder."

"Holly is not a suspect–by anyone, one's investigating! It was her first day in town, and we're not dating seriously. I just enjoy her company..."

"Sergeant, there are a number of facts you are probably not aware of. Her mother's death for one, because it all happened before you moved down here. Hell, my Uncle Teddy was head of the department in those days."

A puzzled Paul just looked at him. "That was what? Twenty years ago?"

"Seventeen. I checked the file this morning. Hester Farrington Corey went out at night to an abandoned mill on her property. After setting the building on fire, she allegedly stabbing herself to death."

"Why is this coming up?"

"It was ruled as a suicide at the time. In the department, we didn't think it was, but we couldn't prove otherwise. Hester Corey to all accounts was a stable woman, with triplets she loved. Her husband had enough motives attached to him and his friends to sink the Titanic, but we couldn't make anything stick, so he was persuaded to leave town. The police could do that with undesirables in those days." He looked directly at Paul. "We can still make people pretty uncomfortable."

"Whatever her parents did, that shouldn't have anything to do with Holly?"

"What her parents were, she is, and she'll pass that on to her children. If you marry her, those will be your children." He paused and then said slowly, "Paul, you're not a local, so you don't know. Holly Corey comes from that 'Old Craft' contingent in town."

"Old craft?"

"Her people are not exactly First Congregationalists."

"What?"

"The Le Feurs. The Hoyt sisters. Some of the Fullers. The Coreys. People into this witchcraft, New Age nonsense for generations. Those herbal shops. Like to run them all in for practicing medicine without a license! I'm not having people like that drag a good officer down, especially a man who has been building a solid career for himself. The department would prefer you didn't socialize with the Coreys."

"Sir..." Paul started. "I already have a dinner date with Holly this Friday."

"You'll have to cancel it. You're on duty Friday."

"I wasn't aware I was scheduled."

"You are working Friday night! And every other damned night this year, if it's necessary. Paul, you can be stubborn. Good trait in cop--within boundaries. But I've got a few years and rank on you. Don't even think you can fight me on this!"

"That's not..."

The chief cut him off. "Did you have plans to marry this lady?"

"I barely know her!"

"Good. If you want your career to continue to advance, I suggest you keep it that way."

"What do I tell her?"

"You're suddenly busy. Very busy. She'll get the idea." Lewis looked tired. " Paul, this is a warning from a friend as well as your boss. As long as the lady and her brother are murder suspects you are to avoid all contact with the Coreys. Consider that an order!"

"Respectfully, sir, my personal life is my own business!"

"It certainly is–unless you continue to sniff after Miss Corey!" Chief Lewis pushed back in his chair. "The Old Crafts are generally harmless people, meditating as they smoke their questionable leaves '*for enlightenment.*' As long as they don't frighten any tourists, they can keep doing their naked minuets in the moonlit woods, but there will not be any officer under my command dancing bare-assed with them! Especially one as promising as you!"

"Is this conversation going on my record?" Paul asked coldly.

"This conversation was not for the record, but if we have to speak about the matter again, it will be." Paul started to object, but Lewis raised a silencing hand. "I've wasted enough time on this matter. Sgt. Travinsky, you are dismissed."

Stiff-backed, Paul turned and left.

Chapter 39

Friday night, Noel and Frost were in the kitchen, with Frost looking in the refrigerator. "Not much here. Open a can of hash and put a couple of fried eggs on it?"

"That sounds okay," said Noel.

Frost looked toward the closed door that leads to the dining room and the parlor with its phone. "This nightly ritual is getting to me. Holly is listening to the day's phone messages and looking like she wants to die when there isn't one from Paul."

"If being a virgin is deal killer for Sgt. Travinsky, he's an idiot," said Noel reaching up in the cabinet for the plates.

"I didn't read him that way," said Frost slowly. "He really wanted her."

"Paul's a ladder climbing guy. He wants a '*college girl*,' who is going somewheres, not someone cleaning out motel rooms," said Noel glumly.

"Holly's a little scatterbrained, but she's smarter than most! She could ace some college courses."

"She flunked out," Noel said. "And she won't try again."

"Like you with swimming?"

Noel ignored Frost's dig and pronounced, "If Holly believes she can't do it, she won't be able to pass a course."

"Before she didn't have us pushing her and Paul to impress. Maybe if she just took one easy course. I could scrape a few bucks together if you can..? The Seaport Museum gives State University extension courses..." He cut off as a sad-eyed Holly came back into the kitchen with Thor rubbing against her legs, whimpering a bit.

For her benefit Noel said, "You know–how about we give that opened can of hash to Thor? And we take my credit card and go out for a real meal tonight? Frost, you must know of a good seafood restaurant around here that's reasonably priced?"

"S&P Oyster Co. by the bridge," supplied a cheerful sounded Frost.

"All in favor, raise hands," Noel commanded.

In unison, three hands raised high.

Running upstairs to change out of her jeans, Holly looked through her clothes. She was so sick of wearing jeans and t-shirts, but she really didn't have any pretty dress or gown. She looked in the closet. Well, there was the bridesmaid dress from Jodie's wedding. It was a princess cut, pale yellow with a faint green-fern pattern, and although the light fabric was more for Summer or Spring, it made her feel feminine to slip it on.

When she came downstairs, Noel looked up at her. "What took you so long?"

"Yeah. Why didn't you wear that dress for Paul. It's wasted on us," said Frost.

Noel glared at him.

Holly drove as Frost directed her to the S&P Oyster Co. downtown, just before the bridge. It was a one-story, white wood building facing the river, with a parking lot in the front and the dining room in the back, with three windowed walls overlooking the drawbridge and the Mystic River.

They sat down to a square table, covered with white butcher paper. Besides the plate and flatware, the table had been set with a water glass filled with crayons. "That's for children," Noel said pointedly, as he studied the menu.

Frost's mischievous eyes twinkled, "Only one red." He grabbed for it, but Holly had it first.

"It matches my eyeglasses!" teased Holly. She started to draw the outline of a cartoon lobster, 'Larry,' while Frost was drawing a great, green bear. Finally, after the waitress left with their orders, a resigned Noel took up a blue crayon and started sketching a very realistic, swooping seagull.

Holly had the lobster salad, Noel got salmon, and

Frost ate crab cakes, as they looked out the window watching the 1920 Bascule, counter-weighted drawbridge lift up. A line of sailboats and motor yachts passing under the bridge, while lines of cars ar patiently waiting on either side. Holly found herself thinking this was great but wishing Paul was with them, or that it was just her and Paul. But she wouldn't ask him to take her here–he was always trying to save his money for his house on the lake, planning for the next college course, his next new truck...his next, non-virginal girlfriend. She looked down at her plate.

"What's the matter, Sis?" teased Frost, as he grabbed away the red crayon she had put down.

"College is such a big thing to Paul."

"Well, it should be," said Noel. "He's a man who wants to get ahead in life."

Holly picked up her fork. "He wants a wife who has a degree."

"Paul said that?" Frost asked.

"He didn't have to," Holly remembered being at the Deli, that feeling of Paul's aura withdrawing from hers when she admitted to flunking out of community college. "But you can learn so much more without sitting in a stupid class."

"College gives you provable credentials. You don't get a high salary just knowing a lot of trivia," Noel finished. "Holly you've got the brains, you can get at least an associate degree. Bet Paul might be happy with that."

"I already flunked out."

But Noel continued, "You didn't care then. You do now! And Frost and I can help you study."

"Yeah, N.C. and I were talking about that," added Frost. "The Seaport Museum is giving an advanced placement course for UConn in Martine History that shouldn't be too hard."

"I-I couldn't...if I flunked, Paul would think I was even more of a dummy."

Noel pushed, "Don't tell Paul you're signing up. If it doesn't work out, he won't know."

"How much would it cost?" she asked slowly as if thinking it over.

Frost hurried with, "I can arrange for you to audit it for free, but I think its worth paying. It's two hundred and eighty dollars if you want it to count toward a degree program someday?"

Sounding discouraged she said, "I don't even have a salary at the moment."

Noel spoke softly, "Between Frost and me we can pay for the course."

Holly didn't understand. "You guys are selling the mansion, and I won't even be living here in two months."

"Where do you plan to go?" Asked Frost sounding surprised.

She looked down at her plate. "I don't know."

"I've been asking around," Noel said. "Rents are high here, but maybe with the salaries from Frost and myself, we can get a two bedroom. And in time we should have the money from the house."

Frost added, "Which will have to go for paying back some of Noel's loans and getting him a car."

"The three of us still living to-together?" She said happily at the thought.

"Of course." Noel studied it. "Maybe we can swing college for you unless you wind up living with Paul. From one of the Aquarium's skiffs, I saw his truck near the building you described over by the south side of the harbor."

"What were **you** doing out on the water?" Frost asked surprised.

"Delivering papers to Dr. Morjessky. She has that small, two-story, gray clapboard houseboat moored over there."

"Think I've seen it. That's tiny," said Frost.

"But you should see the views," said his brother in an amazed tone. "There are French doors on top and bottom on the waterside end."

Holly was finishing the last of her salad. "N.C., you haven't liked boats and water since you were a kid. That time you fell in and nearly drowned because you couldn't swim?"

"Still can't," said Noel.

"What?" interrupted Frost. "You work around those beluga pools, and you can't swim? Isn't it over your head?"

"Being beside the water is okay, being in the water is what I can't do," said Noel. "But Dr. Morjessky wants me to learn to pilot a boat..."

"They let you pilot that skiff to take her papers over?" asked Frost.

Noel shook his head. "No, one of the other guys did. I have to get my Coast Guard water safety training certificate and then get a basic Captain's license before they'll let me take out one of the Aquarium's boats. God, I know Dr. Morjessky wants me to learn but...I can't pilot a boat. It makes me queasy just to be on one." He shook his head.

"And you shouldn't be on the water when you can't swim!" said Frost.

Holly looked up from drawing an orange spotted crab that was biting Frosty's green bear. "You can learn, N.C. Frost can teach you."

Frost got a big, shit-eating grin on his face and started parodying Noel's clipped, command speech pattern: "This is going to be hard, but if you just follow my every command. Absolutely. Immediately. Without question...."

Holly laughed as the waitress started clearing away their dinner plates. Reddening, Noel just ignored Frost and asked, "Holly, are you going to want some dessert?"

She had planned to but now she was looking up, someone was coming in, someone that made her heart beat faster. It was Paul Travinsky, wearing a dark brown suit, white shirt, and gold striped tie. She'd never seen him in anything, but a police uniform or casual slacks and that suit fit his long body so well, he looked so handsome. Paul was holding a foil wrapped, red bowed gift in his left hand.

Had Frost and Noel arranged for him to meet her here?

She looked at her brothers. Frost's mouth was gaping as he was also looking to the man who was walking in the door. Holly looked back. No–it wasn't a man Frost and Noel were looking at, it was a couple. Beside Paul walked a black haired woman in a yellow tent dress, who was laughing and teasingly with Paul, holding tightly on to his arm. She was petite, beautiful and obviously at least ten months pregnant.

Holly wanted to die. "Let's go."

Frost signaled to the passing waitress. "Check please."

Noel's lips had tightened into a straight, tight line. "We should ask Mr. Travinsky to introduce us to his friend."

"In her condition make that 'friends,'" retorted Frost.

"**No!**" Holly wanted to die of shame. "I want to go!"

"Alice said he's not married and not living with anyone," muttered Frost. "And I never read him as that kind of guy."

"You don't have to live with them to get 'em pregnant," responded Noel.

Having seen them Paul was still gently helping the woman settle awkwardly into a table for two by the windows.

The waitress now held out the bill to Frost, but Noel took it. "We're in a hurry, please." He placed his credit card on the folder without checking it and handed it back to their waitress. His eyes icy-blue-green Noel turned to watch Paul. "The gentleman's coming over."

"Yeah," Frost said. "Remember he out weights us both and carries a gun."

"One thing about growing up around military bases," said Noel evenly. "I'm a third-degree black belt."

"With him being 6'4", what if he's a fourth-degree?" Frost pointed out.

"I jus-just want to go! **Now!**" said Holly, miserably.

Paul came over looking a bit harried. "Holly, I saw the hearse in the parking lot. You guys just starting dinner?"

"Actually we're leaving," said Holly with a painted on smile. "Excuse me." She got up, keeping Noel between her and Paul.

Frost also smiled with false friendliness. "That your sister over there?"

"No." Paul looked back to the table where the woman was looking curiously at them. "That's Daphne Mason–her husband's out of town."

Holly was walking away, not looking back.

"Holly! This isn't what it looks like..." Paul started, then stopped when he saw other diners staring frankly at the show.

Frost pointedly looked at Daphne's ballooning belly. "Gee, I would've waited to date her, at least until she delivered."

Paul was still looking at Holly, calling out. "There's an explanation for this..."

"And since you're such a smart, college guy, I bet it's a dandy," smiled Frost bitterly as he got himself between his sister and Paul.

The waitress had returned with the card. Ignoring Paul, Noel signed the credit slip without looking at it and followed his sister and brother out.

Chapter 40

That brief smell of honeysuckle again as Holly was on a step ladder when Noel walked into the parlor. "What are you doing?"

"These curtains have got to come down."

"Don't take 'em down."

"I've got to launder them."

"You can't wash them. They're so old; they'll just fall apart."

"They're dusty!"

"Well, try to vacuum them in place," Noel said doubtfully.

She looked up in frustration. If they were going to be a top level bed and breakfast, they needed so much fixed and replaced. "We need to paint a bit..."

"We can't afford it. Frost and I will work on the replacing some porch boards and some plumbing fixtures. That's it."

The sound of smashing china in the kitchen.

She stopped for a moment and looked at him. "I need your and Frost's help. I want to hold a seance."

"What?"

Frost was coming up in the room. "Seance? To contact who?"

"Our mother," Holly said. They had to agree with her.

Her brothers answered as one **"No! Absolutely not!"**

"All right," Holly gave in. "A seance to try to find out why somebody is smashing those dishes."

"No," Frost said.

"It's dangerous," said Noel. "Look. You're still thinking about Paul. Do you want him finding out you are doing seances? Or any other guy for that matter? He's stopped calling, Holly, maybe this witchcraft stuff is part of the reason?"

Yes. Paul hadn't been calling. It was time she did something. Tomorrow, she'd call him.

*   *   *

And after Noel and Frost went to work, she did.

Feeling sick to her stomach, she dialed his cell phone. He answered guardedly, but she decided to plow on. "Paul, how have you been?"

"Very busy," he said.

"I thought I had a rain check on our date?"

"It's been so crazy here; I really can't..."

"I'm working at the Seaport Museum."

"Full time?" he sounded interested.

"No, just for setting up the Haunted Halloween and then working those weeks as a walking ghost." At least she thought his voice warmed a bit when he heard she had a job.

"Might lead to something permanent, Holly," Paul said sounding encouraging.

"They need other workers; you could pick up something after your shift? Maybe as one of the skeleton pirates?"

He chuckled. "I'm a little too solidly built for a skeleton."

Yes, he did have that broad chest full of muscles. Lord, she'd like to run her hands across it.

But he was continuing; his voice was distancing again. "And with all the extra traffic to mystic, the police will be pretty busy. Won't even get to see the show myself."

Did she hear the regret in his voice or was that just wishfulness on her part? Well, she'd already made a fool of herself, so she might as well keep going, "The museum is displaying my hearse. I'm getting a free family membership for a year and can take in guests. You said you hadn't done the tourist bit at the museum in years? I can get us in for free?"

There was a hesitation on the line, and for just a

second Holly thought he was going to say 'yes,' then, he said, "Holly, I'm sorry. With college and my job, there is just no time for us."

But there was time for his other, pregnant girlfriend? After he hung up, she just stood there, and she swore she heard laughter from the kitchen ghost.

Chapter 41

Monday morning before work, Noel had taken the memory card from the motion activated wildlife camera. Holly followed as he brought it inside, slipping it into the adapter for his laptop. Frost was already getting breakfast, as Noel said, "It'll come up, or we'll have to find the drive." A message popped on the screen. "There it is." She watched as he opened the files. "We've got something."

The screen showed darkly a series of still photos with remarkable clarity: lilac bush branches in ghost white against a black background; white smudged shape; the next showed a head with antlers. "Wow! Five-point buck in our backyard!" said Noel. More shots showed several does following.

Frost looked over his shoulder. "Yhep. When the snow comes, you'll see all kinds of animal tracks."

More pictures: white striped skunk followed by her babies; several more snaps of a lightish dog shape, with pointed ears and a wide tail.

"Is that?" asked Noel.

"Yeah," said Frost. "Coyote, new in New England. That'll cut down the wild turkey population and the cats outdoors. It's like Grand Central out there." He added, "see, it's not that I'm lazy and don't keep up the property, I'm into creating habitats for wildlife."

Noel raised a reproachful eyebrow.

About fifty photos followed, but they did not see their anonymous, red-flannel bag leaver.

Three more nights of photographing got them into a routine. Before bed, Noel set up his laptop on the kitchen table. In the morning, he took let Thor outside for a run and picked up the memory card. Uploading it while Holly and Frost made breakfast. While they ate, the three of them flipped through the photos from the night before. On Thursday morning before work Noel pulled up the last night's file. The same skunk family appeared waddling the brick pathway every night, another feral cat hunting, and two pictures of an owl swooping past the camera, with a mouse in his talons. Then all three Coreys stiffened, single shots of a dark figure moving into camera range, obviously unaware they were being photographed.

"That's a man–in our backyard," whispered Holly appalled.

"No," said Noel. "Look at the short height, thin body, and the narrow shoulder width. A boy?"

"Some prank playing teenager?" Frost mused.

The camera with its frozen downward angle caught just the top of a black hoodie covered head; it was so frustrating, Holly wanted to twist the camera with her hands, see who this intruder was! This person who, came again and again, to place curses on them.

Noel tried to adjust the screen's contrast. "He's walking away."

"Coming from the front of the mansion, and going to the back. Maybe he'll come back up the path," Frost offered.

He did. Three frames later, they had a front view of the dark figure returning with its head down. For a second Holly wondered if it was Miranda searching for her photographs? But why put out red flannel curse bags? More single shots of the dark hoodie, the figure would soon leave the viewing field, but finally--as if the figure sensed the camera in the tree--she looked up full face into the lens.

Frost gasped in amazement. "I-I would've never guessed her!"

But Holly had, and the nasty, meanness of the intruder's little red bags totally infuriated her. "Print out that picture. I want it when I confront her!"

The printer was already beginning to march out its lines of color. "Maybe we shouldn't say anything. We're taking secret pictures of her," Noel pointed out.

"Trespassing on our property at night?" Holly said, her voice filled with anger. "Leaving curse bags to harm us? Yeah, I'm going to worry about her rights!"

Still, furious Holly had to drive Noel and Frost to work.

As he was getting out of the hearse, in the Olde Shopping village parking lot Noel told her, "Wait until we get home. We'll all go to confront that crazy lady together."

Frost was more realistic, when she dropped him off at the Museum Village all he said was, "Take Thor with you. And wear silver!"

Chapter 42

Seeing the wisdom of that, Holly returned home. Knowing the pathway of their intruder, she easily found the latest red flannel 'gift' hidden in a clump of lemon verbena, this she tossed it into her jacket pocket. Back in the house Holly picked up the incriminating printout, put on her grandmother's silver necklace and then at the last moment whistled for Thor to join her. Bernie was not happy with the scratching, clawed Rottweiler in the back of the hearse. The ghost kept sighing which caused Thor to go into wild barking spasms.

Fortunately, it wasn't a long drive to the Hoyt sisters' farm.

Still hot with anger Holly knocked on the extra wide, coffin door, but this time Abby did not immediately open it, and when she did, the tall, older woman started to stand in the way, but Holly pushed past her.

"Miss Corey?" Abby said with annoyance, but not genuine surprise as Thor followed her in. The dog looked around the room, and he obviously sensed or smelled something he didn't like, so Thor bared his formidable teeth and growled deeply taking a wide-legged fighting stance.

Abigail Hoyt's eyes widened to show her whites, but not in fear, in fact, she just quietly crossed her hands before her and stared at the big dog. It was the mighty Rottweiler who slowly stopped baring his savage teeth and growling. Lowered his tail between his legs, Thor whimpered cringingly, her furry defender slunk to the other side of Holly to be protected.

"**Sit!**" commanded Abby.

 Thor sat.

Seeming to ignore this, a tight-lipped Sarah sat at her loom. Today she was weaving a thunderous fabric of dark purple, maroon and black. Leaving the dog sitting by the door

Abby moved to stand protectively by her sister's loom.

Still furious, Holly marched to Sarah, holding the night photograph in front of her. "What did my brothers and I do to deserve this?"

Sarah leaned back on her bench and looked at it. "A picture. A very good one."

"A photograph of you, sneaking on to our property after dark!"

"A photo secretly taken at night. I had a feeling that something had been set up in that tree to watch, but I never thought of a camera." She took the photographic print from Holly's fingers and passed it to her sister. "An amazing likeness for a moonless, cloudy night." Abby looked at it and raised an eyebrow as Sarah continued, "I heard a low sound. I thought it might be a mouse or bat scrambling, but it was so dark, I couldn't see anything in that tree."

"Motion activated infrared light," said Holly.

"What do they say?" Sarah mused. "Any sufficiently advanced technology to the uninitiated appears to be truly magical." She was adding a new color thread to her weaving, in among the indigo blues and inky blacks, she was adding a bright white-greenish color. It gave the effect of lightning in a thundercloud. With a calm face, Sarah continued passing the shuttle between the strings of her huge loom, mechanically depressing the foot pedal and then pulling the beater forward.

What was the matter with them? "Are you going to explain yourselves? All along you've been setting out those spell bags!" Holly demanded, "Whatever did we do that you felt justified in cursing us?"

"No," said Sarah quietly.

She didn't look upset or guilty, and Abby chorused after her, "Not a curse!"

Sarah started again. "Those are gre-gre bags..." She settled back and looked at Holly directly. Holly realized the red-blonde haired Sarah's eyes were a pale, pearl gray and that the chestnut-haired Abby's were the color of burnished steel."Years ago we journeyed to New Orleans. We studied some of their craft down there–at the old church. Attended the hoo doo camp meetings out in the bayous..."

Abby also added, "The hoo-doo rituals were very similar to what we were taught as children, only more flamboyant." Her voice deepened. "Under the full moon, the sweating men, dancing half-naked, in the fire's flames." Her voice took on a sultry tone. "Their endurance was amazing." She came back to reality, finishing a bit primly. "Quite arousing really."

Sarah stared her sister with a raised eyebrow then turned back to Holly. "Santeria, I think they call it now. Not Voodoo or Hoodoo," Sarah absently commented as she began working her loom again.

Holly held out the last red flannel bag. "This is protection against ghosts? Like my mother's?"

Both sisters appeared shocked, as Abby said, "Oh, no. We would never need to protect you from your mother! Dear Hester loved you three so!"

"Then why did she kill herself?"

Abby exchanged a sharp look with Sarah. Again Holly desperately wished she could read these women.

Finally, Abby stated as a simple fact. "Your mother did not suicide."

"Was it an accident?" demanded Holly. Then she asked what she feared most of all. "Did my father kill her?"

Abby sighed. "We know it was not suicide. She loved you babies so much she would never have left you!"

"Then what happened?"

It was Sarah who looked at Holly saying gently, "We really don't know, dear. Over the years we have guessed, but we don't know, and that was such a long time ago. Now we think you should be concentrating on your current dangers!

What's swirling around you and your brothers. We really can't say for sure–but we know that there is greed growing among weak, base people. Because of that danger grows! And because of your digging, it seems to be centering on you three and that house."

"W-w-why put these gre gre's on us..?"

"To protect you, dear. Didn't you sense they were positive energy?" protested Abby.

That stopped Holly, both she and Frost had sensed no harm in those bags. Skye had recoiled from them, but Holly had her suspicions as to just how much Skye Rainbow was a true sensitive, and how much she was just play acting.

Sarah had gone back to concentrating on her weaving. "That murdered man in the bushes, those people you allowed in, or near your house. The questions you are asking about your mother, going to the Millpond, this is all mud and worms and muck–these are not good things to stir up!" Sarah shook her head.

"The emotions from the past are not good and still dangerous," said Abby, nodding her head.

"But it is the new, growing night you must fear," Sarah intoned. "That man shot to death on your land. The greed, loss of control and blindness brought on by hedonism. We feel soon others must die."

"Why?"

"We don't really want to know," said Sarah, "but we do not want you and your brothers focusing this sinfulness here–close to us!"

Holly needed to know something. "My mother was a Farrington, and there are Farringtons buried in your family plot. Are we blood relatives?"

Abby looked to Sarah, who said, "Yes. We wondered when you'd realize that." Sarah looked back to Holly. "Looking at old tombstones is so interesting, but your branch of the family and mine feuded hundreds of years ago. Again, dear, the past is gone. Since we are alive today, and we all stand in danger of being killed by the current affairs, why waste your time on the past?"

"Do you know why Rolf Van Hom was killed?"

"Something he was doing no doubt," Sarah said primly.

"Why was he on our property?" Holly asked.

Abby looked sad. "That's easy. That woman brought it on."

But Sarah suddenly had turned to stare at Holly. She was struggling up from her loom bench, saying angrily, "What have you done?"

Holly felt a searing heat reaching for her. Both of the Hoyt sisters were unconsciously raising their left hands, pointing in her direction, as if they were using some sort of antenna. At this Thor came out of his lock-down. He padded to her with a low growl, prepared to defend Holly.

The sisters ignored him as Abby looked in a distressed manner to her sister. Sarah's eyes were widening, as she looked suddenly aged. "You brought something into the mansion! Something evil!"

Abby accusingly looked from her sister to Holly. "It's the murdered man's–but what is it? Where did you get it?"

"Enough, Abigail!" Sarah interrupted with uncharacteristic anger. "Holly, stop this! Stop asking questions. Stop digging! You're opening up what shouldn't be uncovered!" Sarah sat back on the bench, her face set in harsh lines. "If you don't care about yourself–think of your brothers."

Holly needed their help. "I found photographs that the murdered man had taken. I think he was killed because of them, if I brought them here would you try to intuit why they are so important?"

A frightened Abby looked to her sister, who just stared back with hard, granite gray eyes at Holly. "Dear, at this point I really don't think anything Abby or I can do will save you. Perhaps you should just leave Mystic–all of you!"

"We told your mother that same thing, she didn't listen," Abby urgently added. "So Hester died!"

Chapter 43

When Holly got to the Seaport Museum for her painting week, they had her go for her costume fitting. In the women's locker room the seamstress Katie had a gorgeous gown for her: white crepe de chine, with overlays of floating white-diaphanous veils from the waist, and trailing long sleeves. "I love it." Holly swirled in a cloud of white if Paul could only see her in this!

Changing back into old 'T' and jeans for working, she headed to the boat shed. With her artistic lettering ability, they had set her up painting signs. They gave her a list of what they wanted, and her job was to design each one, so it looked a little different and very scary. The Cafeteria was going to be the '*Davy Jones' Locker Galley,*' which would be selling *strawberry-blood sodas*, *dead dogs* and *zombie burgers*. She had Frost cut her out a special wood sign for the '*Blackbeard's cut finger cookies,*'

The standing tombstones planned for the '*Village Green Graveyard*' were already spray-painted mottled gray. She had to script out names like '*Peg-legged Pete,*' '*Pirate Sam, and Captain Bloody,*' to this list of the dead Holly, added '*Fighting Frost,*' '*Noxious Noel,*' '*Toxic Tarus,*' and '*Putrefying Paul.*'

Passing by Frost studied her work. "No wonder you have trouble keeping boyfriends."

A museum village of the 1830s easily lent itself to a Haunted Seaport theme. Most of the action would take place along the road that leads to the docks, with its small, one story buildings, many of which had avoided demolition by being moved from other New England villages starting in the 1940s. The flat-stone bank was being outfitted with her blood dripping sign signifying '*Blood Bank*' with the docents inside dressed as Dracula and Vampirella. Frost was working on the schoolroom, which would have faked torture instruments and textbooks open to pages on dragons and spiders.

The carpentry shop would be getting a full sized, green-faced Frankenstein, whose job would be to lay still--on a door set up on sawhorses--until the next party of admission paying-terror-victims was lead in. Then Frankenstein would slowly rise, his arms stretched out before him and sit up! With Paul's height and broad shoulders, he could have done Frankenstein and picked up a few extra bucks while having some fun. She could have been his Frankenstein's Bride in her long bridal gown, with a black and white streaked wig. They'd have had such fun together!

She shook off her fantasy. Frost was right, Mr. College Travinski could go take a long walk off a short dock!

Thursday, twenty-two days before Halloween was finally set up. The clock shop with its fragile pieces was staying closed, so they were duck taping cardboard 'planks,' that she painted, over the doors and windows to give them an abandoned building feeling. Same with the Navigational Instruments shop. The print shop will hand out one-page 'tracts' warning of the attack from seagoing pirate vampires. After the paying guests passed the haunted green and its horse pulled 'hearse,' they'd walk past her parked hearse. If some kid stuck a candy-sticky hand on the hearse, itself and Bernie wailed, well everyone would just think it was part of the show.

The final destination was the 'Flying Dutchman' whaler. Joe, the museum's electrician, was testing the amplification of the moaning sounds that would come from the square rigger, while others hung fake seaweed from the rigging lines, Holly watched a line of guys carried plywood coffins up the gangplank.

Later as she frantically worked bent over in paint-spotted jeans, Holly looked up to see Miranda, strolling on some older man's arm. Miranda was laughing gaily with a strawberry lemonade in her hand. She might be just visiting, but Holly figured Ms. Talmadge was probably on the overtime payroll, successfully using her friend to upgrade her to 'supervisory' status.

They were losing daylight, but Holly still had enough light to read Miranda. She was expecting this guy to come through with something big. Great. Holly wanted a cop, who never seemed to call and Frost was following hangdog after this bitch! Now all N. C. had to do was hook up with a professional widow and they'd have the Corey romantic trifecta. Angered, she painted huge, bloody slashes on the tombstone before her.

The final set up was done after the museum closed for the day on Thursday night. They all worked frantically under the generator lights as the Haunted Seaport came 'alive,' or actually 'dead.' They even had a machine rolling out fog across the fields. As Holly proudly surveying her handwork, even Noel had to admit the graveyard was looking pretty eerie! Finishing up, she was listening to a rehearsal of the Zombie Barber Shoppers singing 'My body lies over the ocean' when someone called out to her. "Frost's sister?"

Holly turned.

"Do you know where your brother is?" It was Miranda. Not sweaty or dirty or paint splattered, just standing there looking elegant, with what Holly couldn't see, but knew were perfectly manicured nails.

Not wanting to tell her, but knowing Frost would want to see Miranda, Holly said coolly, "Probably working on 'hauntifying' the whaling ship."

But instead of leaving to find him, Miranda seemed to want to hang around, coming over to look at Holly's handiwork. "You're really quite good as a painter. Can you make a living at it?"

No, Holly had tried. She evaded answering the question by saying, "Are you working Haunted show?"

"Overtime? Oh, yes. I came in for my headpiece

fitting tonight."

Holly moved over to start her next tombstone.

But Miranda was still standing there. "That was so horrible, finding Rolf's body the way you did?'

"Yes." Kind of ignoring her, Holly was pouring red paint into blue for a ghastly purple paint.

"Did you find anything?" Miranda asked hesitantly.

"Find...?" Suddenly Holly realized she was missing something here. Something important.

Miranda was continuing, "Well, Frost said he didn't find anything–but you know how men never see anything. It's the woman who has to see things, has to find money, protect herself."

Holly looked into those brown eyes and felt hunger, a hunger for money and safety that no man could ever satisfy. Holly decided to run a bluff, she stood up and walked to Miranda, saying in a soft voice, "Yes, while my brothers went for the police, I searched Rolf. There was an envelope. I have the pictures of you."

Miranda didn't seem interested in that, asking significantly, "Were there other photographs?"

So the lady obviously knew about the presumed blackmail shots. Maybe even who wanted them and why. "Yes," Holly said confidently like she knew too.

"Did you show them to your boyfriend?"

"The police? No."

She smiled satisfied with that. "Where are they–the pictures?" Asked Miranda, her voice lowering too.

Knowing she had the upper hand, Holly let Miranda wait for a beat then said, "Aren't we getting ahead? I'm going to have to see some m-m-money here before I hand over the envelope over to you."

Holly seemed to have moved up in Miranda's estimation, but the other woman only said, "There's nothing in that envelope that I would pay for."

"But Rolf said somebody else would?" prompted Holly.

Miranda looked at her with calculation in her eyes. "What do you want?"

"To be partners with you, like Rolf was. The same cut." It was another stab in the dark, but Holly sensed she hit home.

At first, Miranda said nothing, then she must have decided half a loaf is better than none. "Okay. Fifty-fifty. Don't do anything with the pictures until we talk again; there is someone I've got to speak to."

Holly managed a smile. "Fine, partner."

Then with a swing of her hips, Miranda coolly walked off, leaving Holly to realize she was playing blackmail games with a possible murderess. But strangely she didn't sense danger from Miranda. Holly intuited greed, fear, cunning, but not the compulsion to kill, and with the police doing nothing but hounding her brother, Holly had to do something to save Frost!

But would she actually trade the pictures for a name? Holly's hands were shaking so much; she couldn't letter the next tombstone. Maybe she had just written her own epitaph?

When she got home, Holly walked over to the phone and dialed in to pick up their messages, nothing from Paul, again, but a man's dry voice said something that made her heart leap. "Miss Corey, this Douglas Holmes from the Leather Bucket. Please contact me as soon as possible. I think I may have something you will be very interested in."

Chapter 44

Two days later she couldn't wait to eat dinner before setting up a family finance conference. As soon as she drove Frost and Noel home, Holly got them sitting around the dining room table. "I've sold something."

"The hearse?" Noel asked hopefully.

"No," she responded in a hurt fashion.

"It's big." Frost studied her carefully, "I can tell that from your aura colors. You've sold the mansion?" he asked.

"She can't sell that without us..." Noel looked back at her closely and becoming excited too, saying, "Holly, if you have a buyer, we have to sell! Please, I need to continue my education! Frost tell her..."

He was still studying their sister and shook his head. "It's something else."

Wanting to keep them in suspense but not being able to hold out any longer, Holly laid out the pale blue check in front of her brothers.

Looking at it, Noel's eyes grew round. "Holy cats..."

"Is that real?" asked Frost.

"Yes, I sold the painting grandmother gave me to a local collector, who may end up donating it to the Seaport Museum some day."

"Painting?" asked a puzzled Noel.

"The Warren John Thomas that originally came from this mansion," explained Holly.

Frost had reverently picked up the check and now passed it to Frost. "It's nice to have a sister with a few bucks!"

"It belongs to all of us," she corrected.

"No," said Noel. "Grandmother gave that painting to you, Holly. You've held on to it all these years. With this money, you can invest for your future, get a condo and pay for a college education!"

"Or," Frost gave an alternative, "she could buy herself violet contacts lenses, get a real car without a ghost, buy some fancy clothes to travel the world, and meet a wealthy bachelor!"

Noel ignored Frost and looked firmly at Holly. "It looks like a lot of money, but it'll dribble away fast if you don't have a plan!"

"I do," Holly said firmly. "We'll start by paying back your school loans, get cars for you guys, and fix up this mansion."

"Holly," Noel seemed sad to stick a pin her bright balloon, "Even this check isn't nearly enough to do all that."

Yes, she had to admit he was right. The check seemed like a lot of money, but they had a lot of bills, Holly reprioritized, "N.C., there's enough to bring you current on your loans, so you can set up your doctorate program. We can pay the back taxes and probably paint this house, and with any money left over, we could have the electricity rewired, maybe even remodel the guest bathrooms?"

"No!" Noel started again. "This mansion has to be sold! We can't afford to keep it up! Frost, you agreed!" Noel turned to him.

Frost was between Noel and Holly, in more ways than one.

Holly had to push him her way. "If we use the money to fix up the house a little, I can try and run it as a bed and breakfast again! Paul says lots of tourists around here prefer the period house atmosphere over the new motels. Frosty, just give me a chance, I can do it!" She looked to Noel. "One year after we fix the mansion to a rentable state, if I can't make money I'll agree to sell."

"We can't live on sentimentality," insisted Noel. "And this place needs constant work just to maintain it!"

She looked from one to the other. Noel hostile. Frost–what? What was Frosty deciding, she couldn't read him. Holly continued to try to push him to her side. "And if we put money into painting and fixing up, our mansion will be in better condition, so if we have to sell we'll get a higher price!"

Her brothers were silent, then Frost pronounced, "I agree. That's the best way."

"Noel?" Holly asked, holding her breath. With one-third ownership, he could take them into court and force a sale.

"One year. And one year only!" said Noel, "So from this check, I get some money for my student loans, and Holly gets her house repairs. Frost should get something?"

His brother looked at both of them, with his usual lopsided smile saying, "Well, the way things are going, maybe bail money?"

Chapter 45

The first night of the Haunted Seaport Halloween was magical for Holly. A cloudy, dark night, warmer than recently, but still recognizable as a fall evening. Barrels of loose candy had been set up at the various scaring stations, so kids in costume--or not--could trick or treat. Grabbing one paper wrapped candy, a contented Holly sucked on the hard raspberry as she headed for the female staffs' locker room.

But as she hurried along the cobble road, she still found herself looking for Paul, wishing to see his broad shoulders above the crowd. He might be working traffic tonight, maybe on duty as crowd control? Supervising? Or if he was off duty, he might have come in as a tourist? He knew she was working here.

In the employee's locker room, Holly slipped into her white lady costume, still twirling a bit as it felt so great. Finishing with her dead white makeup, she took one last look at herself in the mirror and then headed out. She was feeling beautiful and sexy, at least until she saw Miranda's Medusa.

Medusa was the snake-headed monster of Greek mythology who was cursed by the gods so that just viewing her horrible countenance would turn men to stone, but Miranda managed to make her Medusa movie star glamorous. Her hourglass figure was tightly stuffed into a long gown of stretch fitting fabric, printed with a gray snake-skin pattern. The headdress of stuffed snakes that rose themselves from about her head came off as 'coiffured' with carefully coiling serpents framing her face. She looked great, and Holly knew that the Gorilla hamming it up, as he hopped after her was Frost in his costume.

Tarus still wore his khaki shorts, but he had dressed up with a 'bone' through his nose and a string of 'shrunken heads' hanging around his neck. Noel had managed to maintain a little of his dignity, in a seventeen-century sailor's suit with glow-in-the-black-light face paint shaped like a skull. Frost got a little competition for Miranda when Captain Gustav came out in his Flying Dutchman attire with its gold lace trimmed sleeves and high leather boots. In a deep rolling voice, Gustav ordered his zombie crew to, "Move me hardies or be stapled to the mast!"

When the gates opened to the tourists, Holly even recognized more people. Someone called out "Holly," and she turned to see a woman, in a brightly colored, gypsy skirt, who curtsied to her. It took a second to see past the black wig before Holly recognized Alice, the Manager from the Mystic motel. Apparently, the Haunted Seaport was a total town affair, which the locals enjoyed almost as much as the paying tourists.

From a distance, she saw a group of women from Skye's yoga classes, maybe Skye was there with them? Then she looked at two tall female figures that weren't part of the paid costumed actors but wore long, hooded, black wool capes. Sarah and Abigail Hoyt, who nodded to Holly in a neighborly fashion.

As a ghost lady, Holly's assignment was to walk moaning around the tombstones on the Green throughout the night. She made the most of it, only feeling a bit sad when one little girl ran screaming in terror from her. Captain Gustav walked by, holding out a silver flask. "Getting cooler. Real whiskey, my lass. Care for a sip?"

"Nooooooo!" Holly fluttered off in her best phantom fashion. Later she saw Gustav pouring his flask into a plastic cup held by the snake-headed Miranda, and she saw Noel, on his break, walking to the Café. Clinging to her brother's arm was a most bewitching, purple-haired barmaid, apparently hanging on his every word. Tonight, everybody seemed to be making out, except herself, and she was still idiot enough that when she saw a tall man, she found herself looking to see if it really was Paul. It wasn't.

By the end of her haunting, the last guests were filing out, as the ghastly green spotlights were flicked off and the mechanically enhanced wailing died down. She had been told the night guard would let her drive the hearse out after the crowds pulled out of the parking lot. Frost and Noel were to meet her at the boat barn, and then they'd all go out for pizzas with Miranda. Holly joined Noel and headed toward the barn. He was already out of his costume, with the ghoulish makeup scrubbed off his face. She'd have to change, but she wanted to connect with Frost first. Maybe, just maybe, Officer Travinsky might be on crowd control marching tourists out the back gate to the parking lot and see her in the enchanting white gown.

The five-story boat barn was a looming dark shadow with small yellow security lights ringing it, as a ghostly white fog rose off the water. The salt water smell was strong, and in the distance, the three tall masts of the whaler stuck out of the mist, while the wooden docks under her feet rang hollowly. In her long gown, Holly felt she had been transported back to the era of square riggers and whale-boned corsets. She so wished Paul could be here walking beside her, holding her hand in his warm one.

Would he ever ask her out again or even just call? Stop one of them for speeding?

In the fog, she could see Frost was a bit ahead. Her brother had changed out of his Gorilla outfit and now wore his street clothes and was waiting on the dock. He was calling out, "Miranda?"

Again, Holly wished her brother had a girlfriend worthy of him. Noel was coming up the rear. "Let's get out of here."

It was getting cooler, and when the wind blew, Holly shivered a bit in her diaphanous veiled ghost gown. High up the yellow security lights only cast shallow pools of watered paleness on the bleached wood planks, and a remote foghorn was answered by the equally haunting whistle from an inland train. When they reached Frost, he was standing with his hands in his pockets, at the dock's edge, looking out over the dark water.

"She didn't show?" Holly could feel his disappointment at being stood up.

"Not yet," Frost said.

"Time we started getting back," Noel sounded firm.

"We could wait just a little bit longer," Frost pushed. "Miranda might be talking to someone. Miranda's always talking to someone."

"I have to go back and change out of my costume. You guys could stay here until I get back," said Holly softly.

"You should have done that before," muttered Noel. "Twenty minutes only, Holly!"

When she got back, the two of them were arguing about some football team, as they waited in the watery yellow illumination of security lights. It was Holly, who was looking down in the water, saw it first. A dark shape bobbing against the pilings, a darker gray in light-gray water, but recognizable as a body doing the deadman's float. Where the back of the head should be, snakes seemed to be swaying in the water, as the gentle wavelets pushed the body against the pilings.

Holly muffled her scream with a fist. In her Medusa costume, Miranda Talmadge was bobbing dead in the water.

Chapter 46

Not even stripping off his shoes, Frost dived into the freezing water. Noel dropped to the dock, laying prone with his arms off the edge reaching for Frost and the figure he was swimming to. The body's arm Frost lifted to Noel was floppy.

"Get help!" Holly screamed to passing figures, as she scrambled down to grab at the other arm. It took the three of them pulling and pushing as hard as they could to lift the dripping body out of the deadly cold water.

"Frost, get out!" Reaching down Holly cried, watching his movements being dangerously slowed by the frigid water as he fumbled to reach the dock and couldn't. Someone was running toward them, Holly looked up and begged, "Call 911! A woman fell in!" Noel had rolled the body on its back and in the faint security lights from the boat barn, Holly could see the horror of the face. It was a grotesque version of Miranda Talmadge's beauty framed by her stuffed snake Medusa headdress.

Noel was feeling her neck with one hand, her wrist with his other. Holly could see the stranger's face lit up from his phone as 911 came online. "Noel, can you do CPR?" Holly asked.

Her brother shook his head. "It's too late. She's cold as ice."

Frost had swum to the ladder at the end of the dock and laboriously climbed out. Now dripping water he looked down at the woman he had loved. Holly stripped off her jacket and threw it over his shivering shoulders. "We've got to get you inside and dry."

The police came, but not Stg. Paul Travinsky. Officers separated them, and Officer Henry MacKay spoke with Holly, questioning her. Finally, she asked with chattering teeth. "I-I-Is Sgt. Travinski on duty?"

"He's elsewhere," came the evasive answer.

An ambulance arrived. They tried to get Frost to come to the hospital with them, but Tarus had brought him a blanket and a paper-bagged bottle of brandy.

Noel stood protectively near his brother. "You should go to the hospital."

"It'll cost money–I'm fine," Frost's teeth were beginning to chatter.

Holly looked up at a knot of police conferring. "This is the second body the three of us have found."

"Well, at least this one could be an accident," Noel answered, sounding worried.

Holly had her doubts about that. Soon the police were hustling Frost into a patrol car for more 'questioning,' but they let him stay wrapped in Tarus's green wool blanket.

She looked about and saw a police Tahoe, but when she looked at the license plate it wasn't his.

Noel walked back to her. "Still looking for Paul? Holly, forget him!"

"Everybody else is here. He should come."

"I've been talking with Tarus; he's going to drive me over to the police station to wait for Frost. It's getting really cold tonight, and you're still wet, why don't you just go home?"

"Should we get a lawyer?" she asked.

"That's gonna cost money."

"They keep questioning our brother about Rolf's murder because he dated Miranda. Now she's dead."

Noel thought before he spoke. "He's not under arrest, and he's innocent. If he lawyers up, he'll going to look guilty of something."

"But..." Holly felt that Frost was sinking fast, and they weren't doing anything to save him.

"If they hold him tomorrow we'll find a lawyer," said Noel sounding reasonable.

"The guy doing Uncle Ben's estate?"

"No. We'll need a criminal lawyer," he said.

"If Frost doesn't know one?"

Noel shrugged. "We'll go to the library and look one up on the Internet. Here comes Tarus with his truck. I've got to go. We'll wait in the police station for Frost and bring him home. You have to have the hearse out of here before the museum security guy leaves."

She nodded, and he was gone. Holly was cold, but Miranda was even colder. Yes, Frosty would never have killed Miranda, even if she dumped him, but Holly found herself remembering how many times in her life had she been innocent of something silly, then accused by her aunt and she couldn't stutter out a defense. When she finally drove the hearse off the museum village grounds, she knew they desperately needed a plan. They had no friends, no real money for lawyers, but unless she did something, Frosty would be put in a cage and never let out!

Chapter 47

She could go home, or she could try to do something. Alice had said Paul had been assigned night shifts, so that he might be still working. She didn't know where the main police headquarters was, but Holly could start at the community policing station. Leaving the museum, she made a couple of right-hand turns reaching the drawbridge that ran across the river. Driving through the main Mystic town, with its old buildings housing clothing shops, restaurants, and antique stores, they could have turned this front street into a Haunted Seaport, too. It seemed the whole old, whaling port was now one big ye olde tourist trap. She took a left turn then drove along Noank road where the river meets the harbor. Where fine old Victorian mansions, interspersed with the Voodoo Brewery and working shipyards.

The one-room community policing center was on her left. It had no windows, but in the three vertical parking spots alongside it, there was a black and white Tahoe, license plate '609'. Holly suddenly felt a little hope, whether Paul liked her or not he would help her.

If she parked in one of the slots, the long hearse would stick out into the traffic, so she continued on and parked further down. Walking back she wondered should she knock? Or just walk in? What if she knocked and he said not to come in? Holly just opened the door. In this tiny glorified mall kiosk, there was the desk, three steel chairs, a bench and a phone and two doors for closets or something along the wall. Not much room for anything else, certainly not much room for a man of Paul's size.

He was sitting at the desk, studying the screen of a small laptop. Hearing her, Paul looked up and appeared startled. "Holly?"

"You haven't called lately." Of course, he had his pregnant girlfriend. "I was wondering..."

"I've been working," he said, not meeting her eyes.

All what she had wanted to say for so long came rushing out, "I know you didn't want me to be a virgin. You could have fixed that! Paul, what do you want me to do? G-g-go out and find some stranger in some bar? Then if it isn't the first time, will you be okay with it?"

"**No!** That's not it!" He closed his eyes in pain.

"Paul, what did I do wrong?"

"Nothing! Will you stop blaming yourself for everything! You did nothing wrong! I'm sorry, it wasn't working out for us, but it wasn't your fault!"

That wasn't what she was there for. "There was a death tonight."

Instantly he was back to being a policeman. "At the seaport, Miranda Talmadge, and you and your brothers found the body as usual."

"You know?"

"Aaup. They've called almost the whole force down to the museum."

"You didn't come?"

"No." His lips tightly pressed, then he said, "I was ordered to stay here. This phone booth might have gotten stolen."

"They've arrested Frost."

He still wouldn't meet her eyes. "No, they didn't arrest him. The detectives have just asked your brother to come down to headquarters for questioning."

"How did you know?"

"The police department is sort of a close knit family of its own." Now those blue eyes looked directly into her aquamarine ones. "Holly, a woman died tonight. That could've been you."

She ignored that. "I don't think Miranda's death was an accident!"

He closed the lid of his laptop. "I can't discuss any of

this with you."

"Her death was connected to Rolf Van Hom's murder."

Paul sighed. "And both of them are connected to your brother. Which, again, I'm not allowed to talk about."

"Miranda thought Rolf had a packet of photos that somebody could be blackmailed with. I told her I found them on his body and she was going to partner with me, to blackmail a third party."

His eyes widened. "You found pictures on his body?"

"No, but I told her I did. She believed me."

"Did Miranda actually say who Rolf was blackmailing?"

"We talked kinda of obliquely." She tried to explain. "If-If-If she had committed to something positive, I was going to tell you. So you guys could trap her."

"Sounds like somebody beat you to it!" he finished bitterly. "She's dead!"

"Frost said he felt that Miranda didn't love Rolf as much as she wanted something from him."

"She said that to him?"

"No, Frost felt it. That they were more business partners than lovers."

"Felt?"

Holly took a deep breath. "I know you are not going to understand this, but Frost, N.C. and I 'f-f-feel' things, more than most. We understand things others don't. We know in a way that can't be explained..."

"Sort of E.S.P.?" At least he didn't say 'witchcraft,' or 'bunk,' but he sounded highly skeptical. "I know you believe that, but trust me it is not anything someone could take into court, so it doesn't matter." He was packing up his laptop and standing up, looking like if she didn't leave that he would.

She just continued, "I-I think that Miranda and Rolf

may have had something to do with smuggling drugs and that a third party was in it with them. That third party killed them both."

"Who is this third party?"

She couldn't tell him. The man that Rolf photographed getting on those ships was Captain Herald Gustav, but Holly had no proof for the police unless she handed over the photographs. And those photos showed Miranda obviously having sex with the photographer. If Rolf had shown Frost those photographs, her brother might have become enraged and in jealousy killed Rolf. Maybe guessing that Miranda could have confronted Frost and he killed her. At least that was what the police might think.

Paul was waiting. "Who is this third partner? What drugs are they smuggling? And more importantly, how do **you** know?"

Holly tried to visualize those photographs. Captain Gustav climbing on to a yacht called The Lucille. Gustav with a package under his arm. Pant legs that could have been Gustav, walking past that leering statue in the yellow flowers next to the weathered gray door–where had she seen them? Was this vision true clairvoyance? Or just wishful imaginings of a desperate sister? She had to remember where she had seen those flowers! "I-I-I ..."

"Holly, hiding things from the police isn't doing you any good! We're trying to help you."

That angered her. "By arresting Frost? Do you really think that Frosty could kill Miranda? He loved her!"

Paul looked sympathetic. "A lot of guys, when a woman keeps refusing his advances..."

How could he think that about Frost? Frustrated with him, she turned to walk away.

The phone rang. Paul picked up and listened, saying, 'Thanks, Henry,' he hung up. She had the feeling it had something to do with her.

It had. "Your brothers are both on the way home in a patrol car."

She turned to him hopefully. "They've finished questioning him?"

"For tonight," he said. "Holly, the police only investigate a crime. We report our findings to the District Attorney's office and the D.A. decides whether to proceed or not."

"The District Attorney thinks Frost's guilty of Miranda's death?"

"They're still working on Rolf Van Hom's murder! Holly, you have to understand this town's whole income pretty much comes from the tourist industry. Tourist towns can't have robberies or dangerous areas. They certainly can't have reputations for random, unsolved murders, not if you want the family crowds showing up and buying admission tickets."

"Frost becomes the sacrifice to Mystic's bottom line?"

He ignored her hostility. "Have you guys hired a lawyer?"

"W-we haven't found one yet."

He glared at her, then exploded, "You three can't find a lawyer, but you can find dead bodies all over the place! You negotiate with murder victims..." She could feel his constrained fury. "Holly, do you have a cell phone?"

"N.C. does."

"Not helpful at the moment." He glanced at the police phone on the desk, then at his belt. Finally, he pulled out a personal cell phone, seeming to pull up a number from his directory. "You are calling a lawyer named John Hagen. He's a friend of mine, in general practice and if he knows your situation, he'll be reasonable about the bills. You are hiring him right now!"

He stood up and handed the phone to her. It was a

short conversation and when she got off Holly told him, "Mr. Hagen said he would go down to the police station tomorrow." She looked at Paul with frightened eyes. "Do you think they'll put Frosty in prison?"

"It's customary to hold a trial first," said Paul drily.

"I mean before going to trial."

"Holding? If they think they've got a case, they can do it, but your lawyer can request bail."

"B-but even if he could get bail on a murder charge..."

"Holly, you always look at the worse case! If they hold him and they may not, Frost might just get out on his own recognizance. I mean your family's lived here for generations, he's got a job and property in the community. No record. Or a judge may just look at the evidence and say there's no case."

Starting to tear up she had to leave. "We don't have money. We don't have friends," she said miserably.

He was standing close to her even without touching she could feel his strong, protective connection. "That's not true. Frost is a good guy, with a great number of friends in this town. If it comes to it, you guys can go through a bail bondsman; you'll only need to put up ten percent. You could put up your land, but let's see what John can work out for him."

Exhausted, Holly could only turn away, but strong, warm fingers were holding her arm. Psychically she was overwhelmed by his urgent need to be understood.

"Please–that woman you saw me with at the Oyster Co..."

She coolly cut him off. "The very pregnant one?"

"That's not my baby."

"You're denying her child?"

"Of course I am! She's Daphne Mason. Mrs. Rick Mason."

"You're dating a married woman?" Holly was

appalled.

"I'm not dating her! Her husband is a buddy of mine and a patrolman. He's in Washington, taking security training. He calls her every day, and they're really in love."

Holly eyed him suspiciously.

"Look, Rick called me. That night was her birthday, he said Daphne was telling him she was okay, but she really sounded down. He wanted to get her out of the apartment and asked me to take her out to dinner, get Daphne a present and say it came from him. Rick thought it would cheer her up a bit, aaup? I took her to the Oyster Co., I gave her a box of chocolate '*from Rick,*' and she started crying. That's all!"

Holly just looked at him wanting to believe, but why hadn't he been calling?

"I saw your hearse parked outside the Oyster Co. and I still came in. Would I have done that, if I was trying to hide something? Do you really think it's a good career move to publicly date another cop's pregnant wife, while he is away training. C'mon, honey?"

Holly found herself half smiling back. She knew he wanted her, still why wasn't he calling?

Chapter 48

Three days later, Noel had to go in early to the Aquarium, so Holly stayed in Mystic to attend the memorial service for Miranda. It was unofficial, unsanctioned by the museum administration, so it was being held at dawn before the Mystic Village Seaport Museum opened up. A group of her friends walked to the side of the boat building shed near where she died. As Holly looked about, she saw a good sized group standing there. Looking more carefully, she noticed two things: Captain Herald Gustav was not here--she knew Frost had notified him--and Holly also realized she was the only woman among those gathered to mourn for Miranda.

They had assembled on the cement ship lift on the right side of the boat building barn, where someone unhooked the cable that blocked people from walking to the end. Tarus moved toward the edge above the water, and in a green golf shirt and cargo pants, he appealed to the gods in his native language. As Tarus chanted, Frost finished weaving fragrant red roses into a wreath of orange asters, goldenrod and even white chrysanthemums he'd gotten from the Hoyt sisters' garden. Then Tarus spoke in his sing-song English about Miranda. How she would be missed. How frail all humans were, so how we must all forgive and be forgiven, to ease Miranda on her journey beyond these shores.

Frost wasn't wearing his blue tour guide shirt. Instead he was dressed in a casual T with wide navy and white stripes and jeans as he stepped up alongside Tarus. Holly thought she saw tears shine in her brother's eyes, as Frost tossed the brightly colored wreath far out into the lapping green water. It sank a bit, then floated low.

As the mourners broke up and walked off, Holly saw two men standing at a short distance, watching; both looked like policemen, but only one was in uniform. The plain suited officer had a black mustache, Holly had seen him the night

Miranda was killed, and maybe he had been investigating Rolf Van Hom's murder too? Respectfully the police waited until the impromptu service was over.

But with most of the mourners gone, the officers moved toward them. Holly was terrified, but Frost didn't seem surprised and just hugged her. "It's okay, sis. When you were upstairs this morning that lawyer John called. He arranged this with the police to give me time to say goodbye to Miranda."

"You're being arrested?" Terror paralyzed her.

He lightly kissed her forehead. "I've being indicted for Rolf's murder. I'm turning myself in at the police station. These guys are just here to give me a ride, our taxes at work. I'm being held until John can speak to a judge, then I might not even have to pay bail."

That was why he wasn't wearing his blue guide's shirt today. "Why didn't you tell me?"

He smiled. "I didn't want you crying. Remember, this was a memorial service!"

"You and I could have run!"

"Sneaking away in a 1956 Cadillac Hearse? Gee that sounds like a plan, why didn't I think of it?" He hugged her again tightly, but she had the feeling it was to comfort himself, as much as her. "It's okay, Sis." He kissed Holly on the cheek. "See ya, tonight–maybe."

He just walked away to the police, they patted him down, and they left. No handcuffs, just like three friends walking away, but with arresting officers on either side. Holly bit her lip to keep from crying.

She had to get off museum property before they opened to the public, but she needed to talk to someone. Holly walked back toward the boat building shed. Just alongside it she found Tarus. The sun-mahoganied man was sitting cross-legged on the dock, still watching the river's current push Miranda's wreath farther out into the harbor.

She stood above him. "They've arrested Frost."

"He told me this happens. You should not worry. He is innocent." Tarus still was watching those white flowers bobbing on the waves. From his always closed, blank face, for all his unfathomable emotions, Holly realized with a start that Tarus had had sex with Miranda. Now the navigator felt not love actually, more of a sad, empty longing for something that was good and now lost forever.

Holly sat down on the cement boat lift alongside him, saying nothing for a time.

Finally, he smiled as in his sing-song voice he spoke to her. "I feel your disapproval, Holly. Laying with her was wrong? That is because you know little, young one."

"She was with Frost too."

"For him, it is good she is gone. For her, he cared." Tarus shrugged with a crooked-toothed smile. "For the rest of us–only a little sad."

"Who killed her?"

"She fell maybe?"

"I don't believe that. I think she was killed by the same person who killed Rolf Van Hom?"

He said nothing, just looked out to the water. As the harbor tide receded, the fresh-water river smell flowed to the sea.

Holly tried again. "I've got to prove who killed her."

"It is white man's problem. Constables do this."

"They're not." His calmness infuriated her. "They're going after Frost!"

"They are wrong," he said without emotion.

"You call Frost your adopted son yet you won't help him? The police want to pin the murders on Frosty. They want to clean up their town for the tourist trade–he's an easy target!"

He said nothing but Holly could tell Tarus had not really considered that aspect. Finally, he spoke, "Frost would not hurt her, no matter what she does."

"What did she do?"

"She had the sickness."

"Sickness?"

"Yes, my people get it from the whites. You all have it. Now my people have it bad. Miranda, she liked that men give her cigarettes, silk scarves, cars."

"Miranda got those from men? What did she get from you?"

"From me? I had a bag of pearls. Shining little moons-yellow, silver, and black. They almost glowed in my hand as I held them before Miranda. I get lucky too!" He laughed. "Once."

Should she accuse him to see if Tarus' aura showed his guilt? "Because of that, you killed her?"

She could detect nothing, no guilt, no fear, no outrage at being falsely accused. Holly suddenly realized she was sitting alone with a small man who could hoist a wooden beam heavier than her weight up on to his shoulder. Did he kill Miranda here? Would he kill her?

Finally, he spoke quietly, "More Miranda gets, more she wants. A lot of murderers never found. Better that way. No one can blame Frost."

"I have pictures that I think Rolf took. Photographs of ships. Of Miranda. Of Captain Gustav." He turned those impaling, black, bottomless eyes on her. It frightened her, but Holly continued, "Pictures people ask money for. Maybe that's what got Miranda killed?"

He spoke without the sing-song. "Maybe get you killed. Then talking to you gets me killed." Tarus unfolded his legs to stand up. "How they run this museum when we all dead?"

Frost needed his help; she wouldn't let him go. "You know Captain Gustav is smuggling?"

He shrugged. "Everybody get some cigarettes. Some

Scotch. Police not look this way, it's good for all of us."
Tarus said nothing more.

The seagulls called as they swooped over the water.
She could hear waves lapping against the pilings below them.
Even if he knew something, he wasn't going to help her,
unless she could get to him. There was something she felt
would move him. "Tarus, until his trial, they're going to put
Frosty in a cage. After his trial, he may never get out of that
cage." Suddenly Holly sensed Tarus stiffened.

To a man who by choice lived much of his life
outdoors, being imprisoned, being kept away from the sea and
the night sky, was a fate worse than death itself. She'd sensed
before the fatherly bond he had for Frost. "Tarus, please help
me! I think Captain Gustav is smuggling something worth a
significant amount of money, worth Rolf getting killed over
if he tried to blackmail Gustav. Someone, I think it was Rolf,
took photos of yachts, small freighters, fishing sloops, and I
think it was done in this harbor. Can you think of one ship
that you saw Captain Gustav boarding that might be bringing
in drugs?"

Tarus looked out at the green-gray water. In the far
distance, they could just make out the white chrysanthemums
of Miranda's wreath bobbing above the waterline. "One is the
Red Dog, number 491234867. Another has no name, just a
number 89702411." There is Celene, registered 79090108".

"Wait! I need paper! I need a pencil!" said Holly
desperately. "Do you know approximate dates when these
vessels were in port?"

Tarus said nothing. He just got up and walked away,
toward the boat building barn. Her hopes sinking, Holly
followed. "Please." The little man walked surprisingly fast,
but Holly kept up. She'd follow him to the ends of the earth
and keep nagging him if it would save her brother.

Just from inside the door, an unreadable Tarus picked
a clipboard off the wall hook. It had pages of lined schedule

sheets and a pencil tied to it. Tarus handed it to Holly. She pulled off a blank page and then started scribbling, as he repeated the ship's name, registration numbers he had given her and added the arrival and departure dates for each boat in port.

Tarus gave her nearly a full second page of dates, names and ship's registries going back six months. She was stunned. How could he be this accurate over so much time and so many numbers? But Tarus related them with total confidence.

Just to test him, she went back to the front page. Gave him the name of a ship he had given her and asked him what its number was again? Tarus repeated the nine-digit number exactly and just as confidently as he had originally given it to her.

Chapter 49

Frost was already back at the mansion when Holly got home; charged with Rolf Van Hom's murder, but freed on personal recognizance. He didn't want to talk; her brother just went into his room to lay down. Whimpering softly Thor walked to the side of his bed and curled up alongside him.

Holly waited until she drove Noel home before thinking about making their grilled cheeses. With gloves, she already pulled out Rolf's pictures and compared them to Tarus' list and discovered seven of the boat's names or numbers matched! After dinner, Noel had called a family meeting to discuss household expenses. Instead, Holly brought out Tarus' list. "These are ships that he suspects could be bringing in drugs. Tarus will testify that Captain Gustav took his boat out and boarded them."

Frost pointed out, "So? Gustav's a people type of guy; he talks with everybody! Always looking for an angle, a cargo to buy or another group to rent out one of his party boats."

"Seven of these boats appear in this pack of Rolf's photographs. Tarus never saw these photographs."

Noel started, "Firstly, the photographs: you're only guessing it was Rolf who took them, and you're only guessing he was or was planning to use them as blackmail. You're guessing again that he was killed because of that blackmail. Look, if Tarus knows about smuggling, tell him to go to the police."

Frost shook his head. "He won't. For one thing, Tarus goes out to most of those ships to pick up cigarettes and booze himself."

"He can buy cigarettes at the drug store," Holly said.

"Not at the untaxed prices," Noel pointed out.

Holly picked up the list. "One of these ships is in port now, the Argus. It could be searched for drugs?"

"You don't just search a ship without proof!" Noel

yelled.

She looked at the list in her hand. "If the police could verify these ships were in the harbor on these dates that would validate Tarus's memory. And then if those ships came from ports where drugs are trafficked?"

Frost looked to Noel. Her brothers sat there silently.

Holly had to get someone doing something! "Paul shoots with a buddy in the Coast Guard. Maybe he could run a check?"

Noel shook his head. "Are you kidding? You tell Paul you think Gustav is guilty. How do you know–you looked into your crystal ball and intuited where Rolf's alleged blackmail material could be found? Do you think a cop is going to believe in witchcraft? Holly, you like Paul, do you want him seeing you in that light? Do you think you'll have any chance with him after that?"

She pressed to lips. That's exactly what she was afraid of, but Frost was being indicted for a murder he didn't commit. "I don't care. Tarus can give us ships, numbers, and dates."

"So?" Noel shot back. "A shriveled old man, pickling himself in Whiskey says he remembers some boats that came into this port?"

"Actually Tarus prefers to pickle himself in Scotch," Frost coldly corrected.

"Yeah, keep joking!" Noel picked up Holly's sheets closely scribbled with dates and ships. "You're saying that this Polynesian guy has memorized dozens of ships' names, dates, and registrations. How could he?"

Holly had wondered about that too.

Frost dropped his clown facade. "Tarus does not have his doctorate in advanced marine *shipology*, but he is one of last of the elite navigators of Polynesia. He is directly descended from the men that braved the entire Pacific ocean in open outriggers. Without sextants or GPS, they colonized remote island after island across the entire Pacific. Not only did they find these islands, but they could leave and return to them to bring back families, seed and animals to colonize.

"The navigator families were interbred for generations. Men like Tarus are trained from childhood to navigate by complex, moving star maps in their heads. They are trained to see and plot the flight paths of seabirds. To remember the minuet directional changes in wavelets on top of waves.

"Tarus has been teaching me how to form the map of stars in my mind and how to read the colors of the water. I see a lot more now--it was always there--I just never saw it. Tarus' mentors had totem animals that they navigated with, with the same mystical bond you, N.C., have with your belugas.

"Scientists say humans don't utilize ninety percent of their brain. That most people are capable of E.S.P., but since childhood, they've been taught that it doesn't exist, so they never develop anywhere near their potential. Tarus was raised to remember everything related to the sea. He does, that's an indisputable fact."

Holly appealed to them, "Then I should take these pictures to Paul to see if he can trace the ship's routing?"

Noel had a calculating look on his face. "Don't speak to the police yet. At the Aquarium, we have access to several marine databases that I'm supposed to be learning. I might be able to find out what ports these ships came from and where they might be journeying to."

His eyes focusing on the distance, Frost warned softly, "Captain Gustav goes to the Aquarium regularly. Be sure he doesn't know you're looking."

Chapter 50

The next afternoon, Noel handed Holly three pages of computer printouts, listing the home ports and routes of many of the ships on Tarus's list. Noel had high lighted in yellow many of them with ports from Ecuador, India, and Mexico.

"Why are these marked?" Holly asked.

"All these ports are high trafficking areas for cocaine and heroin."

"That proves something!" Holly said triumphantly.

"No, it doesn't. And the fact that a garrulous businessman like Captain Gustav is visiting all the ships in the harbor doesn't prove he's murdering a guy in our backyard. For Frost's safety, our best bet is to just stay quiet and wait to see if he goes to trial."

But waiting wasn't Holly's long suit. That evening she had the packet of Rolf's blackmail photos and was headed into the Community Policing booth over the bridge. With happiness she saw the Tahoe with the license '609' parked outside; she had to park the hearse further down the street and was soon opening his door.

Paul did not look welcoming when she walked in.

"Did you park your hearse in front?"

"No, it doesn't fit well–I parked it down the street."

"This street?"

She couldn't understand. Paul was avoiding eye contact, and he hadn't called her, he'd dumped her, but she still she read in his aura that he wanted her? But it didn't matter; she was here for Frost. "Paul..."

He cut her off. "Holly, I'm sorry, but I can't socialize with you now."

"This is police business," she said firmly.

He briefly closed his eyes. "You know, with the personal relationship between us, maybe you should speak to another officer?" He reached to his belt for a radio. "I have a buddy of mine who is patrolling near here. I'll call Henry..."

"It has to be you! I've got pictures to show you." She thrust the envelope and Tarus' ship sheets toward him.

He looked at the envelope and reddened with anger. "Then what you told Miranda was true–you did find those on Rolf's body!"

"No! I didn't find anything on Rolf's body; I just bluffed with Miranda."

"But now the pictures you didn't find, you have?" He sounded furious.

She lied. "I found them later."

"When and where?" Paul was sounding totally cop.

Holly ignored that. "I think Rolf was blackmailing Captain Gustav with them."

"What did he have on Herald Gustav?"

"Drug trafficking--I-I-I think. I know Gustav has been trading in endangered species items." She thought of Skye. "But I don't think I can say that, without getting someone else in trouble, and selling endangered feathered earrings are not really a great crime, is it?"

Paul sank down in his chair, looking at the envelope and sheets in her hands. "Where did you get these photographs?"

"I don't think that I can say that either."

"Holly!" He sounded and looked stormy.

"I-I found them in the Mystic M-motel."

"Before we searched his room?" Paul looked shocked.

"No. N-not in his room. Outside his room."

"When?"

"J-just a few...."

"Did Alice, the manager know you were there?"

"She..yes."

He sighed. "Did you go into his room?"

"Only after it was unsealed."

"Great." He closed his eyes pain. "Maybe if you found

something there–it's better it stays lost!"

"There's pictures of Miranda Talmadge in there. I was afraid it might look like Frost killed Rolf out of jealousy, but he didn't! And for these pictures, Miranda might have killed Rolf, but I don't think she did."

Paul opened a drawer and took out latex gloves, pulling them on. While Holly stood there, he pulled the photos out of the envelope and started looking through them. "Ships. The bottom of some sort of door with yellow flowers. Gustav boarding the Argus. Boots that could be Gustav's. Pictures of Miranda. Lots of people take dramatic naked pictures with drug paraphernalia to publish on the Internet. None of this proves anything." He looked into the envelope. "You have the memory cards from the camera too?"

"The pictures were probably run off on a computer printer. Did Rolf have one in his room?"

"Aaup, I carried it out when we cleaned his hotel room, but there is nothing unique about a photo run off a mass-produced printer."

"Maybe it inked wrong?"

"Any other printer could also print wrong. And I don't see any distinguishing flaw in these pictures." Frustrated, he looked down at the prints. "You can't tie these home-printed photos to Rolf Van Hom unless there are latent fingerprints. And yours are all over these pictures, right?"

"Y-y-y..." She nodded.

"Yeah. How about Frost and Noel's?"

"Noel used gloves."

"At least one member of the Corey family has half a brain." He stopped, trying to keep control of strong emotions. "Holly, fooling with evidence in a murder investigation can be a serious offense! If they think you are hiding something or lying, you could go to jail!" He slipped the photos into the envelope and pushed it back to her. "If you want it, I've never seen these pictures."

"I don't care about myself." She pushed the package back toward him. "I want to help my brother. If you searched Gustav's ship for the gun or drugs?"

"We don't have probable cause!"

"Tarus has seen Gustav going out to the ships, maybe bringing something in. He gave me a list of ships and dates. He's willing to testify to what he's seen. Look," she reached for the printouts under the envelope. "Some of these ships registrations match with drug trafficking ports."

Paul looked at the computer printouts Noel had gotten. "This looks like it comes from the Coast Guard database. That's classified information. How did you get access to this?"

"I-I-I can't say."

"You can't say." He glared at her. "But we all know that brother N.C. works at the Aquarium and for scientific purposes they have access to a number of restricted databases."

"I'll never tell them where I got it from."

He handed all of Noel's yellowed printouts back to her. "We can check ships on our own."

"But Tarus will testify," she continued, "his ability to remember ships..."

"Is legendary. I'm well aware of that. I am also well aware that Tarus often takes his canoes out to visit a number of ship's captains, and I'd bet a month's salary that those skinny, foreign cigarettes he chain smokes and that booze he's always lapping up has never seen a Connecticut tax stamp!"

"But if there was a drug smuggling ring..." Holly persisted.

"Your brother Frost is always around the docks. He knows Gustav. Frost worked with Rolf and Miranda at the museum. Honey, this could even wind up looking worse for him!"

"Frosty couldn't have been dealing drugs. He has no money."

"That's in his favor." Paul's face looked tired. "But they'll say he just might be hiding his money."

"Then you think we should just dump these pictures?" Her voice held defeat.

With his gloved hands, he started going through the photos again. "It's evidence, for not one, but two murder cases. If it were only Rolf's death I'd say yes, dump it, but with Miranda being Frost's girlfriend and a lot of other peoples'. Miranda showing up dead and Miranda being first found dead by Frost and you guys. All that is damning against Frost. Maybe against you!" He kept looking at each picture. "Still, with these pictures on record, showing Gustav visiting ships, that might actually give Frost's trial attorney something to run a smoke screen with. Counter the jealousy motive with smuggling, but that means as finders of this evidence you will be involved. The detectives are gonna have questions. And you'd better come up with a better explanation of how your found this stuff and why you didn't turn it in sooner. And trust me, honey, you're no good at lying!"

"With these photos, you could search Gustav's ship."

"No." He sadly shook his head. "You read these photos as documentation that Captain Herald Gustav has been going out, buying drugs and smuggling the packages back in port. His lawyer will say the good Captain was out on the ships, trying to collect money for the Seaport Museum's fund for underprivileged children. That package he's slipping out under his coat there is just three cartons of untaxed cigarettes he got as a gift. Which actually would be legal."

"Rolf wouldn't have been killed over cigarettes. Paul, if you could only search Gustav's boat?"

"Holly, he has a whole personal fleet of rental, party boats tied to a dock he personally owns. Without just cause, we can't search any of them."

"If you just went t-there and pushed him a bit..."

"Trust me; Captain Herald Gustav knows his rights. He is not a man the police can bluff or bully. "

Blocked, she stopped and thought about it. "A smart man wouldn't leave a gun and drugs on a party boat where tourists could find it."

"A smart man shouldn't leave any evidence around–but they usually do."

"I thought there was one boat he lived on?"

"Aaup, The Scarlet Lady."

"You're a police sergeant. You could search that." She was desperate, why wasn't he helping?

"Holly, I've ben warned to stay away from you. I'm going to be demoted to beat cop for just talking to you right now!"

She looked down. "I'm s-sorry."

"There you go taking the blame again for something that's not your fault! Honey, your brother, is in trouble, but my instincts say he's innocent. If these pictures tie to Rolf, you are in trouble for hiding them! My instincts say you are telling the truth, but not the whole truth." He was quiet for awhile, and she could hear the normal sounds of passing cars outside. Finally, Paul seemed to make some sort of decision. "I think I should tell my superiors about getting these pictures from you. You swear you didn't find them in Rolf Van Hom's room, while you were acting as a maid there? When we had the room sealed off?"

"I didn't, and I can show you where I found them."

"But?" he asked shrewdly.

"You're not going to believe how I came to find them."

"That's what I thought. Go home. Don't talk about this to anybody but your brothers, and give John Hagen a heads up on why you're going to be questioned, and tell your lawyer the whole truth! You'll be called in, but insist that you must have John present whenever they question you. You have a right not to answer any questions without your lawyer!"

"Will these pictures help Frost?"

"If they don't hang him. Before I hand the photographs over, I've got to talk to some buddies of mine in the Coast Guard. They do random safety inspections all the time. They often have drug dogs with them. Maybe we can turn something up that will save both you and Frost some time in the slammer."

Holly said sadly, "I-I sorry."

"Not as sorry as I am. Prisons don't allow conjugal visits to unmarried couples."

Chapter 51

They heard nothing that night, especially no call from Paul. The next morning Holly was starting to break eggs in a steel bowl for scrambling as an irritated Noel grumbled, "Why did you give those pictures to the police. The photos say nothing!"

"They might help find drugs on Gustav's ships," Holly reasoned.

"What about those ship's database printouts I gave you? They could trace those back to me!"

"Paul gave them back. He kept Tarus's ship list and said they could check them."

"Still no proof of anything," Noel argued.

Frost was letting Thor back into the kitchen. "Tarus had seen Gustav boarding some of those ships. Those ships previously docked in known drug smuggling ports."

"So the police are going to put an old man in a pair of dirty khaki shorts on the stand to claim he remembers the dates and registry numbers of what ten, twenty, a hundred ships?" said Noel sounded exasperated.

"They can test him," Frost said. "Show him a photographs of hundred ship sterns and then ask him to repeat their registration numbers from memory. He can do it. Tarus's memory is on par with Einstein's."

Thor growled at the back door in the pantry and, startled, all three looked up. Who could possibly be way out here this early in the morning?

"Damn," said Frost in a low tone. "With a murderer about, we should be keeping Ben's revolver handy. It's hidden in your rooms, N.C."

A knock and a muffled voice carried to them from outside. "It's Paul. Paul Travinsky."

Holly rushed through the pantry to open the back door, smiling happily. "I w-wasn't expecting you."

In police jacket and navy-blue uniform, Paul walked in slowly, looking reluctant. "This not a social call...well, it's not an official police call either. Frost, where were you this morning? Early?" Paul said, sounding very officer-like.

"Why?" Noel asked suspiciously. "Frost, maybe you shouldn't answer without your lawyer."

But Frost only shrugged. "Got up early. Took Thor out. I rode my bike down to the Deli, to pick up some bacon and bagels."

"Did you guys see him?" asked Paul.

Holly looked at Noel, they both answered unison, "Yes," just as Frost was saying, "No."

The police sergeant closed his eyes in pain. "You guys shouldn't ever try to lie. You're piss poor at it!"

The three looked from one to the other; Frost finished firmly, "They were asleep, and they didn't see me."

As a policeman, Paul pointed out, "But anyone on the road could have seen you on your bike, and the Deli people will probably remember that you were out early."

"So I should admit it?" asked Frost.

"Aaup, don't think you have a choice." Paul shook his head. "You also are going to have to admit I came here and asked you about it. That should torpedo us both! Call John now."

"My lawyer?" Frost objected, "I haven't done anything."

At the same time, Noel was saying, "That's going to raise his bill."

Paul looked angry at their thickness. "Talking to a bunch of detectives without proper counsel is going to cost you more! They already suspect Frost of the murders of Rolf and Miranda."

"It was murder?" Holly asked.

A discouraged Frost could answer that one. "Yeah, my lawyer told me the preliminary report said Miranda died from drowning, but if she remained on land, she'd have died from having the back of her skull caved in."

Holly turned to Paul. "It couldn't have been a accident? She fell and hit the pilings going down?"

Paul looked at them and confirmed, "There were other bruises on her arm, neck, indicating a struggle."

Holly stood up. "But Frost couldn't have done that. N.C. and I had him in sight—all the time!"

"Honey, what did I say about you lying?" Paul said.

"Al-Al-Almost all the time!" she corrected. "The time he would have needed to get her alone and kill her! We were with him. It's was probably Captain Gustav! And he was working the Haunted Seaport too. Miranda must've know Gustav killed Rolf, so he killed Miranda. I know it was him–I can feel it!"

Noel jumped in. "You can't say that! 'Feelings' aren't proof! Gustav could sue us for defamation!"

She ignored him. "I gave you the photographs! Gustav has contact with all the boats in the harbor. He's been bringing in things like illegal ivory rings, that I sold at the Rainbow Realm..."

"Holly–shut up!" her brothers chorused.

"No!" she kept babbling, "I think Gustav and Rolf were trafficking drugs together. Cocaine? Heroin? I think Rolf was photographing Gustav for a reason. Maybe to blackmail him and that got Rolf killed."

Again slipping into the dispassionate policeman, Paul dryly commented, "So Gustav's smuggling in drugs and Rolf's his dealer. They have an argument on the docks, and they start fighting. In the middle, of this dispute, Gustav decides to drive over to some woods, so that he could kill Rolf quietly and, of course, Rolf naturally agrees to this. Then Gustav just happens to pick a property where Rolf's romantic rival lives?"

"Gustav could have just followed Rolf here," Holly

lamely pointed out.

"Why was Rolf here?" Paul asked.

That stopped her; she looked to her brothers, who also couldn't come up with anything.

Paul with weariness said, "It's been noticed in the department that I've been showing a particular interest in you guys."

"Nothing wrong with an unmarried guy dating a pretty girl," pointed out Frost.

"But if you're associating with murder suspects, that's not going to be too good for your career," Noel finished.

"A number of people have pointed that out," Paul confirmed dryly.

"But you were trying to get the Coast Guard to search Gustav's boat?" Holly persisted.

Paul stiffened. Again the policeman won out as he said carefully, "There was a safety inspection. I am not in the loop as to what may have or may not have been found. A drug dog was taken on board."

"Did they arrest Gustav?" asked Holly.

"They couldn't find him," Paul said evenly studying their reactions.

"But if they were looking for him, they must have found something!" finished Holly triumphantly.

Paul looked so tired as if he was struggling against two impossibly conflicting loyalties. "Aaup, as I told you, I've been cut out of this investigation. In fact, I have been ordered not even to talk to you guys, but I just got a call. Since I know this through unofficial channels I'm going to tell you; the police have found a body on the beach. No wallet or watch on him, so it could just have been a botched robbery. The body's not been officially identified yet, but a non-policeman buddy of mine, who shall remain nameless, also saw the body and says it is Captain Herald Gustav."

"Gustav's dead?" Holly asked.

"Aaup," said Paul.

"Maybe he suicided because of guilt?" she asked hopefully.

"Not unless he figured out a way to shoot himself in the back, die, then empty his pockets and hide the gun."

Chapter 52

After telling Frost to call John Hagen again and admit that Paul had been questioning them about a body being found and to say nothing more, Paul left.

With Gustav dead that was the end of Holly's suspect list. With her not working, she was now the default cook and clean-up crew. The bacon and eggs she fried came out a bit rubbery, but as Noel pointed out, "At least this time they weren't cremated."

Frost was looking at her. "What are you doing today, Holly?"

"Working on the wallpaper in the library, if we're going to open up as a bed and breakfast for the December holidays."

Noel pointed out, "You can forget it. You realize all the repair supply money from the Thomas painting will be going to Frost's legal bills?"

Holly was planning to drive both of them to work, but Frost said, "You know, I'd rather not ride confined in a hearse today. I'm taking my bike to work."

"Will you have time?"

"Sure. Going with N.C., I would have been in early."

She dropped Noel off the usual safe distance from the Aquarium, but this time he didn't stride swiftly away from the offending hearse. Instead, he walked to the driver's window and admonished, "Holly, promise you will leave the investigation to the authorities this time? You're just making it worse for Frost. Promise?"

She dutifully smiled. "Yes." It wasn't a problem to promise she wouldn't do anything since she couldn't think of anything to do. Holly wanted so to go to see Paul, but she pretty much knew if it was a choice between his career or her, he was going to give up on the romance. They hadn't had time to grow together as a couple.

Driving back, Holly tried to tell herself Frosty would be okay. This whole thing would blow over. The killer would never be found, and they would open the Corey Mansion Bed and Breakfast and live here together, happily ever after. She had just about convinced herself when she passed Frosty on the bike pedaling toward the seaport. His pale blond-straw hair blew in the wind as he raised a hand to wave at her. He was so happy, so free–soon he'd be locked up in prison.

Not able to do anything else, Holly forced herself into work on the mansion. She'd always felt that in some mystical way its fortunes were tied to that of herself and her brothers. She started to remove more wallpaper from the Library guest suite. Working on the walls, she found about ten layers of wallpaper, and Holly had to add more water to the steamer. Unplugged it, Holly stood up, her back aching, she decided she could use a tin cup of tea and a break for awhile.

As Holy walked through the parlor a faint distant sound of crazed laughter came from the kitchen. The dish breaking ghost was amused. By what unhappiness this time? In the kitchen, Holly filled the tea kettle and was digging out some of Noel's homemade chocolate chip cookies when there was knock on the back door. Could it be Paul again? Holly hurried to open it, but before she reached it, the impatient person had knocked three more times on the door.

Holly opened it to find that in her fashionable suede jacket with its big, curved pockets, Skye Rainbow stood on her doorstep. A light breeze blew her perfect bronze hair, and she was smiling radiantly up at Holly as if she hadn't just fired her. But Holly noted Skye's face had a deathly pale under her carefully airbrushed makeup, and tiny beads of sweat dotted her forehead.

Realizing the time Holly said, "Shouldn't you be at your store? Or did you hire another assistant?"

"Oh, stop talking like that! I didn't really fire you, and you know that I just lost my temper again. And I need you to open the store today, because I'm not feeling very well, in fact, I'm on my way to my doctor." Holly said nothing, so Skye continued with a winning smile. "Could I get a glass of water, I feel terrible. Can I just come in and sit down. Please?"

Reluctantly, Holly moved back to let her in. Actually not working for Skye had made her feel better, Holly didn't know if she wanted to go back. Not looking at her Skye just headed into the kitchen.

Thor growled and started barking, the hairs on his back going up.

"Oh, my god!" Skye staggering back, going deathly white. "He'll bite me!"

Holly hurrying forward, grabbing Thor's rope collar. It took all of her strength to drag the growling dog from the kitchen and pen him up in Frost's bedroom.

When she came back, Skye was recovering. "Oh, this is a wonderful space. When you redecorate, it's going to be marvelous!"

Sitting down at the kitchen table, Skye continued acting as if she and Holly were the very best of friends. "I woke up aching terribly today. It might be the flu." She reached into one of those big, oversized left pockets. "Here, I've come to bring you my key, so you can open up for me. I've written down instructions for the alarm system."

As Skye handed her the key, their fingers brushed, and Holly saw a transparent vision overlaid in the kitchen between them. Holly saw the bottom of the front door, that Rolf photographed to document Gustav's drug trade. The bottom of the gray wood door with its yellow marigold flowers growing alongside the stone stoop, and that smiling satyr statuette. It wasn't a front door. It was the back door of the storage room at The Rainbow Realm!

While Skye was just sitting in her kitchen, she knew Gustav had set up Frost to be the patsy. Skye could have told the police, testified against Gustav! Anger flooded Holly. "You must have customers outside waiting–addicts who need their fixes!"

Skye looked shocked. "How can you say that?"

"The people you bring in the back room? The special herb mixtures, for your personal customers? Gustav had a key to that storeroom to make his deliveries. Boxes you forbid me to open! Drugs!"

The woman looked older but continued nodding confidently, "Yes, drugs. Drugs that should be legal, harmless drugs, mind-expanding drugs. The drug laws in this country are ridiculous! Anyone has a right to use whatever they chose!"

"Cocaine?"

"If used properly, it can expand your mind."

"Did Gustav get you into this?"

"Captain Gustav came to me with some ivory carvings, grave rings, and jade figurines that he couldn't get documentation for legal importation."

"From endangered animals? Ruined archeological sites?" Holly was angry now.

Skye ignored that. "Later he mentioned he could get peyote and ayahuasca, just for the use of my esoteric wisdom circle for spiritual and metal development. I started using it personally to unlock the portals of the soul."

"Ayahuasca?"

"The South American shamans have used ayahuasca safely for thousands of years to reach the other side. To unlock human potential. Those drugs are needed to expand the mind and raise us all to the heights of spiritual enlightenment..."

"Does cocaine bridge the mental gap too?

"Actually it does," Skye spoke carelessly.

Holly took a guess. "And heroin. Is that helping you too?"

Skye reacted as if she had been slapped. Then said, "I told you before. I injured myself in a skiing accident, and the doctor put me on Oxycodone. That helped, but then the doctor refused to give me more. On the black market, it's thirty dollars for just a single Oxycodone pill. One pill isn't going to get me through the day, but for thirty dollars, I can get a day's worth of heroin. Don't look like that! During the Civil War, heroin was sold in this country as a medicine. It's still prescribed in England for advanced pain."

Holly looked at her in horror. "These drugs are affecting your mind."

"I'm not addicted! Cocaine and the rest are all tools I utilize. Tools that give me vastly superior metal processing, spiritual awareness far more advanced than you can understand..."

"And the money for dealing in drugs wasn't bad. It got you the Mercedes?"

"I deserved that money! That car! I have developed my brain far beyond mortal capabilities. My magical abilities are way beyond the puny attempts of you or your mother."

"If your brain is so clear, why did you kill Gustav your only connection?"

"Gustav was crazy! He claimed I was stealing from him! I was taking the real risks. I deserved more! Then he came running to me when he saw the Coast Guard searching his boat, and he wanted me to hide him! He would have turned on me! Now-everything has been happening. Everyones are turning against me. My hands are shaking, I'm sick, and you've been blabbing to your police boyfriend about me!"

"No, Skye," said Holly. "You and I are friends. I wouldn't talk about you." She wondered just how much Skye would believe.

Skye stared at her. "How did you know about Gustav. Did Miranda tell you?"

"No. I found Rolf's blackmail photographs."

"You have them!" That actually seemed to reassure her, and she was quiet for a moment, seeming to be processing the new information. "And you would have told your brother, and he works at the Seaport Museum. Frost must know the same captains that Gustav did. The Argus is anchored out in the harbor. Captain Valdez–I know he was one of Gustav's suppliers. If Frost takes a boat out, talks to Valdez, the captain will give him some boxes for me."

"Drugs?" Holly kept her voice calm and accommodating.

"I'll cut him in, and Frost can take Rolf's place," Skye spoke eagerly as if she had worked everything out satisfactorily.

"You want my brother to deal drugs for you? He can."

"First, I just need a little stuff now, to calm my nerves so that I can think clearly again. And then we can work out an arrangement." Some of Skye's anxiety came back. "You've said you needed money to keep this house?"

"Yes, we do. What do you need my brother to get for you? Cocaine? Heroin?" Holly asked.

"Both, I have the cash I was going to pay Gustav. I'll pay your brother. He can pay Captain Valdez. You can take the money. Half of it is yours–you and your brother's. No. You can keep that half. Don't give it to your brother. I won't tell him. It will be our little secret. We'll give him only two hundred." She spoke in a confident, conspiratorial tone but Skye's auras colors were scatterings wildly, erratically shooting red and flashing black. Her hands were shaking, and her face had gone an even deader white with two bright red spots on her cheeks. Her heart rate must be going through the ceiling.

"You need a doctor..." Holly started to move toward her.

From her large right-hand pocket, Skye pulled out a

revolver. Now her hand was no longer shaking as if holding the gun's power had centered her and given her supernatural strength. "This is Gustav's gun. I found it in his stateroom aboard his ship. He used it to kill Rolf."

A vision flashed before Holly's eyes. The lilac bushes. Rolf Van Hom facing Gustav, but someone with the gun was behind Rolf. Holly said quietly, "No, you shot Rolf."

"I didn't!"

The vision stayed with Holly. Rolf waiting for something from the Captain. "He was trying to blackmail the both of you?"

"Rolf's drug deals weren't making as much money as mine. He had a poorer clientele. He and Miranda were partying, using up the merchandise! Rolf got paranoid, so he thought Gustav was cutting him out."

"Why did you kill Rolf on the grounds of Witch House?"

Skye smiled proudly. "That was my idea. Everyone knew that Frost was in love with Miranda. Hopelessly in love, your brother didn't have the kind of money she demanded. Rolf didn't even have enough money with his drug dealing to satisfy Miranda, that's why Rolf took the photos and tried to blackmail Gustav. He gave us copies and said Gustav had to pay for the camera memory cards."

"How did you get Rolf to come here?"

"Gustav told Rolf that Frost was in on it, too. That your brother would meet him at his house to pay him off."

"Rolf wouldn't believe that?"

"On the euphoria of cocaine he'd believe anything! And to the police, it would just be two jealous males, confronting each other on Frost's property. That was my idea. Two love crazed men fighting over Miranda. One of them bringing a gun."

"Frost wouldn't be stupid enough to kill someone on his own land!"

"Men fighting over a woman don't stop to think. Frost was confronted by his rival and killed him. He could claim self defense. He still can!"

"Frost was at the seaport when Rolf was killed."

"The police can only guess when Rolf died."

"There must have been people who heard the shot," Holly argued.

"From a distance. Nobody looks a clock when they hear a distant shot. They didn't even report it. The way we set it up, your brother could have killed Rolf before he left for his job at the seaport."

"The night of Halloween, how did you get Miranda on the docks alone?" Holly really wanted to know.

Skye hesitated and wet her lips with her tongue. At first Holly thought she wasn't going to admit it, then she said a bit proudly, "Miranda told Gustav she had Rolf's original flash drives, but she would only make the exchange at the museum with people about."

With a sinking feeling Holly realized that if Skye was confessing to her, she didn't plan Holly would live to talk about it. To just keeping living a little bit longer Holly asked, "How did Miranda let herself be out-of-sight of others at the dock?"

She laughed. "Money, my dear. Miranda was so confident she had seduced Gustav like she seduced your brother. Miranda was afraid of me, but she actually trusted Gustav. Stupid girl. So stupid she would have tried to blackmail us again."

"You still have the money?"

"Money?"

"That you were going to pay Miranda? I have Rolf's pictures and three memory cards the photos are on. If you paid me the money, I would just go away."

Syke seemed to think it over, but then, "You'll come back for more."

"No!" Holly promised. "I'm not asking much. Only one payment–just enough to leave here. Go to South Carolina. It's cheaper there to live, and you'll never see me again."

"You'd leave your brother accused of murder?"

What would Skye believe? "You know I haven't seen Frost or N.C. for seventeen years. I mean it was nice to meet my brothers, but now I've got to take care of myself. You understand."

"Get me photos." Skye stuck out the gun toward Holly. "I'll follow you."

Holly had to play for time. "They're not in this house."

Skye gestured with the gun. "Okay. We'll go to where they are." She spoke slyly, "Then you'll have your money. I have it here."

Seeing the lie in Skye's aura, Holly's mind blanked by fear. She knew she must come up with a plan or she'd die. Robotically, Holly preceded Skye out of the kitchen, through the pantry, and out the back door, pretending she knew where she was going. Finally, they were passing the spot in the lilac bushes where they had found Rolf's body, where Skye had shot him to death.

Then it happened so fast. At the same second, Holly got a realization that one of her brothers was near there was the sound of stumbling in the bushes. Skye reacted instantly. Seeing Frost, she gestured with the gun. "Over there–beside your sister!"

Chapter 53

When he was beside Holly cried, "You should be at work!"

"I sensed you were in danger," he said with that lopsided grin of his.

Not a strong enough 'sense' to get Ben's gun apparently, or call the police. Would Noel also sense his siblings' danger? Would he come and be shot by Skye too? Noel's mind was always so focused on getting ahead at work, and he denied his psychic abilities. He might be saved.

Confident she had leverage at last Skye ordered Holly. "Keep walking. Get me the photos, or I'll kill your brother right now!"

"I told you, the photos aren't here."

They had come out to the parking area by the old garage. Skye's silver Mercedes was parked just in front of Holly's hearse.

"What do you mean they aren't here?" Skye demanded.

"They're hidden at Rolf's motel. Let me go and I'll bring the photos back," promised Holly.

"You think I'm an idiot?" Skye sounded offended.

"You're holding my brother. You know I'll come back."

With her mind splintering from drug withdrawal, Skye could still keep a focus. "To save the brother that you said you wouldn't share your blackmail money with?" asked Skye sarcastically.

Even about to die, Frost could still joke, "That's mean of you, Holly. Last night I shared all my potato chips with you."

Angrily Skye ignored him. Instead she glared at Holly. "The police searched Rolf's motel!"

"The photos weren't in his room. I was the maid there, remember! I'd stole a key, and I found them."

"Where?"

"In a secret place. But I left the package there, so my brothers wouldn't find them and cut me out of the deal. We just need to drive there. Then I can get them for you, and you can give us the money."

In Skye's drug wasted mind, that actually might be making sense, but, "Just tell me where they are and I'll let you both go," Skye coaxed sweetly.

After she killed them. "No," Holly said. "You'd never find them. I have to take you in the hearse."

The mouth of the older woman set in a straight hard line. It seemed to be taking her longer to think. "No, my car."

Blocking, Frost made his aura unreadable, but Holly guessed her brother was probably as scared as she was. Holly decided to try again to get him free. "While we get the photos, Frost can take the hearse and get your medicine from Captain Valdez." He opened his mouth to object, but Holly silenced him with a look.

Skye actually seemed to think about that, but shook her head. "He's staying with us! We'll get the cocaine later, you and I will go with him. He'll get all the drugs, and we all be in business together." By her aura Holly could read she was lying, Skye still planned to kill them.

She looked at Holly. "You'll drive my car." With her other hand she pulled out her keys from her jacket and tossed them to Holly. "Your brother will sit in the front, next to you. I'll be in the back. I'll shoot him if you try anything! Frost, stand by the passenger door. You will get in when I do."

After them, Holly slipped into the driver's seat. Skye was crazy enough to march them at gunpoint into the motel. She probably expected to get the blackmail photos, and then shoot them. In her drugged deprived state she wasn't thinking about witnesses, security cameras, and getaways.

Stalling for time, Holly started to adjust the driver's seat.

"What are you doing?" Skye yelled from the back. The thin thread that was holding Ms. Rainbow together was fraying with her drug withdrawal.

"You're shorter than I am. I have to adjust the seat to drive," said Holly moving carefully. As she reached up to adjust the driver's mirror, she caught Frost's eyes. He knew she was going to try something, but he didn't know what. And the horrible part was she didn't know what either.

In the rear-view mirror, she could see the edge of the hearse behind them, and she lowered it so she could see the gun in Skye's hand. It was pointing at Frost. Holly couldn't do a thing.

"Get going!" demanded Skye.

As Holly made a show of putting on her seat belt, Frost automatically moved to click his. Under the cover of the seat back Holly touched his hand briefly to stop him. Getting it, he just went through the motions and braced with his legs. Skye was too strung-out to realize only one seat belt clicked. Holly didn't know what she was going to do, but she wanted him free to get away.

Moving deliberately, Holly depressed the brake and turned on the engine. As it purred to life she shifted into drive. Thought about what she was doing and moved the gear lever again. Not looking at the road ahead, just at the mirror and at the direction of the gun in Skye's hand, Holly slowly released the brake, giving the car a little gas.

They went backwards. In surprise, Skye twisted and jerked her gun hand. Seeing the gun now pointing away from Frost, Holly hit the gas hard–slamming the Mercedes into the hearse behind them.

Chapter 54

At the hearse's impact, Bernie's furious banshee wail of outrage roared in their ears!

In a blind terror, Skye looked everywhere, trying to see where the horrific cacophony was coming from! At the same time, Frost twisted, catching Skye's gun hand as it swung to point in Holly's direction. The gun went off, shooting through the windshield. As he wrested the gun away from her, they shut their eyes against the gray cloud of gun smoke, glass dust and spider webs of the crackling windshield.

Releasing her seat belt, Holly turned and with balled fists plummeted Skye. Gunless the would be murderess slumped back into the leather car seat. Frost ran outside and dragged Skye out on the ground, while Holly scrambled to get the gun off of the car floor.

They were all nearly deaf from the banshee's unrelenting wailing and that ringing shot in close quarters as Holly passed the gun to Frost. A crying Skye was covering her ears, rocking on the grass as Holly ran back to the house to call the police.

The Mercedes back up lights were smashed and rear end mangled, but the damage to the hearse's heavy bumper was minimal and could be easily polished out. Holly kept repeating that, finally getting Bernie's spirit to shut up. He did, just before the police arrived with sirens blasting.

*   *   *

The next evening, Paul showed up to take Holly out. While he waited for her to come downstairs, he was explaining to Noel and Frost, "At least you guys aren't listed as murder suspects anymore. Skye isn't talking, and she's got an expensive lawyer, but the judge just smiled when she tried to claim you guys had attacked her. The detectives managed to turn some of her clients. The gun is still being tested, but it's the right caliber for the murders of Rolf Van Hom and Captain Gustav."

"Do you think she killed Miranda?" Noel said.

"No," Paul thought about it. "To man-handle, a woman bigger than then herself hit Miranda on the head, and dump her off the dock, that was probably Gustav. Although Skye may have been there and might have master-minded Miranda's death. Unless she tries to cut a deal and admits it, we'll never know.

"Skye's in the hospital under arrest, while she is being treated for cocaine and heroin withdrawal." Paul continued, "And they found ten kilos of cocaine hidden behind the paneling in the Captain's cabin on the Argus. Captain Valdez is under arrest, and I hear he trying to cut himself a deal by talking about his smuggling connections."

Noel tentatively asked, "About us finding Rolf's blackmail photos?"

"And your sister not immediately reporting it to the police?" Paul stared sternly at them all for a moment. "I understand the D.A. has been given the impression that she handed the pictures in as soon as she accidentally found them. Anyhow, Dave said he's not going to push it."

Carrying Noel's backpack with her overnight things, a blushing Holly came into the kitchen.

Paul also flushed a little. "We–your sister and I-- thought we might stay out tonight. This weekend, actually."

"Your apartment?" needled Frost archly.

"No," Paul shrugged. "We're driving over to Newport."

"To a motel, a really nice place," Holly said softly. "Paul's showed me pictures on the website. We're going to have the honeymoon suite, with a private hot tub in the bedroom."

"With the special candle and flowers package," finished Paul kissing her on the forehead. "Unless you guys object?"

Noel looked at Frost. Frost said, "Have a nice time."

As Paul took the backpack from Holly, a moaning howl came from outside.

"That's Thor," said Frost. "Must see something outside."

Paul was starting out of the kitchen. "It sounds like the Hound of the Baskervilles just found another body on the moor." Jokingly he asked, "You guys have any more skeletons in the backyard?"

Holly looked at Noel who looked to Frost. Giving his lopsided grin, Frosty just said, "Isn't one enough for you?"

Epilogue

December 4th: First day as the Corey Mansion Bed and Breakfast, their new business. If it succeeded, they would all be able to live here as a family. If it didn't...Holly did not want to think about that.

The scarred dining room table was covered by a heavy, brocade tablecloth that was once a buttermilk cream linen, now a bit yellowish and the Victorian mahogany parlor furniture was polished until it shone. On the Greek revival mansion's porch, Holly had set out large flower pots of artificial poinsettias. If she could just keep the poltergeist in the kitchen from smashing dishes about, they'd be okay.

Now Holly stiffly sat, in an ironed, pink flowered dress waiting for Witch House's first guests.

Nervously waiting, her hands twisted in her lap. She wished Frost or Noel had been able to stay with her to wait. Sensing her nervousness, their Rottweiler came over and laid his massive head in her lap, and she stroked his warm fur. Would these guests be afraid of a big dog like Thor? Allergic to dogs? She should tie him outside near the woods.

No. That would be too cruel; he'd think he was getting punished for something he did. Holly stood up and reached down for Thor's red collar. "C'mon, you have to stay in the kitchen wing, fella. Just for this weekend."

But just as she turned to lead him away, the old brass knocker on the front door hammered.

Holly stiffened. Forgetting Thor she released his collar, smoothed her dress and headed to the door. What would she say?

Why couldn't Frost be here? Noel?

She stopped at the heavy door and took a deep breath. These were people, coming to share this house's loveliness for a short time. They were her cherished guests, soon to be new friends.

She pulled the door open.

On the porch was a tall, red-haired, freckled guy of about twenty and a dark-haired woman smiling near him.

"Hi! I-I-I'm here." That was stupid. She held out her hand. "Welcome!"

The guy reached down for their suitcases. "We're the Simmons. Andrew and Kate. We've got the Library room, right?"

"Yes, sir. To your right."

He walked right in front of the young woman, and she looked down, not meeting Holly's eyes. Feeling something strange, Holly held out her hand, blocking the woman's way. "I hope you like it here."

The woman nervously glanced up at the two-story hallway. "My husband says we will," she said in a quiet, beaten voice trying to avoid contact, but Holly deliberately stepped to block Kate, so she almost had to take Holly's hand to shake to get past.

As Holly closed both her hands over Kate's, she was overwhelmed by the emanations from the gold ring the brunet wore. It radiated coldness. Hate. An ancient curse poisoning this young woman. Holly nodded. "Yes. I think you will be happy here."

Especially, after she negated that pulsing, poisoning curse, but first Holly had to find out who had laid it and why?
 The End

If you enjoyed this book, please put a comment on your favorite social media, so that I can continue to write more Mystic triplet mysteries.

Thank you, Lynn

OTHER BOOKS BY LYNN MARRON

CHECK www.lynnmarron.com

FOR PURCHASING INFORMATION AND

PUBLICATION DATES

OTHER WITCH TRIPLETS' SEAPORT MYSTERIES:

MURDER AT THE ALTAR

When the triplets reunited in Mystic, Connecticut, Holly Corey found both the Old Craft worship of her witch family and a handsome police sergeant, Paul Travinski. The shadow of her mother's untimely murder still haunts them, but now her serious-minded brother, Noel, is suddenly suspect in the murder of one of his fellow beluga trainers at the Aquarium! She investigates, finding immediately that the mysterious Hoyt sisters have been keeping a secret that might get Holly killed. And despite Paul's orders, Holly decides to hunt a murderer, skyclad, at a midnight gathering of Grace Le Fleur's Coven!

MURDER AT THE MILL

GRACE FARRINGTON'S OYSTER RIVER GENETICS RESEARCH MYSTERIES:

ORR: THE NOBEL PRIZE MURDER

While working at Oyster River Research, Grace Farrington is passed over for this year's Nobel Prize, and then the DNA pioneer finds herself accused of murdering the man who stole her first shot at the Nobel. With the formidable mental powers that Grace normally uses to unravel complex DNA puzzles, she is forced to solve a triple murder. In her efforts she is helped or sometimes hindered by her eclectic group of friends: a psychic Viking named Freya; a old money patron, who seems more interested in Grace's body then her body of work; a hot-tempered research assistant who can't stop punching; and a very politically incorrect marine biologist who wants her on the back of his bike when he goes midnight partying with his motorcycle gang.

ORR: FATAL DNA

ORR: MURDER GENETICALLY ENGINEERED

ORR: THE TELL TALE Y

ANTHOLOGY OF ADAM MARTIN'S LAW PRACTICE REPRESENTING WEREWOLVES, DYADS, GORGONS , THE REINCARNATIONS SISTERS, ETC.:

ADAM'S UNORTHODOX, UNNATURAL LAW PRACTICE

Inheriting his Great Uncle Quentin's unusual law practice, Adam Martin finds himself defending the rights of water witches, a semi-senile seer, mermaids, zombies, and gorgons. He also finds himself writing contracts for werewolves, consulting with ghosts, as he struggles to protect unfairly accused fire starters. Rough duties, but Adams must do this while trying to stand up to his six foot '*Cherokee*' law secretary and dealing with his staid, disapproving family of conservative lawyers led by the formidable 'hang 'em high' Judge Jeremiah Martin!

CENTAURESSES OF THE SILVER DRAGON

The Regiment follows the hoof prints of Jace, a ruggedly handsome centaur of Clydesdale proportions. Winning on their last field, but betrayed by treacherous princes, these sword-wielding mercenaries are outlawed. Now as he hunts a patron to keep his band together, he must hide a worsening leg wound, knowing a challenge to his leadership will end in death!

Stumbling on to a dying bazaar, this legendary fighter finds a patron in the stunningly beautiful Silver Star, a tall, gray centauress with sea foam white hair, luxurious tail and ominous cloven hoofs. Star promises a vast treasure if the Regiment frees her rich mines from a rampaging dragon. But there are problems: Jace does not believe in dragons, and the lady has not told him of her real enemies, the deadly Scarlur.

With the free-ranging lifestyle of centaur society, Jace has always had many lovers. But none truly have touched his heart, since he was forced to slay Ginger on the battlefield. Slashing his sword down to give his true love a merciful death, he killed his heart too. Yet now Silver Star, this skilled healer and intriguing fast running she, awakens old desires within him. Beyond just mounting Silver Star, he must possess her! Even if her kin forbid their love and his warriors fear this silver siren is leading them all to their deaths!

CENTAURS OF THE JEWELED SPEAR